WYVERN AND COMPANY

SAA THALARR SERIES, BOOK TWO

CONNIE SUTTLE

Print Second Edition (2018)
Print ISBN: 1-63478-077-9
Print ISBN-13: 978-1-63478-077-3
eBook ISBN: 1-93975-930-7
eBook ISBN-13: 978-1-93975-930-6

Published by:
SubtleDemon Publishing, LLC
PO Box 95696
Oklahoma City, OK 73143

Cover art by Renée Barratt @ The Cover Counts

To Walter, Joe, Larry, Lee, Dianne, Sarah and Mark.
Thank you.

A very special thank you to Renée B., Richard K. and
Amy S.

ACKNOWLEDGMENTS

As always, this book is the result of collaboration. If it weren't for the support of my editor, my cover artist and my beta readers, it would be less than it is. All mistakes, as usual, are mine and no other's.

About the Author:
Connie Suttle lives in Oklahoma with her husband and a conglomerate of cats. They have finally banded together to make their demands, which has proven disconcerting to all humans involved.

You may find Connie in the following ways:
Facebook: Connie Suttle Author
Twitter: @subtledemon
Website and Blog: subtledemon.com

ALSO BY CONNIE SUTTLE

Blood Destiny Series:

Blood Wager

Blood Passage

Blood Sense

Blood Domination

Blood Royal

Blood Queen

Blood Rebellion

Blood War

Blood Redemption

Blood Reunion

Blood Destiny Series Boxed Set (Books 1-10)

Blood Recall

Blood Alliance*

Legend of the Ir'Indicti Series:

Bumble

Shadowed

Target

Vendetta

Destroyer

Legend of the Ir'Inditi Boxed Set

~

R-D Series:

Cloud Dust

Cloud Invasion

Cloud Rebel

~

Latter Day Demons Series:

Hot Demon in the City

A Demon's Work is Never Done

A Demon's Due

~

Seattle Elementals Series:

Your Money's Worth

Worth Your While*

~

BlackWing Pirates Series

MindSighted

MindMage

MindRogue

MindMaster*

~

Black Rose Sorceress Series

The Rose Mark

Rose and Thorn

Black Rose Queen

Queen of Thorns and Roses

Future Wars Series

Buffer Zone

Black Zone*

Other Titles from SubtleDemon Publishing:

Malefactor

Transgressor

Underhanded*

by Joe Scholes

*Forthcoming

CHAPTER 1

"*H*ey, Justin."

Marilee Short walked up behind me as I pulled my English homework from my locker. It was Friday after our first week of school and Marilee was on the prowl. Her fake, sultry voice might work on the rest of the football team, but I wanted nothing to do with her.

I can't explain that—Mack almost pants around her if she speaks to him at all. And Short? What an oxymoron of a name. Marilee is five-eleven in her socks.

"Marilee." I acknowledged her presence by saying her name and slamming my locker door. She began to walk her fingers up my arm the minute I turned to look at her.

"Whatcha doin' tonight, Justin?" she asked, turning the pseudo-sultry up a notch.

"Helping my dad," I said, "At a construction site." I stared at the fingers walking up my arm. She dropped her hand and her eyes.

"We-ell, if you get done early," she looked at me again, "A bunch of us are getting together at my parents' lake cabin to get drunk. You're more than welcome to come."

"I'll think about it," I lied. I hate to lie, but sometimes there's just no other way. Marilee waited for me to say something else. When I didn't, she took the hint and walked away.

"See you there," she called behind her.

"Not in this lifetime," I muttered before turning to walk out a different way.

The hallway was deserted and dim that afternoon—most kids couldn't wait to get away from school on Fridays. I heard sounds of car engines starting outside; seniors were allowed to drive themselves and they were squealing out of the school parking lot, just to make the others envious.

I had to walk all the way around the building to get to my car, but by the time I got to it, Marilee and her crowd were already gone. Climbing into my six-year-old Honda, I shut the door and got the engine going.

The weather was as hot as you can imagine Fresno might get in late August, and I hoped the AC would get the car cooled fast. While I waited for that to happen, I pulled my cell phone from beneath the seat to check for messages. There was only one—from my best friend, Mack.

Mack's real name is Martin Walters, Jr., but his family calls him Mack because his dad goes by Martin. Mack is better than being called Junior any day of the week. Punching a button, I called him back.

"What's up, JAG?" Mack asked.

JAG is code for my initials, Justin Adam Griffin. Mack is the only one who calls me that. Actually, he's the only one who'll get away with calling me that. If anybody else did, I'd be pissed. It's just like calling my dad sweetie. Mom can get away with it, but if anybody else said that to him, they'd be acquainted with a wall in short order.

"Not much happening here," I said. "What's up with you, dude?"

"Marilee just called. I got invited to her parents' lake cabin tonight." Yeah, he was excited. Mack was smitten with Marilee Short—the top of his head came up to her chin, but that didn't stop him for even a second.

I also recognized Marilee's game—if she convinced Mack to go, then maybe he'd convince me to come, too. "You goin'?" I asked.

"Hell, yeah."

"Have a good time. I'm helping Dad at his new construction site tonight."

"Groovy. Uh, sorry you can't go," he covered his mistake.

I laughed. "No prob, dude. Have a good time. Don't get too drunk. You have to drive home, you know." Mack knew Marilee had her eye on me, and couldn't understand why I kept shoving her away. If I didn't go tonight, maybe he'd have a shot.

"See ya, dude," Mack said.

"Later, dude," I responded and ended the call. At least our conversation allowed time for the Honda's AC to work. I drove home only semi-moist from the heat.

~

"Mom, what the hell?" I said, dumping my cell and my backpack on the kitchen island. She stood in the middle of the island, her feet bare, stretching to reach the light fixture hanging overhead.

Dad, who'd walked into the house a nanosecond after I did, now stood beside the island, watching Mom's attempt to change a light bulb while he scowled at her. When he folded his arms over his chest, that was a signal—that somebody was doing something that didn't meet with his approval.

"Adam, it's a good thing you didn't build this house," Mom grumped as she stretched on tiptoe to reach the burned-out bulb.

"And if I had built it?" As always, he sounded calm. I recognized the tone, however—it said *I'm not taking much more of this nonsense.* If I'd been on that island, I'd have gotten down. *Fast.*

"If you'd built this, I'd smack you for putting this light fixture where you can't reach it with a ladder," she said.

Yeah, it was time to defuse. "Hi, Mom," I said, walking to the opposite side of the island and lifting my cheek for the traditional kiss. Mom smiled and leaned down to do just that.

I pulled her off the island the minute she leaned down, setting her on the floor while Dad hopped onto the island like it was three inches instead of nearly three feet off the floor. He had a new bulb in the fixture before Mom could draw breath to yell at both of us.

"Effing fine," Mom snapped when Dad jumped off the island with a grin. Except she didn't say effing. She said the actual word. Then she added something about tag team crap, only the S word was used instead of the C word.

Dad and I waited for her to leave the kitchen before we started laughing.

"You still planning to clean up the site tonight?" he asked.

"Yeah."

"It shouldn't take long. Joey wants to go to a late movie afterward, if you're interested."

"I sure am. Why?"

"Just didn't want to put a crimp in your social life," he teased.

Dad has a faint accent when he speaks—either British or Australian—I can't really tell. His birth certificate says he was born in London, but he says he moved around a lot before he met Mom and settled in Fresno.

Miss Channing, my eleventh-grade History teacher, sighs and bats her eyelashes at Dad whenever she sees him at one of my basketball or football games. Dad pretends he doesn't see her.

Mr. Jameson, the assistant principal, was the one I worried about, though. I overheard him saying he wouldn't mind effing my mom, only he said the actual word, too. I didn't tell Mom about it—I told Dad. I mean, that's just creepy.

Dad had a look on his face that I'd never seen before when I told him, just before he went to have a talk with Mr. Jameson. I don't know what Dad said, but whenever Mr. Jameson saw Mom after that, he ran in the opposite direction.

"I think I can get the site cleaned up before dinner," I said when Mom walked back in the kitchen.

"You have three hours," she said.

"I can handle it." Pulling my shirt over my head on the way to my bedroom, I grabbed work clothes, dressed and was out the door in ten.

~

"How bad was the worksite?" Uncle Joey asked as we stood in line to get popcorn at the theater.

"Found a bunch of roofing nails in the flower bed. Good thing I had the nail magnet with me—Dad told me to take it before I left the house. I'd still be there if I hadn't."

"How did it look?" Joey stepped up to the counter to order popcorn and drinks for both of us.

"Good. Dad's crew did a great job and the interior is finished— they're only waiting for carpet, now. The tile is already down."

"How's school? Two large popcorns, please, and two bottles of water."

"School's school," I shrugged as we watched the clerk fill two tubs of popcorn. "May need your help with calculus. Mr. Draper is just as boring as everybody says he is. I hope I don't fall asleep during class."

"I'll help," Joey agreed and handed money to the clerk.

"I got invited to a beer party tonight. Didn't want to go," I added as we walked down a hall toward our theater. "Mack went. He really doesn't like beer—he wanted to go so he could drool on Marilee Short."

"She really bothers you, doesn't she?" Joey opened the door and let me walk through first. Commercials were already playing on the screen, but the previews hadn't started yet.

"I don't know why. She's pretty and popular. She isn't stupid, but she lets everybody think she is. I guess she just doesn't try," I floundered.

"That bothers you too, doesn't it?" Joey nodded as we walked up carpeted steps toward a high seat.

"Yeah. The other guys tend to eat that up, but to me, it's just dumb. Why hide what you are?"

Joey chose that moment to choke on a mouthful of popcorn. He coughed for a minute or two before going up the steps again.

We'd gone to an action/adventure movie. It was strong on action and special effects, but rather deficient in story. Joey and I complained about it on the drive home.

~

Saturday is my laundry day. Since I was twelve, I've been washing my own clothes and bedding. Mom said it was good practice for later, when I went to college or looked for a girlfriend. Who wants to be invited to a dirty apartment or dorm room?

Actually, I was looking forward to a little mess, but not so much it couldn't be cleaned in half an hour. At least I knew how to clean and do laundry—Mom made sure of that. That's why I was carrying an armload of sheets and pillowcases toward the laundry room when I heard the television going in the media room.

Normally, Mom and Dad seldom watched television—especially so early on Saturday morning. At first I ignored it, choosing to stuff the sheets in the washer, add soap and get it started before walking into the kitchen for a glass of orange juice.

That's when I walked into the family room, carrying my juice and looking to find out why the TV was on. That moment set me on a track I'd never known existed. I froze, my glass halfway to my mouth, as the huge, flat-screen television came into view.

Splashed across it was Mack's photograph from last year's yearbook—the one he hated so much. A reporter blathered some nonsense while I read the caption at the bottom of the screen—the one that said *arrest made in party massacre at Shaver Lake cabin.*

The glass of orange juice fell from my fingers and shattered on the wood floor.

CHAPTER 2

"*H*e didn't do it. Mack wouldn't do that," I repeated. I think I'd said it at least six times.

"Son, we know that," Dad said, putting an arm around my shoulders. "We just have to convince the authorities they have the wrong person."

The landline rang while Dad did his best to reassure me. Mom answered.

"Hello?" she said. "Yes, this is Mrs. Griffin. Why do you want to know whether my son is home? Of course you may question him, but only with his father and me present." I knew then Mom was dangerously close to letting whoever was on the other end of that conversation have it. "Yes, that's our address," she confirmed. "We'll be waiting." She hung up.

Dad can sound deadly, but when Mom gets that quiet and deliberate, somebody is in real trouble for sure. "The police are on their way," she announced. "It seems Mr. Jameson named Justin as Mack's coconspirator in everything he does, and suspects that he was at that party last night."

"I will take that bastard apart," Dad rose, his voice barely above a growl.

"Adam, calm down. There are other things that require our attention first," Mom said. "Mack is in real trouble. We can't have that."

"They won't arrest me, too, will they?" I asked. Honestly, being implicated in multiple murders wasn't even on my radar until that moment.

"You will not be arrested," Mom said firmly. "We will handle this, one way or another."

Two police officers showed up twenty minutes later. Dad frowned as both of them walked into the house. Mom politely (and stiffly) offered coffee when they sat across from me at the kitchen island. Both accepted a cup.

"Now," the taller of the officers, whose nametag said Francis, turned to me and began. "We understand that you and the suspect are inseparable."

"We don't sleep together," I snapped. Well, it just came out of my mouth—that's the only excuse I had. "He went to the party last night. I cleaned up a construction site for my dad, then went to a movie with Uncle Joey."

"Do you have proof of this?" The second officer—Barton—asked.

"I have the ticket stub," I said, slapping the tiny square on the island. "Luis, my dad's foreman, was at the construction site last night, too, to lock up after I got done. I called my mom on the drive home, to ask what was for dinner. We had manicotti."

"How did you know Martin Walters, Junior, went to the party last night?" Barton asked, saying Mack's full legal name. Mack would have been pissed if he'd heard *that*.

"I called him before I drove home from school, yesterday. He said he was going. I told him I didn't want to go because I promised to clean up the construction site."

"Is that the only reason?"

"I don't like Marilee Short," I blurted. "And I don't much like beer."

"Is that why you plotted with your friend to attack her and the others at her party?" Officer Francis asked.

"He told you he wasn't at the party, and he provided proof and witnesses. That should be the end of it," Dad hissed. His voice was so compelling, it rattled both policemen, I could tell.

"Did Mr. Walters inform you of his plans, then, to attack those at the party?" Barton tried another tack.

"Mack is five-six and weighs one-twenty. Do you think for a minute he could take on most of the football team, half the basketball team and the cheerleaders, too?" I huffed. "I saw the news—somebody leaked information that the victims looked like they were attacked by wild animals. Tell me how Mack could do that all by himself without somebody pounding him to a pulp, first. Why don't you talk to the survivors? I hear there are eight of them."

"They're not speaking," Francis snapped. "Too traumatized, according to the doctors. Two are in critical condition, and may not live."

"Then answer my son's question," Mom snapped. "Tell us how they were attacked from close range by someone strong enough to do that kind of damage, without anyone attempting to fight back?"

"We don't have an answer, ma'am," Officer Barton muttered. "But the assistant principal said your son and Martin Walters, Jr. are best friends. We're obligated to investigate."

"Where is Mack, now?" I demanded.

"In jail," Francis said. "He's eighteen—he'll be charged as an adult."

"He's not guilty of any of that," I said. "Mack would never do that."

"He says he tried to call for help, but we can't find any record of the call and his cell phone is missing," Barton said.

"Wait," I said, standing. "Let me get my phone to see if he tried to call me. I turned the ringer off last night for the movie and forgot to turn it on again."

"I'll come with you," Barton stood and nodded to me.

"We don't have any guns in this house," Dad said, his voice soft and deadly.

"How did you know?" Barton's voice wobbled as he blinked at Dad in confusion.

"I know a damn sight more than you," Dad said. "We'll both go with

Justin to his bedroom. He's seventeen and is not considered an adult yet. At least in the eyes of the law."

"All right," Barton held up a hand, as if he were attempting to fend off my dad. "We'll all go."

My hand shook when I lifted my phone and entered the security code. I had three voice messages from Mack. All three were practically the same, except the last one, at the end.

"Dude," Mack shouted into the phone, his fear-filled voice creating the crackle of a bad connection. "I can't get through to nine-one-one. Those things are eating people. Send help. Please!" A growl sounded shortly after, and the message cut off.

I wanted to shout at Mack to run.

It was much too late for that.

Somehow, he'd gotten away when most of the others hadn't, and the police arrested him for it. Guilt ate at me, too. If I hadn't gone to a worthless movie the night before, I'd have heard Mack's call for help. Surely, somebody could have helped him.

I just didn't know who.

"This puts a new spin on things," Officer Barton sighed after listening to the message a second time. I slumped on the side of my freshly made bed and covered my face with my hands.

Officer Barton's radio blurted a message.

"Inmate attacked at county jail," the woman's voice said. "All available officers respond."

"I have to go," Officer Barton said and ran from the room, taking my cell phone with him.

"Adam?" Mom appeared in my doorway. I looked up—the sound of her voice was strange. Like she was terrified. She was as pale as paper, too, and I had no idea why.

"What is it?" Dad asked, his voice betraying concern.

"We have to get to the hospital. Mack's on the way. Adam, they tried to kill him."

∽

I'll never forget the next three hours as long as I live. Mom and Dad ran out of the house, leaving me behind. Joey showed up ten minutes later, offering me a ride to the hospital.

I couldn't ask if Joey knew anything. At that moment, I fully understood Schrödinger in a way I never had before.

If I didn't ask, then Mack was alive.

If I asked, he could be dead.

I hung in limbo, too afraid to know the truth.

Adam's Journal

We had to leave Justin behind. Kiarra folded space to the hospital —there wasn't much time left for Mack.

I managed to clear the room where they'd taken him—whoever had beaten him didn't intend for the boy to live.

"I don't think I can save him—his injuries are too extensive," Kiarra wiped tears away. "I can't let this happen," she added, before saying a name that sent a chill down my spine.

"Pheligar."

He appeared without bothering to disguise himself. My wife is the only one who can call the tall, blue Larentii Liaison without raising his ire.

"Kiarra?" he asked, meeting her eyes briefly before going to the boy. Mack's bloodied and broken body lay on the gurney—there wasn't anything the doctors could do except watch him die.

Kiarra was extremely talented as a healer, but even she couldn't reverse the damage done to Mack's body.

"Will you help me?" Kiarra begged Pheligar, her blue eyes filling with fresh tears.

All of our race know that Larentii are the finest healers—if they choose to heal, that is. Generally, they do not interfere, preferring to observe only. The boy wasn't connected to our race, therefore the Larentii wasn't obligated to do anything for him.

Pheligar gazed steadily at Kiarra for only a moment. "I will," he said, his voice deep, his words measured, "if you will return the favor, someday. I will not ask you for anything you cannot give, and my request will not break the rules or any laws. You must promise to do this."

"I will do what you ask," she replied with a brief nod. "My word is law."

I stiffened. For her to say those last four words meant she was committed, no matter what Pheligar asked. I knew she loved Mack as if he were her own, but this—I had no idea what a Larentii might ask in return for a healing.

"Good," Pheligar said. "I will begin."

If I hadn't placed a shield about us, the brightness of the light might have blinded everyone in nearby rooms. Nearly an hour it took, too—Pheligar placed the body in stasis so it wouldn't die before he could make necessary repairs.

I knew my son sat in the waiting room with Joey, terrified for his friend. I cared for Mack—almost as much as Kiarra and Justin did. I wasn't about to argue with her decision, although I worried for her. I knew, too, when Martin Walters arrived at the hospital, ready to explode. That's when I left my shield in place and went to him.

I knew what he was.

He knew what I was—or as much as he was allowed to know. He never worried if Mack spent time at our home, because he knew his son would be protected.

My shoes squeaked as I ran down tiled floors, bent on stopping Martin before he stormed into Mack's emergency room cubicle. He didn't need to see what was going on there. I caught him before he entered the hall leading to the room.

"Martin, I think he'll be all right," I gripped his arms to keep him from tearing into the doctors and nurses following him. They hadn't caused the damage to his child—careless and vindictive employees at the county jail had done that. We also didn't need hospital security to intervene—Martin was angry enough to take someone down after his son was injured.

That, of course, would have to be dealt with and Martin needed to stay out of it. If he didn't, he could also be arrested.

"But the detective said," Martin growled.

"Look, he's receiving the best care anyone can hope for. Give it a few minutes, all right? I think you can see him after that."

"Dad?" Justin's voice wavered as he appeared behind Martin Walters.

"Son, Mack will be all right, I think. We just have to wait a little longer."

"He is fine."

I knew the physician who'd walked up to us was the Larentii in disguise, but I wasn't about to let anyone else know. "You may see him, now." Pheligar, wearing a human disguise as well as unneeded spectacles, nodded to Martin and me before walking away.

"Come on," Justin grabbed my arm and pulled me after Martin, who'd taken off in a near-run.

～

Justin's Journal

"Mack?" I said his name tentatively, still worried that he might not be awake, much less whole.

"Dude?" His voice croaked, like it was hard to talk.

"He needs some water."

How did Mom get here ahead of us? It didn't matter; she held a glass to Mack's lips and helped him drink. I couldn't figure out why she looked exhausted; Uncle Joey led her out of the room after Mack got his water.

"Thanks, that's better," Mack sighed. "Man, I'm tired," he added.

"Son, you're covered in blood," Martin said, stepping toward the bed and taking Mack's hand.

"Yeah. Most of it's mine. That wasn't fun," he said.

"You'll need an attorney, Martin," Dad said, giving Mack's dad a nod. "I believe you'll find that Mack was placed in a cell with that evil bastard on purpose."

"What?" Mack and I said at the same time.

~

I'd have stayed with Mack at the hospital if they'd let me. Instead, his dad, his sister and a couple of his dad's friends intended to take shifts. The funny thing? The emergency room doctors were calling Mack's recovery a miracle.

Yeah, he still had a bunch of bruises and some cuts, but no broken bones. That was sort of weird, too, because at least two doctors swore he had multiple fractures when he was brought in. At least one of them mentioned massive internal injuries, too. I guess they were wrong.

Didn't matter; Mack was alive and that's all I cared about.

We watched the late news together, that night—Mom, Dad and I. The reporters were now saying it looked as if those kids at the party had been attacked by wild animals of some sort, but couldn't say for sure what sort of animals.

I also learned that four students who'd attended the party were missing, although there was evidence at the scene that indicated their bodies had been dragged away—toward the north. Mack had run south—in the opposite direction.

Mack's messages from my cell phone were played, too, on both local and national news. I got sick of hearing them after a while. At least Mack was no longer considered a suspect. The other thing that happened was this—a police officer was suspended for putting Mack in the wrong cell with a violent offender—nobody was supposed to be locked up with that guy.

The trouble was—I recognized the officer's name. Mack and I went to school with his son—Randall Pierce. If Officer Pierce were anything like Randall, it didn't surprise me that he'd deliberately put Mack where he had.

Randall was a bully, in every sense of the word. He didn't bother me, because I was taller and outweighed him. That didn't stop him from taunting Mack every chance he got, though.

"When will Mack come home?" I asked.

"In a day or two, I think," Mom said. "I hope this doesn't traumatize him too much. He went through a terrible ordeal—not only at the party but in that jail cell, too."

"Yeah." I shook my head—Mack's mom lived in Colorado with her second husband. She'd left Mr. Walters when Mack was eight; that was traumatic enough for him to deal with.

"What do you think attacked those kids?" The rest of them began to weigh on my conscience—I hadn't really thought about all the classmates who'd died, or the others still in the hospital with injuries—I'd only thought about my best friend at first.

"Son, we can't say for certain," Dad said. "Don't worry about it—I'm sure someone is on their trail. I only hope they can do something about it when the monsters are found."

"I'm going to bed," I announced. "Mom, how long will the police keep my cell phone?"

"I don't know. It's evidence and that means they may hold onto it. You can borrow mine if you want—I seldom use it—until we can get another one for you."

"Okay."

"I'm more concerned about Mack's phone," Dad said. "I don't believe the investigators looked hard enough for it before arresting him and stuffing him in a cell with a repeat offender."

"I could go look for it," I offered.

"You will not go looking for it," Dad said. He used the voice that accepted no argument, too.

"Honey, we don't know whether the monsters are still out there," Mom said. "It's too dangerous."

"Yeah. Well, maybe the police will look again. In their next life."

I stomped toward my bedroom, angry about the many things I couldn't resolve or define.

Sunday's news broadcasts were filled with names of the dead. Warren

James, Matt Brown, Brett Brinkley and Travis Duncan were on the list —all starters on the football team. I considered them friends, although we didn't hang out together much.

Trace Linn and Clay Holder's names only ramped up my anger— Mack and I played video games with them. They'd been to the house plenty of times. Clay loved Mom's brownies.

"I know, baby," Mom sat beside me in the media room while I watched names of classmates crawl past on the bottom of the screen. I'd tuned out the reporter after a while—he was only spouting what everybody else was about Mack's brush with a criminal, when he shouldn't have been in jail in the first place.

Six survivors were listed, too—two of the initial eight died during the night. Marilee Short's name was on the survivor list. Yeah, I sort of blamed her. She'd had a party at her parents' cabin while they were out of town and didn't know. They were refusing interviews or to make statements to the press.

Well, I'd be mad, too, if something like that happened on my property without my knowing.

"Do we know how bad the six survivors are?" I turned to Mom, then.

"Honey, I can't say," she said, but there was worry in her eyes. That worried me in return. "They're under medical care at the moment, but none of them are speaking."

"They're not talking? That doesn't sound like Marilee," I huffed. "She never shuts up."

"We'll find out eventually," Mom said, rising from the sofa we occupied. "Want breakfast? I think we can see Mack this afternoon at the hospital if you want."

"Of course I want to," I said, hunching my shoulders. "How did he get away?"

"Honey, Mack's special. We both know that. Come on, I'll make biscuits and gravy for you."

"With bacon?"

"With bacon."

I followed her into the kitchen to help.

~

"Dude," I said, handing an iPod to Mack, who took it eagerly. I could tell he wanted out of that hospital bed—bad.

"Thanks, man," Mack said, fiddling with the attached earphones. "Hi, Mrs. G, Mr. G." He took a moment to grin at my parents.

"Mack, hon, are you all right?" Mom went to the side of the bed and brushed dark hair back from his forehead.

"Yeah. I guess." Mack lowered his eyes and the smile disappeared. That's when I knew all the crap that happened to him in two-and-a-half days had taken a big toll.

"Stop worrying about it," Mom soothed, stroking his hair. Mack let out a breath when she did that, as if a weight had been removed from his shoulders.

"Thanks, Mom," he sighed and closed his eyes.

Yeah, Mack sometimes calls her Mom. I wasn't about to argue with that. His Mom was hundreds of miles away, and I didn't see her standing in his hospital room, taking care of her son.

My mom was.

"I brought something for you, too," Mom said when Mack opened his eyes again.

"What?"

She pulled a cold bottle of Dr. Pepper out of her purse.

"Thanks." He had the cap off and was drinking when his older sister walked in. Mom doesn't let us drink soda at the house very often. She says it should be an infrequent treat instead of a several-a-day habit.

She knows Mack loves Dr. Pepper. She'd brought him one. Mack's sister, Beth, grinned as he emptied the bottle, then smacked his lips. "Good vintage," Mack said. It sounded so normal, I laughed.

"The doctor says he'll be released tomorrow, if he continues to improve," Martin Walters walked in and shook hands with Dad.

"Awesome," I breathed.

~

School was canceled for three days; Mack came home on Monday afternoon. His dad had already replaced his lost cell phone, so he called me the minute he could.

"Dude, we need to talk," Mack said.

"Okay," I hedged.

"Really. We need to talk."

"I said okay."

"Can you come over?"

"Yeah. I think so. I'll tell Mom."

Ten minutes later, I was on my way to Mack's house. His dad does specialty cabinetwork and sometimes my dad hires him when a job requires the fancy stuff. Martin Walters is an artist—according to Dad, and Dad would know—he's an architect.

Mack met me at the door, so I followed him to his bedroom. It always looked rumpled, but his dad makes him clean up at least once a week.

"You okay, man?" I asked the minute he shut the bedroom door behind us.

"Yeah. For the most part. I just wanted to talk about a few things with you, first. I think they're hallucinations, mostly, but," he shrugged.

"What hallucinations? After that guy almost killed you?"

"Some of it," he said. "Look, sit down. This may take a while."

I sat. Mack didn't say anything for a while; he just leaned against his headboard and stared out the window.

"Those—things," he began, "they looked half-lizard and half-human."

"Huh?" I stared—I know I did. "Which half was human?"

"No. That's not it—they looked like grayish-brown humans with scales and nasty teeth," he said. "Geez, maybe it was all a hallucination."

"Dude, I've never seen you do that. Keep talking. There has to be an explanation for this."

"They just walked out of the trees. A bunch of them. Most of the football team was already drunk, but when one of those things

18

jumped Matt and bit him, the rest of the team jumped on the thing. That's when all of the things went nuts. Blood started to fly. When they started eating people, that's when half of us were either taking pictures with cell phones or calling nine-one-one."

"What were the other half doing?"

"The ones that weren't being eaten? Running. They didn't get far. I guess the monsters figured the rest of us were too stupid to run, and they didn't want anybody getting away. They were too fast for just about everybody."

"Who were they not fast enough for?" I thought to ask after blinking at Mack for several seconds.

"Me. They weren't fast enough to catch me," Mack whispered. "Dude, I can't explain that either—because I have a memory of running on all fours."

"That can't be," I shook my head at him. "Nobody runs that fast on their hands and knees."

"I don't remember hands and knees."

"Have you talked to your dad about that?"

"Would you?" Mack sounded terrified at the idea—as if somebody, somewhere, was waiting to lock him up again because they thought he might be crazy.

"I guess you're right—that does sound kinda weird," I acknowledged. "Maybe it was because of the circumstances that you're making something up—some reason for you to get away when most of the others didn't."

"Yeah. Dude, I don't think they'll find anybody else alive," Mack said softly. "Those things—monsters—were just too vicious."

"Then you are one lucky dude," I said.

"You think I don't feel guilty about that?" His words surprised me.

"Yeah. I guess you would," I sighed. "You can't let this rule your life, man. Out of all the people who could have gotten away, I'm really glad it turned out to be you."

"Do you think it's weird that I want to hunt those things down and kill all of them, now?" he asked.

"I think that's normal," I said. "If it were possible, I'd help."

"I'm not sure either of us would live over it if we did. That doesn't mean I don't want to, anyway."

"I feel guilty, too," I confessed. "I should have been there with you and I wasn't."

"Look, if you'd died, I'd feel worse than I do, now."

"Too bad we're not superheroes. That could solve everything."

"We're not superheroes," Mack sounded depressed. "Man, I wish your mom was here."

"I think she's your mom, too," I shrugged. "She sure left the house the other day like a bat out of hell when she heard you got hurt," I added. "And pissed—man." I shook my head at Mack.

"She made me feel better yesterday—for sure," Mack said. "Like the weight was lifted for a while."

"Want me to call her?" I lifted the cell phone she'd lent me.

"If you don't mind."

"Hey, you think your dad will let you come home with me? I don't think Mom will mind if you stay with us."

"I want to," Mack nodded. "Dad's got a job going in Visalia, and Beth's classes at Fresno State take up most of her time."

"Then call and ask," I nodded toward his cell phone. "I'll call Mom."

Twenty minutes later, I drove Mack to my house. Mom met us at the door. "Honey, how are you feeling?" she held Mack's face in her hands. He let out a sigh, as if the weight were lifted again.

"I have your bedroom ready," she said. "But you and Justin can play video games in his if you want."

"I do," Mack nodded and offered her a lopsided grin when she let her hands fall. "Thanks, Mom."

"Anytime, baby."

Normally, Mack would consider himself too old and way too macho to accept baby as an endearment. He didn't mind a bit when Mom said it to him. "I'll have dinner ready in two hours," Mom said and shooed us toward my bedroom.

"Let us know if we can help," Mack called out.

"What are we having?" I asked.

"Fried chicken."

Mack stopped in his tracks and turned around to walk back to Mom. "I love you." He flopped his arms around Mom's neck and gave her a hug.

Mom cooks meat for Dad and me, because we're carnivores. She's vegetarian. Yeah, it sounds weird, but that's the way it's always been. Mack's favorite meal is homemade fried chicken, mashed potatoes with gravy and fresh green beans. Mom wanted him to be happy and get his mind off recent events, so she was cooking something he loved.

I was all for it.

~

Adam's Journal

Sweetheart, Lion and Dragon are coming for dinner, I sent. *We have to discuss this mess and what we should do about spawn in the area. What the hell are they doing here, anyway? This is a breach of the agreement.*

You can't ever rely on their complete compliance, she sent back. *Maybe somebody didn't get the memo after Corpus Christi. I'll cook extra chicken for Lion and Dragon. Mack is here to spend the night with Justin, and if I have my way, he'll stay until Martin is done with that job in Visalia. He's too far away if Mack happens to need him, right now.*

Are you prepared if things happen with him? I asked. It was a valid question.

I think I can handle it, she responded. *He's having trouble dealing with the emotional fallout from that pile of spawn-induced shit. I'm more concerned about those six kids they have locked up in a mental ward at the hospital,* she went on. *You know they were bitten.*

That's why Dragon and Lion are coming—we have to discuss this and come to some sort of decision.

Adam, I'm really not feeling good right now.

Sweetheart?

I think I'm going to be sick.

On my way.

Ten seconds later, I held my breath and my wife's hair while she vomited in our toilet. This hadn't happened in more than eighteen years. I sent mindspeech to Joey, telling him to get here quickly. He folded in, took one look at Kiarra bent over the toilet and put his hands on her forehead.

She stopped dry heaving immediately.

I flushed the toilet while Joey pulled Kiarra away and set her on the dressing bench nearby.

"Let me check," Joey's hands went to her abdomen. "Yeah, Adam, you're gonna be a papa again. I'll ask Karzac to come so we can confirm, but this looks like a done deal from my perspective."

"Fuck, shit and damn," Kiarra cursed before shaking her head at Joey. "Right when we have to deal with the fucking spawn from fucking who knows where."

"Sweetheart, you're cursing in front of the baby."

"Look, you're probably five or six weeks along, if that," Joey attempted to placate my wife. "You still have six more weeks or so to smite spawn if the need arises."

"I don't like that idea," I snapped.

"I don't care," Kiarra snapped back. "Getting pregnant again wasn't exactly in my plans, Adam Chessman."

"You're blaming me?" I tapped my chest with a finger.

"Enough." When Karzac appears and growls like that, it's time to shut the hell up. He put his hands on Kiarra. "Yes," the Refizani physician nodded. "Yes. You are correct, young Joey. Pregnant. Six weeks. Kiarra, please tell me that this does not upset you. After all, Lion and Marlianna would love to have children, yet they cannot. So far, you are the only one among us who has overcome the necessary obstacles."

"Fuck," Kiarra hung her head. "I'm not upset about another baby. I'm upset about the timing." Her eyes begged Karzac to understand.

"Then I understand. It is not, as you say, the best time for a little one. We will work around that, won't we?"

Karzac has light-brown hair, green-gold eyes, stands at roughly six feet and has a soft spot for my wife.

"I guess," she mumbled.

"Has your stomach settled?"

"Yes. I need to get back to the kitchen to finish dinner. I promised to make fried chicken for Mack."

"Would you like me to take a look at the young one?" Karzac lifted an eyebrow.

"Sure. I've already squashed Mack's memories twice. He really needs somebody better suited to handle the emotional side to this."

"Then I will talk with him. Come, I will follow you to the kitchen, gather soft drinks for your son and his friend and we will have a talk."

"Thanks, Karzac."

"You are very welcome."

CHAPTER 3

*J*ustin's Journal
I seldom see Uncle Karzac. He showed up that afternoon. Yeah, I knew he was a doctor and plenty busy, but somehow, Mom and Dad got him to make a house call. He brought two bottles of Dr. Pepper to Mack and me, then sat on my bed and talked to both of us while Mom cooked dinner.

He had good things to say, too. He told Mack that feeling guilty about surviving was natural. Lots of people felt that way in traumatic circumstances. He said what I did, too—that it wasn't Mack's fault that the bad stuff happened or that he'd miraculously lived over it.

We also discussed people who did bad things for reasons known only to them, and that Mack wasn't responsible for any part of that, either. I could tell Karzac wasn't happy that Randall Pierce's dad stuck Mack in the same cell with a homicidal lunatic, but he didn't come out and say it.

When Mom knocked on the door and said dinner was ready, I could tell Mack felt better, and it wasn't just because fried chicken waited in the kitchen.

That night, we had dinner with Uncle Karzac, Uncle Lion, Uncle Joey and Uncle Dragon, something that seldom happens except at

Christmas. Uncle Lion grinned and teased Mack and me, but it was a gentle teasing—about stuff that really didn't matter and made us laugh.

Uncle Dragon watched both of us with guarded attention. He does that a lot—as if he's making sure everybody is safe. Mom always says Uncle Dragon does it out of habit. I have no idea what that means, but it's nice to know.

Mack admires Uncle Dragon a lot—he's only seen him a few times, but since Dragon is Asian and has a long, black braid down his back, Mack says he looks like an ancient, Japanese warlord or something.

After dessert, which was banana pudding, another of Mack's favorites, Mom, Dad and my uncles went to Dad's study to discuss business. Joey didn't go to the meeting; he helped Mack and me clear the table and load the dishwasher instead.

"Want to see the latest?" Joey held up a flash drive when we were finished in the kitchen. He'd been working on his own video games, and the last one looked pretty cool.

"Yeah," Mack said, his eyes shining. Joey was working on what might prove to be the coolest game ever, and Mack and I couldn't wait to try it. Joey did all the computer work for Dad's business, but he did this on the side and wanted to start a gaming company someday.

This game would be a good start on that dream. Joey had serious talent in that area—he'd graduated with honors from MIT. That's why he could help with all my math and science homework—those subjects were never a problem for him.

Mack and I followed him as he led the way to my bedroom and my computer.

∼

Adam's Journal

"I don't like the idea of waiting," Dragon said before sipping the bourbon I'd poured for him. "We only need a plan to get them out of the hospital before taking care of the situation. They're not human any longer—we all know that. I know their parents will be devastated, but devastation is better than being bitten and turned to spawn by your own children."

"I agree with Dragon," Kiarra said. "Who has ideas on getting them out?"

"You will do nothing of the sort." Thorsten appeared in a brief flash of light, wearing a huge frown. "I command that you allow this to play out as it will," he added.

"What the fuck?" Kiarra bristled. She disagreed with Thorsten more than half the time, and often argued against his decisions. The rest of us let her take point on things of that nature—it was her right to assert her opinions, after all.

"Kiarra, I will hear no arguments this time," Thorsten huffed. "This is the way it will be. Watch and wait, then take them down when it becomes necessary and not before."

"And that could happen in a crowd of people, just like Shaver Lake," she protested.

"Most of those are dead," Thorsten hissed. "I trust Adam can place compulsion on the boy if it becomes necessary."

Right then, I knew my wife wanted to hit Thorsten. She didn't, but only because Pheligar appeared and held her back from our superior. The Larentii didn't harm her; he merely wrapped a blue arm about her body and pulled her against him. I couldn't think of anyone who might escape a determined Larentii, and that included Kiarra.

"Kiarra, he has spoken," Pheligar said. It wasn't difficult to tell that Pheligar disagreed with Thorsten's decision, too—he merely wanted to keep Kiarra safe and away from the minor god's wrath.

"There," Thorsten jerked his head at Kiarra and Pheligar. "I have commanded this. You will not hunt them; you only have permission to take them down if they attack. That's the end of it," Thorsten muttered and disappeared.

The room was quiet for several seconds after Thorsten left.

"We'll stay to fight spawn," Dragon offered, nodding toward Lion. "We don't have assignments coming up for a few weeks."

"Then we'll let things play out, just as commanded," I growled.

Pheligar released Kiarra, who looked very much like a ruffled and offended hen at that point.

"Allow this to play out as it will, my ass," she muttered as she stalked out of my den.

"Pregnancy will not improve her temper during this volatile time," Pheligar observed dryly once she was gone. "I will be more vigilant—it is my guess that this spawn epidemic will spread quickly if we cannot actively hunt them, and she will be tempted to use her abilities past the twelve-week mark."

"Does that mean we'll see more of you, then?" Lion asked.

"Logically speaking, if I am present more often, then the likelihood of your seeing me also increases."

"Save me—he's employing logic," Lion pretended to be choking.

"I assume that was an attempt at humor. I assure you it was wasted effort."

"He said let things play out as they will. That means we can go if we hear or see evidence of spawn, right?" Dragon asked. "I swear I will go at even the hint of spawn. The six in the local hospital? We wait and watch. I have already visited the hospital to prevent the personnel from drawing the blood of those spawn-infected teens—it was to save the lives of the staff. You know the newly-made spawn will see such as an attack and kill as a result. It is also my fear that Kiarra is correct—these may turn in front of a crowd when the time is right and their hunger for human flesh takes over. I have no idea why Thorsten has decided thusly. The results of this decision may serve to panic a nation that has no idea what may be attacking it."

"We may have other worries, too," Lion pointed out. "While I can't say for certain at the moment, those who sent the spawn may have formed alliances with humans. Perhaps that is why Thorsten made this decision."

"We have another problem, too," I said.

"Yes." Pheligar agreed. "Justin's eighteenth birthday is approaching."

"Three weeks," I said. "If things should happen with him, they will likely happen then."

"Not the best of times to teach a fledgling," Dragon nodded.

"Kiarra is keeping an eye on Mack, too," I said. "We may have two fledglings."

"When will you tell your child of the impending birth of his sibling?"

"We'll have to tell him soon, I suppose. We should keep it under wraps until he and Mack are in a better place emotionally, I think."

"I agree with that decision," Pheligar said.

That surprised me—the Larentii acted as if he were a member of our group instead of an aloof superior. I refused to blink or show my confusion. Perhaps it was that he stood with us on this, instead of blindly accepting Thorsten's latest decision.

"May I suggest," Pheligar went on, "a larger home? If you find suitable land to purchase, we can have the home built to your specifications quickly. If you buy enough land, you can build a guesthouse where Lion and Marlianna will reside. With Thorsten's command, I believe this could take weeks or even months to conclude. Make sure to build a house with many bedrooms; Dragon will want to move in with Karzac."

"Why would I want to do that?" Dragon asked.

"The Wise Ones approached me. They say Kiarra is carrying your mate in her womb," Pheligar shrugged.

"Here," Lion said, pointing to several acres that once were part of a local strawberry farm.

"That's ideal—nothing close-by except more farmland," Dragon agreed. I was busy *Looking* to see what would be required to build an English manor-type home with three stories and a larger garage.

Dragon didn't express it, but hope shone in his eyes for the first time since I'd known him. Our daughter—Kiarra's and mine—already belonged to the former Falchani Warlord.

"I will take your plans and with Dragon and Lion's help, it will be accomplished swiftly and with little notice," Pheligar said. Yes, the Larentii was still there. Kiarra had no idea what we were plotting—

she'd gone to bed already, claiming she had a headache. Joey took care of it and placed her in a healing sleep afterward.

"Can you expedite the sale? I can pay cash, but we need paperwork done and building permits filed."

"I will see to it," Pheligar said. That's one of the things he did—smoothed the way for us to walk into any situation or onto any world and fit in easily. Pheligar had a talent for it, actually, and I was grateful for the cool efficiency of his race.

"I already have plans drawn up to rebuild the house in England, but it's owned by the bastard's family now and they won't sell it, either. I hear they're hoping for a title to go with the land, but that won't happen. The title died with my brother, after his heirs moved to America. It won't matter how many royal rings they kiss, they're not going to get a title out of it."

"Where are the plans?" Pheligar asked, interrupting my huff. *Pulling* the rolled-up plans to me, I placed them in his hand. I'd made changes for a massive remodel of my ancestral home, hoping one day I'd be able to make those changes. I had no idea whether that would ever be.

"I will see this done—in a week," Pheligar said and disappeared.

"Fuck me," Lion breathed and shook his head. "I've never seen that Larentii so determined before."

"I don't think he's ever disagreed with Thorsten so actively, before," Dragon observed. "This is his way of making sure things are taken care of without drawing Thorsten's ire."

"So he's placing us on Earth for a reason," Lion slowly nodded.

"We have to be ready to go at a moment's notice, wherever spawn crop up," Dragon rose and *Pulled* his sheathed blades into his hands. "My friend, we'll be ready. Adam, I hope you have a place for me to spend the night."

"I do," I agreed. "We'll just have to move a cot into Justin's room for Mack."

~

Justin's Journal

I don't know where the extra bed came from, but Dad and Uncle Dragon moved it into my room because Uncle Dragon was spending the night in Mack's bedroom.

Mack didn't care—in fact, he was relieved. His twin bed was shoved against the opposite wall after Dad moved my desk and beanbag aside. We hadn't slept in the same room since junior high, after I outgrew my twin bed.

At six-four, I was as tall as my dad and looked a lot like him, too, except for my hair color. It was a sandy blond and I figured the lighter shade came from my mom, whose hair is pale blonde.

"You gonna be okay?" I asked Mack when the older folks left the room.

"This is fine," he said, wiggling into a better spot. Mack looks a lot like his dad, too, with dark hair and eyes. Marilee was stupid for not seeing past his height—Mack is awesome in my book.

"Good-night, then," I said, turning off the bedside lamp. Sleep was slow to come, that night—too many things swirled inside my brain and I couldn't shut it down.

~

Hearing the television in the media room on my way to the kitchen was turning into a regular event. This time, Mack followed me as we walked in to find Dad, Mom, Uncle Dragon, Uncle Lion and Uncle Karzac watching TV at seven-thirty on a Tuesday morning.

We saw images of sheet-covered bodies scattered across a field in Yosemite. That was bad enough, but the sound that came from Mack's throat as he watched?

It sounded almost like a growl.

"Dude," I whispered and elbowed him. He turned fast to blink at me.

"Sorry," he shook himself. "Man, what happened?" He turned back to the screen.

We saw images of collapsed tents, with long shreds of waterproof fabric lifting in the breeze. Some of that fabric was stained; I knew it had to be blood.

Journalists at the scene were already comparing this attack with the one at Shaver Lake—the similarities were eerie. At least Mack hadn't been anywhere near Yosemite, so they couldn't blame this on him.

"Another attack; this time at a campsite in Yosemite," Dad sighed. "They found sixteen bodies, but three others are missing."

"Not good," I muttered.

"For damn sure," Mack breathed beside me.

"Want breakfast?" Mom stood and stretched before walking around Dad's feet and heading in our direction.

"Yeah." I'd been plunged right back into depression at the sight of the murders.

"Honey, don't think about that, all right?" Mom linked her arms through Mack's and mine to pull us toward the door.

Adam's Journal

"This is unacceptable," Kiarra huffed. I agreed with her. Yes, we'd gone to kill spawn in Yosemite the night before, but sixteen humans were already dead and the last three were spawn bitten and dusted when they died.

We'd killed the spawn responsible and gotten rid of spawn dust afterward, but the whole situation was as unacceptable as my wife claimed. Thorsten's command held us back from actively hunting spawn, and that's exactly what we should be doing instead of dealing with them only after they'd attacked a campsite filled with college botany students in a national park.

I didn't like the fact that Kiarra was pregnant and insisting on fighting, either. We'd waited to have this conversation until after Mack and Justin were back in Justin's room, playing video games with Joey.

Karzac had to pull Dragon back, too—he'd been ready to voice his opinion on Kiarra's involvement in the spawn hunt. Already he was protective of his mate, although she wasn't much more than a collection of cells inside my wife's womb at the moment.

"She doesn't have a name," I said aloud.

"What?" Kiarra stared at me. I'd just derailed the train, in her opinion.

"Our daughter. Dragon's mate. She doesn't have a name."

"Adam, Karzac says I'm only a few weeks along. A name is something for later. Besides, shouldn't she have a choice in this, too?"

"You know how M'Fiyahs work," Griffin appeared inside our kitchen. I wasn't sure I wanted him there, but didn't say anything. He'd retired from the Saa Thalarr, giving up his spot so I could take it. I didn't want to fight with him in my own kitchen—retired Saa Thalarr held onto their abilities and I wasn't in any mood to test his.

"I don't give a damn about how M'Fiyahs work," Kiarra slammed a pot into the dishwasher. "She gets a say. End of discussion. Now, back to the fucking spawn in fucking Yosemite."

"How is Merrill?" I asked politely, turning to Griffin. We liked Merrill—that was a certainty. Justin liked Merrill, too, and called Franklin Grandpa Frank. Franklin grinned every time Justin said those words.

Franklin was the one who, with Merrill, had arrived to help after Kiarra was injured at Justin's school. That day is still a bit foggy in my mind, but Franklin went right to work, cleaning house, cooking meals and doing laundry.

Merrill and I kept Kiarra entertained and off her feet for two weeks. That's all she'd give us. They'd gone home after three weeks, but I know Justin and Franklin keep in touch by e-mail and the occasional phone call.

That doesn't concern me at all. Justin will never have grandparents, and that is a shame. If he wants to think of Franklin as his grandfather, then he couldn't have made a better choice.

"How about Anna Kay?" Kiarra straightened after loading plates in the dishwasher.

"Anna Kay?" I stared for a moment at my wife before nodding.

That's who I thought Kiarra was when I first met her—Anna Kay Madden, a psychic detective in Port Aransas, Texas.

I didn't know at the time that the real Anna Kay was dead—killed by the enemy. Kiarra had taken her place to disguise herself while tracking spawn in the area; it was a good cover to utilize many of her talents.

With the help of Dragon, Lion, Joey, Merrill, Daniel Carey, several vampires and the Corpus Christi Pack, we'd successfully fended off an invasion of spawn, Ra'Ak and a nasty monster called a kapirus.

That success had also pulled Earth back from its status as *Not Worth Saving* in the eyes of our superiors. With the recent spawn attacks, it looked as if someone were trying to put it on the list again.

I knew Kiarra wouldn't let that happen, as long as there was breath in her body. It made me wonder at her pregnancy—she'd led the charge last time, but this—after three months, she wouldn't be able to fight and I didn't intend to let her; use of her power could kill the child. Thorsten's edict, too, had placed a crimp in any efforts we might make to defuse the situation before it had time to take hold and spread.

That concerned me—too much.

"Sweetheart, I'm really beginning to worry about those teens in the hospital. Will they keep them there, do you suppose, because they no longer speak?"

"Whether they keep them or let them go home is moot—either way they'll cause death and destruction." She sat on the barstool next to mine with a sigh. I rubbed her back gently and was surprised when she buried her head against my shoulder. "Adam, what are we going to do?" she moaned.

"I'm not sure," I kissed the top of her head. "We'll take this one day at a time."

～

Justin's Journal
Mack and I thought Thursday would be like any other day at

school, forty-three classmates' deaths and counselors combing the hallways and setting up appointments with students notwithstanding.

Boy, were we wrong.

Piles of flowers lined the fences surrounding the school, and the only blooms that weren't dying in the heat were the artificial kind. Those were slowly being bleached by the early September sun in Fresno. Notes, too, were stuck in the fence, along with stuffed animals and anything else someone thought to give to honor the students who'd died.

Mack was traumatized enough that he'd seen what he'd seen and felt guilty for surviving, but I can't begin to describe the nasty looks and nastier comments aimed at him for exactly the same thing—that he managed to survive while the others were either dead, in the hospital or missing.

I discovered that Randall Pierce, whose dad was still suspended from the police force, was fanning the flames with his Mongol horde of henchcreeps.

A school assembly was held at the end of the day to announce a memorial service at the first football game, which was slightly more than a week away. Mack and I took seats high up in the gym, and nobody sat near us. That didn't stop the talk and whispers, though, which Mack and I heard easily enough.

Valley High had shunned us without the usual, accompanying silence.

The Principal stepped to the podium on the gym floor and cleared his throat before announcing the memorial service and telling us that the football coaches had chosen replacement players for those who'd died or were in the hospital. I almost gagged when Randall Pierce and two of his friends joined the other players on the floor.

"I'm quitting the football team," I mumbled. Not only were they taking Randall Pierce, I was included in the backlash aimed at Mack, merely because we were friends. The friend part didn't bother me. What bothered me was that there was a backlash to begin with, and Randall was leading the charge.

"Dude, you can't quit," Mack whispered. "They don't have any decent players left as it is."

"Then they'll have to cancel the season," I said. "I'm not playing. If they can't get their heads on straight about any of this, I'll be damned if I fraternize with the enemy."

Mack followed me when I went to find Coach after assembly. "Justin, practice is in ten," he said.

"I'm not going," I told him. "I'm sorry, Coach, but I'm quitting the team." Coach's eyes slid to Mack, who stood right beside me, before clearing his throat. "I, uh, well," he shook his head. "The decision is yours, obviously."

"Yeah." I turned and stalked off, with Mack right behind me.

Coach knew Mack was being bullied and he chose to ignore it, like everybody else. "Well, screw all of 'em," I whispered as I headed toward the doors and the parking lot beyond.

Mack and I had ridden together in my car, so both of us fumed silently on the way home.

～

"Son, you don't have to explain it to me—I understand why you did it," Dad said when I told him about quitting the team. "Some things are more important than a game, and a lot of people fail to see that."

"My Friday nights just got freed up," I shrugged. "I may quit basketball, too, if things don't improve."

"I spoke with Mack's father," Dad said. "Mr. Walters is coming to work for the company as my construction manager when his job in Visalia is done. He knows everything about the business, and he says cabinetwork is spotty this year anyway."

"I didn't realize you were so busy," I said.

"It's not busier than usual, but I wanted to be closer to home. Son, your mother and I decided to go ahead and tell you now—you'll be getting a baby sister in seven or eight months."

"What?" Of all the possible things Dad might have said, that wasn't even on the list.

"It was a surprise for us, too," he said. "We didn't think it was possible."

"Uh, Dad," I said. He knew before I said it. How many people are creeped out when they learn their parents aren't too old for sex? I tried to squash that thought. They still looked young. Really young, actually. I thought it was because they were healthy and made healthy choices.

Dad knew exactly what I was thinking. "We've had the talk, son, and I assume you recall your lessons at school?"

"Yeah, but," I mumbled, ducking my head.

"It's natural. Do you remember me saying that?"

"Yeah. But everybody else treats it like a big secret. A big, dirty secret." I remembered Sex Ed in school, and how most of my classmates were laughing in an embarrassed sort of way after the classes.

"With the proper person, it shouldn't be that way. Between consenting adults, sex can be many things, including a way to relax and enjoy your partner and yourself. You show your feelings that way —it's a forum to drop all those taboos and leave them behind."

My voice hadn't broke in at least two years. It was breaking, now.

"Dad," I croaked. "Enough, okay?"

"All right, but think twice before believing anyone is too old to have sex," he said. "Talk to me in forty years, and we'll discuss this again."

"I sure hope not," I muttered and headed for the door.

Friday at school was worse than Thursday, due to the confrontation with Randal Pierce and his Mongol horde in the parking lot Friday afternoon.

Randall and three friends were blocking the way to my car. I guess if you have enough people, you think you're invincible. I didn't want a fight, and I sure didn't think Mack was in the mood after what happened a week earlier.

I have no idea how the cavalry knew to show up but they did, in the form of Uncle Lion and Uncle Dragon. Both of them—tall, muscled and frowning, looked as formidable as two Mount Everests as they walked up beside Mack and me. Together, we stared down Randall and his friends across a hot patch of bare concrete in the parking lot.

I could feel the rising heat washing over us in waves and couldn't help thinking of a few westerns I'd seen on TV.

"Who are they?" Randall demanded, nodding toward my uncles. The fact that his voice rose a pitch or two told me he was about to crap his pants. I would, too, if I were on the other side of the stare Uncle Dragon leveled on Randall and his friends.

"My uncles," I said as evenly as I could. Randall's buddies started backing away, which pissed Randall off.

"Time to go, man," one of them—Todd Mann—grabbed Randall's arm to pull him away.

Randall tried to shake him off, but that didn't work. Todd is taller and heavier than Randall, so he just got a better grip and held on. Randall, who didn't want to show weakness although his knees were probably knocking together, let Todd pull him away.

The minute they loaded into Randall's almost-new Chevy and drove away, I heard Mack release a sigh. "Thanks," he nodded to Uncle Dragon and Uncle Lion. "I'm not sure we could have come out of that alive."

"Someday, you may surprise yourself," Dragon patted Mack's shoulder. "This just wasn't the time or the place for that. If any of those used the brains they had, they'd never have accosted you here to begin with. Security cameras are focused on this parking lot."

"I'm glad you came," I said, shaking my head at the circumstances. "Somebody would have gotten hurt for sure."

"Want to ride home in the Jeep?" Lion asked. "We can get your car home later. The Jeep's running and cool inside."

"I'll vote for that," I nodded. "Mack?"

"Yeah." Anytime he could ride with my uncles, that was all right with him. He hero-worshipped both of them, especially Dragon.

We walked to the street in front of the school, where Mom's Jeep was parked and running. It was cool inside, and that came as a welcome relief—both from the situation we'd found ourselves in and the high temperature that sent heat waves lifting off the concrete.

Lion drove, Dragon rode shotgun and Mack and I sat in the back on the way home.

∾

Mom and Dad were in the kitchen when we got there, and Mom had made brownies. The kitchen smelled good.

"We'll be moving next week," Dad announced. "We bought a bigger place, Dragon's moving in and Lion and Marlianna will live in the guesthouse."

"We'll have a guesthouse?" I squeaked. "Wow." The fact that we were moving hadn't even settled into my brain, let alone having a guesthouse big enough for Uncle Lion and Aunt Marlianna.

"The guesthouse is bigger than this house," Dad said, and almost smiled.

"Should I pack?" I asked, still feeling stunned. "What about Mack?"

"Mack will have his own room, and he can stay whenever he wants," Mom said, moving forward to give Mack a hug. He ate that right up, I could tell.

"Your father is going to be my new construction manager," Dad told Mack when Mom moved away. "He says you can stay with us as much as you like, just check in with him every day. He'll be back from Visalia on Monday—he thinks if he stays there over the weekend, he can get the job done by then."

"Cool," Mack said. "What's for dinner?" he turned toward Mom.

"I thought we'd go out tonight, unless you have other plans?" Mom offered him a big smile. "Feel like Italian?"

"Steak and spaghetti?" Mack asked.

"If that's what you want."

"Yeah." Mack gave the idea an enthusiastic thumbs-up.

"Mack, do you think your sister would like to come?" Dad asked.

"We'll get your car on the way home from the restaurant," he turned to me, then.

"I'll call," Mack said and pulled out his cell phone.

Beth said she had a date, so she couldn't go. Mack just shrugged at the news after he hung up. "She's seeing somebody from Sacramento," he said. "It just feels weird, I guess, that she might marry him. I haven't met him, yet, but Dad has."

"Steak and lobster?" Dad quirked an eyebrow at Mack. "With spaghetti?"

"Oh, yeah," Mack nodded. Maybe it was my imagination, but his appetite appeared to be increasing, lately. Maybe it was stress eating, but what did I know?

"We'll leave in an hour—since it's Friday night, the wait will be less if we go early," Mom said.

"Suits me," Mack grinned.

CHAPTER 4

*J*ustin's *Journal*
There was a wait at the restaurant anyway—Giorgio's was always super busy on Friday and Saturday nights. What surprised me was who waited on us after we were seated—one of our high school classmates, Gina Allen.

"Gina?" I blinked at her when she showed up at our table in the standard Giorgio's uniform of red, monogrammed polo and black slacks.

"Hey, Justin, how are you?" she smiled at me.

Yeah, my heart rate went up several notches. Not only was Gina pretty, she was smart, too. She was in my English and calculus classes, but we seldom talked—I wasn't sure why, because she was so interesting. Truthfully, I was surprised she knew my name.

"I'm good," I said.

"Hi, Mack," Gina nodded to him, too. "Are you okay?"

"I'm fine," Mack dropped his eyes.

"Look, those kids at school are morons," Gina said. "Don't pay any attention to them."

"Easier said than done," Mack said, but at least he was looking at her, now.

"I know. Just remember they have little sympathy and fewer brain cells," she said. "What can I get you to drink?"

"I'll have a Dr. Pepper," Mack said immediately, and things went back to normal. Sort of.

Dinner was great; Mack ate a huge plate of food, Gina was the best waitress ever and at the end, she handed me a slip of paper with her phone number on it.

I had no idea how hard it would be to act cool instead of like an idiot when that happened. I thought Uncle Lion's grin might outshine the sun as we walked out the door.

I do know that Dad gave Gina a huge tip. She deserved it, after waiting on a table with eight people—Joey and Karzac were with us, too.

"You dog," Mack elbowed me before I could climb into the back seat of Dad's SUV. We'd been forced to bring both vehicles in order to haul all of us.

"Not a dog," I claimed, tapping my chest. "She made the move, man."

"You didn't push back. I've seen you push Marilee back a hundred times."

"Dude, I didn't want Marilee."

"That's fine. More for me," Mack sat back on his half of the seat, a smug expression on his face.

"Marilee is still in the hospital," Dad pointed out as he started the engine. "Things may never be the same with her, Mack."

"Yeah. I know." Mack sighed and stared out the window.

"Honey, don't worry. Things will work out," Mom swiveled in her seat to talk to Mack.

"I sure hope so," he mumbled.

We drove past the exit to get to our house and went even farther east. I hadn't bothered to ask Mom and Dad where the new house was, so I was about to find out.

Mack and I stared as a tall, arched metal gate swung open when Dad hit the button on a remote. We drove past and the gate closed behind us. The gate turned out to be the least amazing thing there—a three-story house waited, and it looked like something out of a picture book.

It had peaked roofs, two turrets, two chimneys and was built of pale, gray stone. There wasn't anything else like it in Fresno. "This is ours?" I breathed as I took it in—a four-car garage was attached to one end, and a connected circle drive bordered the front of the house.

"The guesthouse is behind this one," Mom explained as Dad stopped the car and Mack and I tumbled out of the back seat.

"Can we go in?" I asked. Yeah, I couldn't take my eyes off it. It was new, and yet it felt familiar in some way.

"We have keys and a security code," Dad grinned. I'd never seen him this excited about anything before, and he'd built a ton of houses and businesses.

Double doors led into the house, and a wide, tiled entryway lay beyond that, with a double staircase on both sides, going upward to the second floor.

"Dude," Mack mumbled in awe as we walked inside.

The rest of the house was just as amazing, from the huge kitchen to the dining room and the bedrooms upstairs. Dad had a bigger study and the family room was enormous. The biggest surprise lay at the back of the house—an indoor pool.

"I can't wait to get in that," Mack breathed. The water was clear; with the pool lights on, I could see the bottom of the pool. A filter hummed somewhere, keeping the water circulating and clean. I couldn't wait to get in it, either.

"Next week," Mom said. "We have a few things left to do, but it's ours."

"What's left?" I turned to Dad.

"Some electrical and plumbing, plus a few things on the third floor. It'll be done by Monday, I think, so we can move in sometime after that."

"Do we need to pack?" I asked.

"We have movers coming—it'll happen in one day," Mom said. "I hope it's done by the time you get home from school on Thursday. We'll drive over and make sure everything is where you want it."

"Are we going to the football game next Friday?" I asked. I had mixed feelings about it; Mom, Dad and Mack were usually there, but I'd always been on the field while they watched from the bleachers.

"I think we ought to go," Dad confirmed.

"Okay." I shrugged. "Mack?" I turned to him—he might not want to go, and I wouldn't blame him if he didn't. The thing was, they'd planned the memorial service before the game, and I felt I needed to pay my respects at least, by being there for my teammates who'd died.

"If you're going, then I'll go," Mack decided.

"Good. I wanted to get the move done before that," Dad said. "Ready to get your car and go home?"

"I guess. I really like this place," I added. "It feels like home." Dad ruffled my hair and headed toward the front door.

It shouldn't have been a surprise, but still it made me so angry I could have hit something. My Honda was covered in eggs and multiple colors of spray paint. "Dude, it looks like the Easter bunny dropped his load on it," Mack muttered.

It did. Dad held onto Mom as they surveyed the damage. The last insult? All four tires had been slashed. "We'll get it taken care of," Dad said and pulled out his cell to call a towing service.

"Three guesses who did this," Mack growled. Yeah, it was a good growl—one I wished I could make. Dad talked to the tow service about picking up my car, and told them it would have to be hauled—it couldn't be driven anywhere with four flat tires.

"Trouble?" Joey drove up in Mom's Jeep—he'd dropped the others off at the house, looked like.

"Take Kiarra and the boys home; I'll wait for the tow truck," Dad said.

"I'll let Justin drive; I'll stay with you," Joey suggested.

"Fine. Justin," Dad jerked his head toward the Jeep.

"Thanks," I nodded to Joey.

"It's time for another car," Joey shook his head at my Honda.

"I think I need a tank or the bat mobile," I muttered.

~

I understood completely why Dad didn't want the police involved in the vandalism of my car. After all, one of them almost killed Mack—indirectly, of course. Still, it was a crime and somebody ought to pay for the damage.

I had a good guess who should do that, but felt powerless to do anything about it. I'd probably get thrown in jail if I went after Randall Pierce, and there's no telling what would happen to me after that.

"Sometimes we have to let the small things go, to preserve the greater good," Mom said, sliding a plate of brownies toward Mack and me. We'd sat at the kitchen island after we got home, but I was mad and depressed at the same time.

"My car is a small thing?" I blinked at her.

"Honey, I know it's a big thing to you, but you have to remember what started all this. Those monsters may still be out there, just waiting to attack again. Randall Pierce is trying to get revenge against innocents, when he has no idea how to combat the guilty. His father, on the other hand, failed to do his job. That was intentional. Whatever punishment he gets, he will deserve. Does that make any sense?"

"You're saying he can't blame his dad, so he's taking it out on us?" Mack said.

"In a way. He lost friends, too, in that attack, so he's going after the only survivor, plus the survivor's best friend. He hasn't realized yet that doing so will not solve his problems. He only feels the need to lash out at something or someone. He hasn't thought it through well enough to discover how his emotions are manipulating him. He may end up in deep trouble over it, if I'm not mistaken."

"That's messed up," Mack grumped before reaching for a brownie.

"Want milk?" Mom asked.

"Yeah."

~

My car was towed to the new house and left there; I couldn't drive it anyway, so Dad said I could borrow Mom's Jeep. I hoped Randall wouldn't recognize it when I drove it to school on Monday.

The rest of the weekend was quiet—Mack and I played Joey's video game—it was in three-D and it felt real as we made our way past warriors and obstacles to get to the prize at the end.

It wasn't easy, either, but it was fun. Joey had done a great job, but he still insisted it had a few bugs and intended to work on those. I liked it and failed to understand what it was he wanted to tweak. Grudgingly, we stopped playing it Sunday afternoon to work on an English assignment.

Mack and I dreaded going to school on Monday, although his dad said he'd come to the house after school to see Mack—he was finishing the job in Visalia and should be back in town by then.

Mack stood for a few seconds outside Mom's Jeep in the school parking lot, steeling himself to walk into the building.

"Don't worry about it," I said. "Come on, we'll be late."

Mack followed me into the building, where things hadn't changed much. I ignored Randall, Todd and the others as we walked past them, until Randall asked about my car. My temper was white-hot when I whirled to face him.

No, I'd never threatened anyone before—hadn't really needed to. I stalked angrily toward Randall Pierce, who took one look at me before turning and almost running down the hall, the noise they made sounding as if a small herd of buffalo trampled their way across the tiles. Several people poked their heads out of classroom doors to see what was going on as a result.

"Wow," Mack breathed as he watched Randall and his friends scoot away. "Why didn't we know before how easy that might be?"

I had to shake myself to get rid of the rage that threatened to overcome me. "Man, that was close," I muttered. I doubted Mom and Dad would understand if I got expelled from school for fighting, even if the fight was with the jerk who'd vandalized my car.

"Justin?" Gina Allen came up beside me and took my arm. "We'll be late for class if you don't come now," she said and led me away. Mack wore a bemused expression as he followed us to English class.

~

Mack and I ended up having lunch with Gina—plus several others. I couldn't have predicted that—no way. Mack was just as surprised as I that he had supporters in school; we'd thought all of them were against us.

I guess not everybody swallowed what Randall Pierce was dishing; some of them thought for themselves. Tactfully, nobody asked Mack about what happened at Shaver Lake, and it would have upset him to talk about it anyway.

Someday, he might get to a point where he could, but he'd witnessed a lot of murders before running away. His recollection of running away wasn't exactly logical or sane-sounding on top of everything else, so I was grateful nobody asked.

"Look, it's Goober Griffin, and he's got an army. A really ugly, geeky army," Randall stopped by our table. Yes, he'd waited until we were in the cafeteria and watched closely by several teachers to do his digging. At least he was attacking me, now, instead of Mack.

The problem, of course, is that some of those teachers watching from the sidelines might agree with Randall and ignore his bullying. I hated to think that, but worried that it might be true.

"Look, it's Ratface Randall, whose grades will probably get him off the football team faster than he got on it," I snapped, standing up to defend us.

"I second that," Gina rose beside me.

"Yeah. Me, too," Mack stood. His words, however, definitely contained a growl. I'd have to figure out how he did that—it was becoming seriously cool.

The rest of our lunch table rose to show their solidarity. Randall, Todd and the other bullies decided to leave. For once, we actually outnumbered him and his horde.

"You know he'll try to get back at us—again," Mack said, shaking his head before sitting down to finish lunch.

"That's guaranteed," I sighed.

"Don't worry about him, he's a jerk," Gina said, taking her seat at my side.

"Oh, he's more than just a jerk," I said. "He's a stupid jerk. Feckless. Moronic. Ineffective. Unproductive. Injudicious."

"I'd add dense and slow to that list," Mack said. "He doesn't understand multi-syllable words, you know."

Gina laughed. It sounded amazing and was just what we needed to hear.

"If my mom's Jeep is in one piece after school, want a ride home?" I asked Gina as we headed toward calculus class after lunch.

"Yeah. I'll let Mom know she doesn't have to pick me up today." Her eyes shone and she giggled—she was excited to be riding with me. For the first time in my life, I considered that I might have a steady girlfriend.

Sure, I should have thought twice about stopping at the local hangout for a soda, but hey—it was expected if you had a girl. Besides, Mack was all for it—he wanted a Dr. Pepper.

We pulled in and placed our order at the kiosk. That went just fine. What didn't go fine was the four who waited at the end of the drive-through, blocking our way. Randall and his horde had eggs, paint and a baseball bat with them.

Honking did no good at all. They approached the front of Mom's Jeep. Eggs and paint flew while Randall took his frustrations out on the vehicle. Gina cowered in the front passenger seat as rocks joined the eggs and both headlights were broken by the bat. A hailstorm might have competed with the noise of the pelting rocks and eggs as they pounded the metal vehicle with regularity.

Honestly, I was so mad I could have taken all of them on, but the police showed up in less than thirty seconds. I have no idea how they got there that fast, but I was more than grateful to see Officers Barton and Francis get out of the first car to respond.

More police arrived as Randall and his friends began to back away. Did he think his dad's being a member of FPD, even a suspended one —would get him out of this mess?

Mack and I exchanged looks before opening our doors and getting out. Randall was resisting arrest, it looked like, while his friends stood quietly, waiting to be loaded into nearby police cruisers.

Gina got out, too, and came right to me. I wrapped my arms around her while we watched; Randall was shoved to the ground after he kicked Officer Barton. He was handcuffed after that and still fighting when he was pushed into the back of a patrol car by four officers.

"We had a call on this attack, plus the footage from the school parking lot," Officer Francis walked up to talk to us. "You all right? Do you need assistance?"

"I think we're okay," I said. "Gina?" I tilted her face up with a finger.

"Yeah. Just a little shaken," Gina's smile wavered.

"I'll need information on this vehicle to file an incident report," Francis said. "It'll help with the insurance company, too. Know any reason why he wanted to attack you?"

"Just a guess, and I have my license here," I pulled out my wallet. "Insurance stuff is in the car."

"I'll get it," Mack offered and went back to the Jeep.

"What's the guess?" Francis asked, writing the information from my license on a piece of paper.

"He's mad because some of his friends died and Mack didn't. He started out bullying him," I said. "Then his dad got suspended for putting Mack where he did at the jail. Since I was with Mack all the time at school, I got included in Randall's attack. He upped it when he egged and spray-painted my Honda, then slashed all four tires."

"Why wasn't that reported?" Barton joined the conversation.

"Because we weren't sure who we could trust on the police force," I said bluntly.

Barton cursed softly. "Son, this isn't an attack against you, your family or your friend, here. Emotions were running high when we were sent to question you, but there's proof now that Mack wasn't involved. He's lucky to be alive, the more I see of the evidence coming from Shaver Lake and Yosemite."

"I feel lucky that he's alive, too," I agreed.

"I hate that you feel you can't trust Fresno PD now," Francis said. "If you have any more problems, give me a call." He handed me a card. "Is your vehicle drivable or do you want me to have it towed?"

"I think I can drive it—it's still running and the tires aren't flat—Randall didn't have much time to do damage before you guys came. Thanks for that, by the way."

"It's our job," Barton said. "Randall knows better. I have no idea why he's blaming either of you for the circumstances in his life."

"I don't think he knows who to blame, so we became his targets by default," I shrugged. Gina blinked up at me, then hugged me tighter. I didn't mind one bit.

"I wish the kids at school didn't believe him," she said. "He said Mack was involved in that mess somehow, or he'd never have gotten away."

"That isn't true in any sense," Barton shook his head. "It's a miracle he was able to get away at all. Those kids don't have access to the forensics. What we're finding is evidence of animal attacks, just like he told us when we questioned him in the beginning. We should have paid closer attention."

All of us watched as Dad's SUV pulled up and parked nearby. He, Uncle Lion and Uncle Dragon climbed out and walked in our direction. "Officers?" Dad said the minute he reached our side.

"Randall Pierce and four of his friends attacked your wife's vehicle," Officer Francis said. "They've been arrested. I'm sorry we didn't arrive in time to keep them from doing so much damage."

"This is the second of our vehicles they've vandalized," Dad pointed out.

"I understand that. The school sent us the video footage from the school parking lot after an anonymous tip came in. We have the whole act of vandalism recorded," Barton said. "Would you like to come to the station and file a report?"

"Yes," Dad said. "Do you need anything else from my son?"

"No, Mr. Griffin."

"Justin, take Gina home. I'll catch up with you at the house. Mack's dad is waiting."

"Thanks, Dad," I breathed. I'd forgotten all about Mr. Walters meeting Mack at the house. "After I drop Gina off, we'll go straight home."

"Good. Officers," Dad nodded to Francis and Barton.

"It only took thirty seconds for the police to show up. I still can't figure that out," I said, dropping my backpack on the kitchen island with a sigh. Mom was waiting, and the first thing she asked was whether Mack and I were hurt. "We didn't even have time to think about getting out of the Jeep."

Mack's dad sat at the island, having a glass of tea and a sandwich when we got home, so he was content to let Mom ask questions.

"I heard from a sergeant at the police station. He said Randall told an acquaintance that he intended to follow you after school and cause trouble. The boy called the police. I'm grateful they took the call seriously," Mom said. "Sit down. Are you hungry?"

Mack and I had a sandwich, while Mack's dad had a second one. "Did they arrest that Pierce kid?" he finally asked Mack.

"Yeah. Had to handcuff him—he kicked one of the officers and fought with the others."

"Good. Maybe they'll hold him for a while so he can't cause more trouble."

"I hope he's not at school tomorrow," I blew out a breath. "It would be nice not to see him around every corner, and even better not to have to listen to his crap."

"Mack, why didn't you tell me this before?" Martin Walters turned dark eyes on Mack, who wriggled uncomfortably.

"Honey, I know you think it'll go away after a while, but sometimes a lot of damage can be done, even if it does go away. You can't count on that," Mom told Mack. "That's why we're here—to help you fight your battles when you need that help."

"I feel the same," I said. "I'd help fight your battles, too."

"Justin's helped me fight my battles lately," Mack admitted. "I couldn't go to school if he wasn't with me."

"You'd stand with me," I shrugged. It was true—we'd stood together most of our lives. Granted things had never been this bad before, but I didn't intend for anything to be different because of it.

"Is there any way he can see Dr. Karzac again?" Mr. Walters asked Mom quietly.

"I'll arrange it if that's what you and Mack want," she said.

"I'd appreciate it," Mr. Walters said.

"He's here now, let me see if he has time," Mom said before walking out of the kitchen and down the hall. She was back in five minutes with Uncle Karzac.

"Young one, would you like to settle on your bed while we talk?" Karzac asked.

"Yeah—I'm comfortable there," Mack agreed. I watched as Mack followed Karzac toward my bedroom.

"I can't say thank you enough for what you've done for him," Martin Walters told Mom.

"I'd do anything for that boy. He feels like one of mine, Martin, and I hope you're not offended by that."

"Offended? Hell no," Martin muttered. "I'm just glad he has such good friends."

"He has good *family*," Mom corrected. "I'd like to think we're part of it. Justin sees him as a brother—you know that already."

Talk turned to the new house after that, and I was glad. I hoped Uncle Karzac was helping Mack, too, because he wasn't talking much after the events of the afternoon. Getting attacked by Randall Pierce, even though he was only hitting the car with a bat, put both of us on edge.

"Honey, you haven't said what you want for your birthday," Mom interrupted my thoughts after a while.

"Oh. Man, I forgot all about it," I shook my head at her. "It doesn't matter," I said. "A cake and ice cream. Mack will like that for sure." My birthday was less than two weeks away and with everything else that had happened, it slipped my mind. I'd be eighteen. Mack had already turned eighteen the first week of August, so for just a few weeks, he was a year older than I was.

This year, he'd been so preoccupied with the attack and everything else that followed, he'd forgotten to tease me about it.

~

Mack talked to Karzac for more than an hour, then took a nap afterward. He woke up around six-thirty, just in time for dinner. Mom made chicken and dumplings, another favorite meal for both of us.

Mack's dad liked it, too, I could tell. He'd stayed to eat with us because Beth had classes and would grab something on campus to eat. He and Dad talked during the meal about the construction manager job with Dad's company. I could tell Mr. Walters was going to do just fine.

~

"You going to the football game Friday?" I asked Gina when we walked to class together the next morning.

"No. I have to work," she said. "I'm saving for college. I have a scholarship lined up, but it doesn't pay for everything."

"Understood," I nodded.

"I don't have to work Sunday night," she smiled shyly.

"How about dinner and a movie?" I asked.

"That sounds great."

"Pick you up at six?"

"Yeah."

I probably wore the goofiest grin ever as we walked down the hall, but it was worth every second of potential embarrassment. *I had a girlfriend and I was going on a date.*

The only thing that came close to making me that happy was this; Mack and I learned that Randall Pierce and all four of his friends were suspended from school for two weeks for what they'd done to my car in the school parking lot.

For as much as my Honda had suffered, it turned out to be for a good cause. Gina told us the news at lunch, and I watched as Mack shifted in his seat. I could almost see the weight dropping off his shoulders, and only realized then what the bullying had cost him.

My thought about the whole things was that Randall had to be the worst prick ever to pick on Mack when he'd already been traumatized enough.

More news came on Thursday—the six who'd been hospitalized after the attack would make a brief appearance at the memorial service before the game. So far, they still hadn't spoken, but were responding to directions and commands well enough that their doctors thought it safe for them to go out with their families for a while.

Mom had a strange look on her face, though, when Mack and I told her after school.

"This isn't good," she shook her head. "Look, why don't you order pizza for dinner. I need to find your father and your uncles."

Adam's Journal

"The timing is close enough—what do you suggest we do if they turn at the memorial service?" Kiarra asked. Joey, Dragon, Lion and Karzac had joined us for an emergency meeting in my study. Justin and Mack were waiting for a pizza delivery and had no idea how much danger the school could be in.

"Whose bright idea was it to let them attend the memorial anyway?" Joey scoffed. "That's lunacy."

"It was lunacy to arrest young Mack," Dragon pointed out. "So far, I have failed to detect an overabundance of clear and prudent judgment. These humans have short memories and shorter attention spans. Just because they haven't seen further evidence of spawn, they believe the problem eliminated. Nothing is farther from the truth."

"We're so used to seeing this on other worlds," Kiarra said. "And the attacks are never this soon after a previous infestation. It has only been twenty years for us since the events in Corpus Christi."

"Things are changing," Pheligar appeared. "I dislike what may happen at this confrontational sporting event. Therefore, I shall be there in disguise, in case shielding is needed to keep your efforts from prying eyes."

"Thank goodness," Kiarra's shoulders sagged in relief.

"Do not become overly stressed," Pheligar rubbed her shoulders gently. "While your pregnancy is not evident at this time, it is never good to allow anxiety to rule your life while in this condition."

I lifted an eyebrow in curiosity when a large blue hand wandered to Kiarra's belly, where he stroked and comforted her body carefully. "The child is growing nicely," he said softly. "We will make sure that continues."

I'd never seen the Larentii show this much affection to anyone, and it surprised me. Where was it coming from? Was he so angry with Thorsten that he was allowing other emotions to surface?

Before I joined the Saa Thalarr, I would have been eaten alive with jealousy if someone else touched my wife. Once you become a member of that tiny, exclusive race, any jealousy you have is removed. As long as it's with Kiarra's permission, it doesn't bother me. The same goes for me, but I have no desires in that direction.

I'd found what I wanted.

The move Thursday happened with help from Dragon, Lion and Pheligar. Everything we needed at the new house was transported with power while Kiarra and I made suggestions as to placement.

Most of the furniture wasn't making the move—I wanted to redecorate, so Kiarra let me know what she wanted and I arranged for it to arrive at the proper time.

Clothing was sent over and landed in closets and inside drawers. The pantry and garage were emptied. I was satisfied with all of it when it was finished, and draped my arms about my wife while we surveyed the new house. For me, this was home—the one from my early days with my family.

To Kiarra, she was stepping into the world I'd known so long ago.

"I hope you like it," I said, leaning down to kiss her.

"I do. I know Justin likes it, too. That's all that matters."

Justin's Journal

The new house waited Thursday after school, and Mack and I wandered through it when we arrived. His bedroom was already furnished, and he liked the new king-sized bed Mom and Dad bought for him.

Joey donated a laptop for Mack to do his assignments, and he was happy with that. The pool waited, too, and we got to swim before dinner. The only thing that put a damper on all of it was the game and memorial service the following day.

On Friday, the school was decorated as it usually was for the first football game of the season, but a somber mood stalked the halls behind squeaking athletic shoes and student conversations.

A huge poster hung in front of the trophy case, depicting the students who'd died in the attack. Room was left at the bottom for other students to offer their condolences and it was already covered with words.

Mack wouldn't even approach the poster, as so many others were doing. He'd watched those people die, in horrible ways. Gina linked her arms with ours and led us away from it toward English class.

At least Dad managed to get the headlights fixed on Mom's Jeep before we'd had to drive back to school, but the dents and dings from the baseball bat and rocks remained as evidence. We found a crowd around the Jeep when school let out.

At least they politely got out of the way when we arrived and climbed in to drive home.

"This sucks," Mack mumbled as we drove through the gate and onto the street outside the school.

"Still planning to come with me tonight?" I asked.

"Yeah. I'll come. I'm just glad your dad will be driving us."

"Me, too," I said. "Gina, do you have a ride to work tonight?"

"Mom takes me," she shrugged. "I'll be thinking about you tonight."

"Thanks."

Early evening that Friday was hot, and I hoped it would let up for the memorial service and the game afterward.

"Dress light," Mom poked her head inside my new bedroom.

"On it," I said. I had a nice pair of cargo shorts and a white polo laid out on the bed. Somehow, I felt weird, like the air and rising heat in Fresno was going to stifle all of us when we got there, but that thought was shoved aside.

I think Mack was just hoping to get through the night without breaking down.

We rode to the football field in Dad's SUV in near silence—Mack and I stared out our windows in the back seat, seeing the roads and traffic without registering any of it. I couldn't explain how I felt—like something was about to happen and I had no idea what it was or how to stop it.

"We're here," Dad said, pulling into a parking spot and shutting off the engine. "If you two want to sit higher up on the bleachers, you can. Your mother and I will sit farther down."

"We'll sit with you," Mack said before I could answer Dad.

"Good enough," Mom put an arm around Mack's shoulders.

Surprisingly, a comfortable breeze blew through the stadium, which was unusual for the middle of September. We found seats right behind the railing on the first row, by the goal line. I have no idea why Dad chose that spot, but he evidently had some purpose in mind.

I didn't argue. The air was cool enough to keep us comfortable, and I wasn't about to question that. Most of the crowd had already arrived, so it was less than ten minutes before the memorial service began.

The football team stood with their helmets off on the sidelines as six students, Marilee the tallest of them, were led toward special seats on the field. The band was nearby, as were many teachers, the Principal and Vice-Principal.

The school board was also sitting on the field, waiting for the state Superintendent to begin the short service.

She never got past the first few words of her speech before Marilee and the five others stood, their skin dripped and split off them and the ugliest, nastiest creatures fell on anybody close enough to get caught.

CHAPTER 5

*J*ustin's Journal
Pandemonium is the best word I can find to describe what happened.

As it turned out, there weren't just six who became monsters. Others were mixed in the crowd and they did the same thing Marilee did. So many things happened at once—so many deaths—that I can't sufficiently describe the carnage that ensued.

Instead of running toward an exit like everybody else, Dad pulled Mom against him and leapt over the railing to the football field below. I blinked at Mack for only a nanosecond—he was growling and his eyes were going strange.

"Come on, dude, let's go with Dad," I shouted at him. He let me grab his arm and drag him over the rail, where we dropped onto the field and struggled past fleeing tuba players to get to my parents.

By the time we got there, things had certainly changed.

Dad had claws at least a foot long on his hands, and he was using them to cut heads off a swarm of creatures attempting to get to him.

Mom held a glowing sword in her hand—I had no idea where that came from—and she was doing the same thing.

Mack?

He no longer stood beside me. A tall, almost shoulder-high black wolf had taken his place. I watched in stunned surprise as the wolf growled before leaping at one of the creatures that rushed Mom.

Okay, that pissed me off. Those things were after Mom and Dad? While I had no explanation for that, it made me madder than I'd ever been.

More creatures were coming, too, and I was terrified they'd hurt Mom. She was pregnant, after all, and that hit me like a ton of cinder blocks.

I went after the monsters, then, shouting at them to leave her alone.

Except that wasn't what came from my mouth. To my ears, it sounded like a roar, and a really loud roar on top of that.

There had to be at least two hundred creatures there. The wolf took down his share. Dad killed many of them while Mom's blade flew faster than the eye could follow. I had claws similar to Dad's, but where he remained human, I saw my claws at the end of the most unusual appendages ever.

Folded wings were held tightly beneath what I considered my elbows, while I clawed, bit and spit out chunks of creatures before ripping heads from their bodies. Beheading was the best way to kill them, I learned, but I used my tail to protect my back.

It whipped back and forth in angry, jerking motions, knocking creatures toward Dad, Mom and the wolf. I didn't have time to question anything—I only had time to protect my family and hope the other people got away.

People screamed, sirens screeched; someone from the press box announcer's booth yelled that the southern entrance was the best way to escape. Dad shouted at Mack and me, but his voice was lost in the confusion.

I kept fighting—I didn't know what else to do—until there were two monsters left. Dad killed one of them while the last creature thought to attack Mom from behind. I lunged, swatting him with my tail toward Dad, who neatly beheaded him as he sailed through the air. That creature, like all the others, exploded in an angry, forceful blast of black sand.

The ensuing silence was more frightening than the noise during the attacks. I worked to catch my breath, my lungs sounding like a bellows as I panted on the fifty-yard line. The wolf came to sit before me, his golden eyes blinking at me in curiosity as I struggled to even my breathing.

"Justin?" Mom's blade disappeared in her hand—to where, I had no idea. She approached me slowly, her hand held out in a calming gesture.

"He doesn't know how to turn back," Dad said, walking toward Mom. "Young Mack, are you all right?" He dropped a hand on the wolf's head.

The wolf turned toward Dad and whined.

"Just think of being human again," Dad said gently. The wolf disappeared and Mack reappeared—completely naked. Mom covered him up with a blanket that magically appeared in her hands.

"Justin? Son?" Dad came toward me. I didn't know what to do, and I suppose my brain was too addled to think clearly. I had no idea what I was and was only then beginning to feel like a monster myself.

"You are no monster," a very tall, blue man appeared before me. "You will stop thinking such erroneous thoughts immediately. Now, I will help this time, but next time, you must do this on your own."

He held out a hand and I dropped to the ground. My arms were back to normal, at least—because I hugged myself while my breaths remained ragged and uneven.

I was still dressed, which came as a surprise.

What was I?

What was Mack?

For that matter, what were Mom and Dad?

"This is not the time to ponder those questions," the blue man continued. I figured that he was at least eight or nine feet tall. "You must come with me before the authorities arrive and attempt to arrest you."

One minute, I stood on the grass of the football field, surrounded by family and my best friend, who'd just become strangers. The next, I knelt beside the indoor pool at the new house.

Without blinking, the blue man held up a hand and Mack was dressed again, the same as he was before the attack. "I suggest watching the local news. I shielded your participation in the event," he said. "However, I did not disrupt the broadcast of the turnings or of those that came from the seats to assault attendees. It is time these humans knew what was attacking them."

He disappeared, leaving me staring after him in shock.

Joey, Karzac, Uncle Lion and Uncle Dragon were all there when we had our meeting. Joey brought boxes of pizza. Somehow, he knew Mack and I would be starving. The last person to arrive, oddly enough, was Mack's dad.

"I'm proud of you, Son," Martin Walters ruffled Mack's dark hair. "Most werewolves don't acquit themselves so brilliantly on their first two turns."

"What?" Mack stared at his dad. I'll admit, I was staring, too.

A werewolf? Mack was a werewolf? How did that happen? Was he bitten?

"Werewolves are born, not bitten," Joey patted my arm. "Mr. Walters is the Fresno Packmaster. They don't tell the young ones until it's time—it's easier to fit in with humans that way."

"But Beth," I floundered. Beth was Mack's sister. She had a boyfriend. How did that work?

"Beth is also a werewolf, and as female werewolves are rather rare, she is promised to the Sacramento Second. At least they like each other," Mr. Walters sighed.

"Dude?" I turned to Mack. "Is this how you got away?" It was dawning on me, then, just what it all meant and how he'd survived. It also accounted for his memories of running on all fours to get away. He'd done exactly that.

"It is," Mr. Walters confirmed. "I believe he may have killed one or two of those monsters at Shaver Lake, but the wolf knows when he's outnumbered. He ran; that saved his life. I've been waiting for signs of the turning since then. It happened tonight. I'm glad he was with you and your parents. Of all the people who'd understand," Mr. Walters said.

"But," I began.

"We weren't sure about you, Son," Dad said. "You don't realize what you are, either, because you couldn't see yourself. You impressed Pheligar—he spoke to you directly."

"But," I repeated.

"Justin, we had no idea what you'd be, or whether we could be certain that you'd turn. You're a Wyvern, honey. A red-gold Wyvern. I wish you'd seen yourself. You were amazing against those spawn." Mom gave me a tired smile.

"Can you tell us now what those—spawn things—are?" I croaked. Somebody had kept those things secret. "Why were you fighting them? Have you seen them before?"

Dad smiled at Mom and patted her hand.

"It's what we are and what we do—we fight spawn and the ones that make spawn," he said. "Living in Fresno and running a business is just a cover."

"Joey, am I dreaming after a really bad sci-fi movie?" I turned in his direction.

"Nope." He grinned at me. "I'm their healer." He pointed toward Mom and Dad. "I don't have much to do, usually, because they're good at what they do and don't get injured much. That leaves me time to do all the computer work for your Dad and design video games on the side."

"What about Uncle Lion and Uncle Dragon?" I asked.

"Tomorrow, after we recover from tonight, we'll take you to the beach house we talk about sometimes, and show you how your uncles fit into the equation," Dad said. "Let's watch the news as Pheligar requested. I'm sure we'll see something unexpected."

We did.

Vice Principal Jameson was attacked by the monster that used to be Marilee Short. I almost gagged when that thing bit out his throat and gobbled up the flesh before devouring his arms and part of his chest. Others died in the attack, too, but that was the one shown in detail on the news.

"Dude, that's just sick," Mack huffed beside me. Yeah, he'd already seen it before, just not from Marilee.

"That thing isn't her," Dad said, as if he'd read my mind. "She died the moment one of those creatures bit her. It takes thirty seconds for the saliva to infect and destroy a human after the bite."

"Are you going to talk about your claws, Dad?" I turned toward him and ignored the carnage being shown on the eleven o'clock news.

"Tomorrow. You'll hear it from me—and your mother —tomorrow."

I turned back to the television then, in time to see the screen go fuzzy and hear the journalist announce that all cameras, including cell phone cameras and video cameras, stopped working at the same time.

Eyewitness accounts were also spotty after that. It made me wonder about the blue man and how he managed to do all that.

Adam's Journal

Pheligar appeared in our bedroom as Kiarra and I were preparing for bed. He was exhausted, although his eyes held a bit of anger. "I had a lengthy meeting with Thorsten," he explained, holding up a large, blue hand. "Thorsten claims you went looking for those spawn tonight, instead of reacting as he asked. We must all tread carefully from now on. He made threats." Pheligar shook his head, as if he were confused.

"What the hell is going on?" Kiarra demanded.

"I fear that if you react to further attacks by spawn, there may be consequences. I fail to understand this, as that is why your race was created in the beginning. I know not what has precipitated this reaction."

"What are we supposed to do, then? Let them take over?" I snapped.

"Let me think on this," Pheligar sighed. "Perhaps there is a solution. We will discuss this again very soon."

He disappeared, leaving us in confusion.

～

Justin's Journal

"Did you sleep last night?" Mack asked as he shuffled into the kitchen the following morning. Neither he nor I usually got up before seven-thirty on any Saturday morning. Today, we were both up at six.

"Nah. Too much to think about." He scooted onto the barstool beside mine and stared at the refrigerator opposite the island.

"Want cereal?" I asked.

"Yeah. Dad says that now the wolf has made his presence known, I'll be hungry because I'll be growing."

"Seriously?" I turned to blink at him.

"That's what he says. We talked for a long time last night after you went to bed. I saw his wolf. Man, he's huge."

"You were no slouch," I pointed out and stood to walk toward the pantry. I pulled out a box of cereal, then got milk from the fridge and set it on the island before grabbing spoons and two large bowls from the cabinet.

Mack and I were crunching away on crispy rice squares when Mom and Dad walked into the kitchen.

"How are my boys?" Mom asked, giving us both a hug.

"Better now," Mack offered her a grin.

"Good." She ruffled his hair affectionately before heading toward the fridge and the coffeemaker.

"Dad, are you British? Is that why you always drink tea instead of coffee?" I asked.

"I am. I was born in the mid-eighteenth century," he said. "This house was built from the same plans used to build my family home back then—on a smaller scale."

"What?" Mack stared at Dad.

"I'll tell you soon enough. Your father said you could come with us to the beach house for the weekend. He has Pack business to attend to this weekend anyway. He wants his wolves to go hunting for spawn, since our hands are tied on that, at the moment. The Sacramento Pack may join the Fresno Pack, to help track these things."

"Seriously? They can do that?" I said.

"Werewolves are the best trackers," Mom said. "A friend of ours, Daniel Carey, is coming from Corpus Christi to help out. He has plenty of experience tracking spawn, so he'll work with Martin and Thomas Williams on this. We set it up last night, after everyone else was in bed." I could tell there was more to the story, but didn't ask. If I needed to know, she'd tell me.

"So *we* can't track them?" I asked Mom.

"Your dad, your uncles and I are prevented at the moment," she said. I could tell she wasn't happy about that, either. "We can't hunt them; we may only be able to react if they attack us directly. As you probably know, that is far too little and much too late."

At least a hundred questions circled my brain, most of them dealing with who would prevent the hunting of those monsters—and why. "Where are they from?" Mack sputtered.

"They can be from anywhere. As you've probably guessed, the spawn need a host to perpetuate their race. Humans are especially susceptible. They incubate in the host for two weeks or so, then slough off the outer skin like a chrysalis, to become a newly-hatched spawn, hungry and prepared to attack any food source available," Dad said. "They are supernatural creatures and generally, humans are too slow to combat them with success. It takes another supernatural creature to fight them."

"I saw you take their heads, so that's what I did, too," I said. "Is that the only way to kill them?"

"Yes. Guns don't work. You'd have to have a really big bomb that covered a lot of area to make that an effective option, and the side effects of that sort of attack are just too risky. They move too fast, otherwise. You can toss a grenade at them and they'll outrun the blast.

65

Same thing with rockets, and weapons such as that. Only a few weapons exist that will take them out, and those haven't been created yet on this world."

"Damn," Mack muttered.

"What do you mean, this world?" I whispered.

"Son, Earth is only one of many and not very advanced compared to others," Dad said. "Get your clothes on; we'll show you what we mean."

"I remember this, now," I said as Mack and I took in the huge space that was part kitchen, part dining room. On one side was a wall of glass at least thirty feet tall, and beyond that, far below the house, was an ocean with tall, sharply spiked rocks standing in the water. I watched in fascination as waves boomed and broke against those rocks.

"I thought this was in Australia," Mack whispered.

"Me, too," I whispered back.

"This is a private planet. It belongs to your mother," Dad said, settling a hand on my shoulder. "She brought me here shortly after we met."

"You own a planet?" I turned to face Mom.

"I own three," she said and shrugged, like it was no big deal.

"You own three?" Dad asked. "You never told me that."

"You never asked," she replied. "They have to be uninhabited, and I had to do something worthy of the award."

"Which ones, pray tell?" Dad sounded confused and angry at the same time. I moved away from him. When he's mad, I prefer to be as far away as possible. Mom, on the other hand, never backs away.

"One doesn't have a name, and it's pretty dead. All I get from it is the minerals, gems and precious metals. The other is Tiralia."

"What the holy fuck?"

Dad never swears—at least when I can hear it. He was swearing, now.

"What does that mean? What's Tiralia?" Mack mumbled beside me.

"Tiralian crystal," Dad growled. "The most precious and expensive gem in the known universes. That's what." He stalked toward Mom. Mack and I backed up a second time.

That's when Joey appeared from nowhere. "Time to go to the beach," he announced and pulled Mack and me away with the same traveling trick that Mom and Dad used.

Adam's Journal

"I own the planet," she shrugged and walked away from me.

"You have that much money at your disposal?" I growled.

"It's my savings account," she said. "You haven't told me about all the accounts you have everywhere, after all."

"Is that what this is about? Full disclosure?"

"No, it just never came up and you never asked. I don't care about your money. I don't care much about my money. I own Tiralia. End of statement. If you want Tiralian crystal cufflinks, I can oblige that request."

I could see she was upset. I couldn't stop myself from pushing anyway. "I want Tiralian crystal cufflinks, cut and spelled by Grey House," I snapped.

"Will that get you off my case?"

"Mostly."

"I'll have them ready by your birthday in October."

"Good."

"Will you stop being an insufferable asshole, now?"

"I'm an insufferable asshole?" I pointed to my chest in self-defense.

"That's what I'm seeing from my perspective."

"I'll have a record of all my accounts, profit and loss statements and anything else you might want delivered to you on Monday," I huffed. "Is there anything else you haven't told me in the twenty years we've been together?"

"Plenty," she shrugged.

"Fuck," I muttered and stalked away.

Pheligar found me pacing the deck outside the house ten minutes later. "There are some things she finds it difficult to tell anyone," he said, forming a chair with power and pointing me toward it.

"Sure, tell me that now," I snapped.

"She earned Tiralia after she saved it, when it was classified as not worth saving. Unfortunately, the remaining population killed itself anyway, so the planet came to her afterward. It still has a cloud of poison about it, so one has to be heavily shielded in order to visit it. Tiralia's atmosphere would be toxic to most humanoids, no matter how well they believe their suits will protect them."

"She goes there?" I stood again. Pheligar forced me back onto the chair.

"She knows where all the veins of crystal are, and *Pulls* what she needs or wants away."

"All right," I muttered and scrubbed my face with both hands, as if that would scour away the image of my wife going into a known poisonous environment. Tiralia had killed itself with chemical warfare; that fact was widely accepted. Nobody attempted a landing there—not if they wanted to live.

"The crystal and the profits from it, instigated the war to begin with, if you'll recall," Pheligar pointed out.

"I remember."

"She hasn't told you how old she is," he said, forming a second, much larger chair and sitting beside me.

"No," I said. "She hasn't. I didn't ask, because it's custom not to ask another vampire his age. It doesn't matter to me."

"She's nearly fifteen thousand years old," he said. "Time was bent to collect her, then bent again to deliver her to the proper place. She has existed for nearly one hundred fifty of your Earth centuries."

I choked and coughed, until Pheligar put his hand on me to relieve the onset.

"If she reveals her past to you, I hope it is with more acceptance than what you displayed earlier," he said. "I regret not picking her up myself, all those years ago. I sent Lion and Dragon, instead. It is one of their favorite recollections. Perhaps you should ask them to tell it, sometime."

"I overreacted, didn't I?"

"Yes. And now she is upset—over nothing. She bears your daughter. Does that mean nothing to you?"

"I don't know why I picked the fight," I admitted.

"You are frustrated. She is frustrated—with the way things are and an unplanned pregnancy. No, do not think for a moment she doesn't want your daughter," he reached out and placed a hand on my arm. "She does. As she stated before, the timing is inconvenient."

"There's something you're not saying," I said.

"I worry that this is an arranged pregnancy," Pheligar sighed. I'd never seen him so frustrated before.

"Arranged? By whom?" I was ready to stand and begin pacing again. The Larentii held me down.

"I worry about many things," he said. "Perhaps they are baseless. Perhaps not."

Yes, I worried, too, about the timing. This—this just seemed wrong, somehow. All of it, from being forbidden to actively combat spawn to this.

Justin's early turning worried me, too. "I thought you had a power ward on Justin to prevent his turning—if it were possible," I said.

"I did. I removed it yesterday. Soon, too, I wish to discuss things with you and Kiarra, which will involve your son. I should wait until his birthday for that discussion."

"You're thinking of putting him into this fight, aren't you?"

"I see few ways around it. He does not belong to the Saa Thalarr, but he has the ability to destroy spawn. You saw it yourself last night. He and the werewolf child, too. Perhaps there is a higher hand in this, gently unraveling the ties Thorsten has placed upon you."

"I hope we're shielded right now," I muttered.

"We are. I would never say that outside the strongest shield any Larentii might place upon a conversation."

"Thank you," I sighed. "I worry for the race as a whole, if spawn and their makers are allowed to run amok throughout the universes and all we're allowed to do is react against a direct attack, instead of being proactive."

"As do I," he replied. "I will do all within my power to see that the race survives. You should go to Kiarra, now, to make your best apology. She does not feel well."

"Fuck." I was out of my chair like a shot and shouting Kiarra's name the moment I folded into the house.

After pulling her away from the toilet with Pheligar's help, we settled her onto the bed with a cold compress on her forehead. She'd never been this ill with Justin; Joey said so.

This child was different, in so many ways. "I don't feel good," Kiarra mumbled as I stroked hair away from her face. "Adam, somebody needs to get Justin and Mack and explain things to them."

"I'll get Lion and Dragon to do it," I murmured. "You need rest, my heart. I'll stay with you."

"Joey can take care of me," she said. "Justin needs his father right now."

"I will stay," Pheligar said. "I will ensure that the sickness does not return."

I folded to the beach to catch up with Justin and Mack—at least Joey had called Bearcat to stay with them until I could get there.

Joey's Journal

Shortly after Adam left to find Justin and Mack, I watched in shock as Pheligar lifted Kiarra and held her like a baby in his arms. What surprised me next was the sound he made. It was a beautiful humming noise, so restful that my eyes closed and I fell asleep in seconds.

~

Justin's Journal

"Dad?" I said the minute he appeared beside me. Mack was busy tossing bits of shell into the water, after he carefully examined each piece. Few of them resembled what we'd find on any of Earth's beaches.

"Your mother isn't feeling well—morning sickness," I explained. "I wish she'd tell me these things before letting me pick a fight with her."

"That sort of upsets me," I admitted.

"I know. Nobody is going to hurt you, Son. Not your mother or me, anyway. I think I send out vibes when I'm angry, and you pick up on them. That's my fault. There's no way I'd hurt your mother, either. You'll understand, someday, that people have disagreements, sometimes over things that don't mean anything."

"Okay." I hung my head. "It just upset me to see Mom so upset," I added.

"I know." He pulled me into a hug. "This is supposed to be a good day for you. I'm sorry for ruining it so far."

"We have lots of questions," I mumbled against Dad's shoulder.

"I know." He let me pull away.

"First," I said, doing my best to look Dad in the eye, "What the heck are we?"

"Your mother and I belong to the Saa Thalarr. We're supposed to be sterile. That makes you a miracle," he said. "And your baby sister is a miracle, too."

"Seriously?" Mack had come to stand beside me—he was just as curious as I was. "You and Mrs. G are gonna be parents again?"

"Yes," Dad nodded. "But that means several things, the most important of which is this—your mother can't take her other shape or use much of her power past three months, or it could harm the baby.

71

Therefore, she will not be fighting these creatures after another month has passed."

I could tell Dad didn't like the fact that she was fighting them, now. I let that go.

"The next thing," Dad said, "is that we're immortal, unless the enemy finds a way to kill us."

"What?" I'll admit, I was surprised. As in *I almost came out of my socks* surprised.

"Dad told me werewolves live to be two hundred or so, unless they get killed," Mack grumbled beside me. "Immortal? Wow, dude." He elbowed me.

"What's Mom's other shape?" I asked.

"I'll let her show you. Here's mine." He changed.

Boy, did he change.

A huge, black Gryphon stood before us, looking fierce even before he flapped his wings and his eagle head screamed a battle cry. Mack cringed beside me, it was so loud.

In a split second, Dad was back. "Holy crap," I shook my head.

"Here comes your Uncle Dragon," Dad nodded toward the ocean behind us. Mack and I turned. Yeah, Dad is impressive, but there's nothing like your first sight of the biggest red dragon ever, flying low over the water.

He landed nearby and breathed fire before he turned. Mack dropped to his knees in hero-worship. If he'd idolized Dragon before, it was just multiplied by ten, at least. "Meet the former Falchani Dragon Warlord," Dad said beside us.

"Falchani?"

"Falchan is a world hundreds of light-years from your own, young werewolf," Dragon said and offered a grin after turning back to himself. "Lion is coming."

He did come, arriving in his other form, a huge, black lion. He roared for us and that's all it took.

"So Aunt Wolf and Aunt Tiger and Uncle Lynx?" I asked.

"Are named after what they are," Dad said. "Your mother is the only one who didn't choose her animal name for herself, at least in some way. I chose Griffin as my last name instead of the first, for obvious reasons."

"Yeah. I can see that," I agreed. "The school might have a problem if I listed my dad's name as Griffin, one name only."

Mack snickered.

"Bearcat?" I asked. I'd only met him when Joey introduced him on the beach. He'd wandered farther down, giving Dad and my uncles time to talk.

"Is a shapeshifter, and was before he came to the Saa Thalarr as a healer," Dad said.

"Wow," I said. "That's sort of awesome."

"It is," Bearcat suddenly appeared beside us. "I have great hearing, thanks to what I am," he added. "It's called folding space, by the way. You may be able to do it yourself, someday."

"It's really folding space?" Mack blinked at Bearcat.

"Yes," he shrugged.

"Anybody hungry?" Joey appeared beside Bearcat. "I am."

"Pheligar is with Kiarra?" Dad asked.

"He said to feed the young ones; he has things under control," Joey said. "So I thought spaghetti might be a good idea."

"I'll help cook," Uncle Lion offered.

"Good," Joey's shoulders sagged in relief. "I was hoping somebody would volunteer. I make good garlic cheese bread, but my sauce isn't the best."

"Let's go," Lion grinned and Mack and I were transported back to the beach house.

Mom slept most of the afternoon, and I saw what Joey could do when she woke up feeling nauseated. He had her feeling better and eating in just a few minutes. We didn't get to enjoy the whole day like I thought we would, though.

Spawn attacked another cabin at Shaver Lake, and Uncle Dragon transported us straight there in a blink.

CHAPTER 6

*S*pawn ran from the carnage the minute we arrived, but it was too late to save anybody. Half-eaten bodies were strewn everywhere, but the birthday cake? It sat pristine and untouched atop a white tablecloth that someone had spread over a picnic table.

The worst part?

The birthday party was for kids. They couldn't have been more than eight or nine, and most of them had been devoured. Only bits and pieces remained, while the adults were dismembered and only partially eaten.

I felt sick—and then I felt angry. Strange, too, that all those emotions ran through me in three blinks. "Son, let's go after them," Dad tapped my shoulder.

"Yeah," I nodded. I wanted to take something apart right then, and the ugly, heartless creatures that did this? They were my chosen targets.

"I want to," Mack growled beside me. I knew his wolf was only waiting for a target after seeing what was left behind following a spawn feeding frenzy.

"Change now," Dad nodded to both of us. "I'll fold us in front of them. Dragon, Lion and your mother are already chasing them."

I took one more look at the bloody carnage surrounding the cabin before allowing my anger to force the Wyvern into existence. Mack was out of his clothes and turned to werewolf almost as fast. Dad folded space with both of us.

There! I heard Dad's voice inside my head. Jerking my snout in the direction he'd indicated, I saw them.

They were running straight at us. It didn't take a genius to figure out why after a few seconds—Uncle Dragon's Dragon, Uncle Lion's Lion and—wow. All I could think was *wow*. A unicorn, nine feet tall at the shoulder and shining white in the late afternoon light of a California day, raced between Dragon and Lion.

That's your mother, Dad informed me. *Anything touched by her horn dies. Get ready, we're about to kill spawn.*

I'm ready, I thought. I was ready. My breathing sounded like a bellows as I allowed my anger to become white-hot. Mack's wolf growled beside me.

You have mindspeech already—very good, Dad responded to my thoughts. *Here they come.* His claws formed on his hands, but he kept his human shape. I could see we still needed to have a conversation about that.

Not now, the spawn—twenty-four of them—hit us like a storm.

Mack and I allowed instinct to take over. I'm glad it was available to us—our animals killed the spawn that thought to attack or run past us. What we didn't get, Dad did. I'd never seen anything move that fast before. The spawn were fast, but he was faster.

Spawn dust exploded around us whenever we made a kill, and I can only imagine that it resembled a black cloud to anyone who might have seen it happening from a distance.

The only sounds, however, came from us—grunting, growling and hissing. Spawn are eerily silent—when they attack and when they die.

Mack's shoulder was sliced by one that got too close, but Dad killed it before it could make a second strike.

That's when Dragon, Lion and Mom joined the fray. They trapped the spawn between us and it didn't take long after that.

I blinked as Dragon became himself and lifted a hand afterward.

Piles of black spawn dust disappeared around us while Mack and I watched.

"Mack," Mom became herself again, "Let me see your shoulder." She walked toward us. "Justin, turn back, honey. Mack needs your shirt."

Joey arrived in seconds with a pair of pants for Mack, while I shrugged out of my shirt and offered it to him.

He took it with his right hand while Mom and Joey healed the slice on his left shoulder.

"Wow, I can barely see a red line," Mack said as he studied the mark on his shoulder.

"You did so well," Mom hugged him. "Your wolf is an amazing fighter."

"Thanks, Mrs. G," Mack's face went pink at her praise.

"You, too, honey," she came to me. "No wounds?" she looked me over, paying attention to my arms and head.

"I don't feel anything," I croaked. "Can we get some water?"

"We'll go home. The authorities will arrive at the cabin any minute, so Dragon will erase any evidence we were there," she sighed. "Come on, I'll take you this time."

We landed in the kitchen of the new house, and I realized then that we really hadn't spent much time in it. Too many other things had happened, when we should be enjoying our new home.

Pulling glasses from the cabinet, I filled them with cold water from the fridge and set them in front of Mom and Mack before getting some for myself. Dad, Joey, Dragon and Lion came in shortly after, so they got water, too.

"Thirsty business," Lion nodded his thanks when I set his glass down.

All of us avoided the subject of dead kids at a lake cabin. I didn't know whom to blame now that the actual perpetrators were dead, but somebody needed blaming, in my opinion.

Instead, I said, "Dad, tell me about your claws. Does everybody else have those?"

"No," Dad sighed. "I have them because I used to be a vampire.

Before you ask, the old stories are true—real vampires die in the sun. It's a way of killing them."

"You lived in the dark?" I began, after shoving aside my initial shock. *Dad was a vampire?*

"For more than two hundred years," he nodded, his eyes meeting mine. "That's how things were for me when I met your mother. I keep my vampire abilities—they come in handy quite often."

"But what about," Mack began. He was werewolf; I guess it only made sense that there were vampires, too.

"You want to know about the blood, don't you?" Dad turned his gaze on him. "It's true—vampires drink blood to survive. Most drink bagged blood nowadays—it's safer for everybody that way."

"But," I said.

"Yes. If you're wondering, your mother doesn't mind if I bite occasionally," Dad said. "Although not while she's pregnant, unless I want to die. I believe Karzac or Pheligar would be happy to make that happen if the rules are broken. Before you ask, I don't bite anyone else. End of statement and no more questions."

"I guess it's not every day you learn your dad's a vampire," Mack observed philosophically. "Or a werewolf."

That made me laugh. Just a few days earlier, I'd have said someone was lying if they'd said that to Mack and me. The truth of it was now slapping us in the face. We went to school with humans, but we'd never been human. It was almost too much to consider.

"Should we watch the local news, or have we seen enough tragedy for today?" Mom asked.

"I'd say we've seen enough," Lion said. "Marlianna is coming tomorrow—we'll move into the guesthouse then."

"I'll look forward to that," Mom said. She hesitated for a moment. "Actually, Lion, can you ask her to come now? I have something for her."

"I can if that's what you want," he said.

"I do."

"Marli, my love, can you come?" Lion said to empty air. I gaped as Marlianna, Uncle Lion's wife, appeared from nowhere at his side.

"Kee says she has something for you," Lion grinned and put an arm around her waist. Aunt Marlianna's skin is the color of warm caramel, and she is so pretty that people stare if she goes anywhere with us. She leaned down to kiss Uncle Lion, who still sat at the island. It's not hard to see that they love each other a lot.

"You have something for me?" Marlianna smiled at Mom. "Congratulations, by the way, Lion told me about the baby." She couldn't keep the wistfulness out of her voice when she said that.

"That's what I have for you," Mom offered her a tired smile. "As First among the Saa Thalarr, I am giving you permission and the ability to get pregnant. To both of you. My word is law."

A brief flash of light followed her statement. I have no idea what all that meant, but Dad, Joey and Dragon perked right up and Marlianna turned to Uncle Lion with a happy squeal.

Lion stood really fast, hefted Marlianna into his arms and they disappeared.

"Kiarra, what did you just do?" Pheligar, the tall, blue man appeared, his arms crossed over his chest in disapproval.

"What should have been done a long time ago," Mom snapped at him.

"You are dangerously close to overstepping your authority," Pheligar pointed out.

"But I didn't. Admit it—this is only fair," Mom defended herself. "If I can get pregnant, it's fair that someone else should, too. Especially since they want that more than anything. Marli is a healer. It shouldn't affect much with her—Joey can fill in for her when needed when she's too far along. Nobody deserves a baby more than those two."

"I would like to argue this with you, and you should have consulted with me before doing it," Pheligar grumped.

"What's stopping you from arguing now?" Mom demanded.

"This has been a trying day for you and the others. A better time will come and we will discuss this use—and potential abuse—of your position."

"You have to ruin everything, don't you?" Mom snapped.

"I realize your hormones are affecting your body and your temper. As I said, a better time will come for us to discuss this."

"You are an insufferable blue ass," Mom shouted.

"As all of my skin is blue, it is only logical that my ass, as you so inappropriately put it, is also blue."

How often does this happen? I sent mindspeech to Dad.

With frightening regularity, he replied.

Can we go out to eat tonight? I think Mack's gonna cave in.

We can, if we can pull your mother away from the Larentii.

"I'm hungry," I announced, interrupting the argument. Mom had stood and started shaking a finger while yelling at Pheligar, and that didn't look safe to me.

"Look," Mom said, "If you want to continue this argument, you can make yourself look human and go out to eat with us. Mack and Justin are starving."

"I did not start this," Pheligar huffed.

"Then either come with or take a hike," Mom flung out a hand.

Without blinking, Pheligar caught her hand, patted it and put it at her side. "I will accompany you," he said. Mack and I gasped as he transformed himself. He looked like someone who could be your neighbor, with glasses and everything. I clapped a hand over my mouth—I'd seen this guy before—right after Mack's life was saved.

"Holy cow," I mumbled between my fingers.

Please do not let your werewolf friend know his life almost ended. He has enough worries, a strange voice—Pheligar's voice—sounded in my head.

Sure thing, I sent back. Oddly enough, he didn't seem surprised that I had mindspeech. My curiosity about the Larentii reached an all-time high at that moment, and I was determined to learn all I could about him and his race.

We didn't go to Giorgio's, which disappointed me, but it was just as well—Pheligar, Mom and the others wanted to talk business. We ended up in a private room at our favorite Japanese restaurant instead.

If Mack had turned to werewolf, he'd have wagged his tail because he loves sushi.

"The young ones are curious, and as little information was given them earlier," Pheligar began.

Mack and I learned about the Saa Thalarr that night. We discovered that Saa Thalarr meant *Hope and Vengeance* in a long-dead language. We heard how they were a race created specifically to combat spawn and those that made spawn—the Ra'Ak. I hadn't heard that word before and wanted to ask questions immediately.

"Here." Joey held out a hand, where a tablet appeared. The thing was, I'd never seen a tablet like that one before.

"It's a comp-vid," Dad said. "You'll learn more about that later. Joey has images of Ra'Ak. Understand those are difficult to come by," he added.

Holding the comp-vid so Mack could see, too, I studied the giant serpent depicted on the screen. "How big?" I asked.

"Average size runs twenty to forty feet, with younger ones smaller and older ones longer—they grow all their lives," Mom said. "Three to four feet thick at their widest. If you meet one of the longer ones, then you know he's one of their strongest and most cunning fighters to have survived so many centuries. When they're not fighting us, they fight each other."

"You fight those things?" Mack shook his head.

"Everything about them is poisonous," Joey said. "Scales, teeth, spikes, all of it."

"That takes the term *snake* to a whole new level," I breathed.

"It's part of our job to heal scale poison—that's the least harmful," Joey explained. "Teeth or spike injuries can be fatal if they're not treated immediately after the Ra'Ak dies."

"Why does the Ra'Ak have to die first?" Mack asked. I hadn't realized how valid that question might be, and felt a chill seep through me when Mom answered.

"Every challenge we make against the Ra'Ak is to the death," she said. "Worlds depend on the outcome of a challenge. If we win, the planet lives. If the Ra'Ak win, they devour and destroy it. They haven't won a fight in more than fourteen thousand years. They'd love to take one of us down because of that."

"How many of you died before that?" I asked. I had to know—I was beginning to realize that my parents had a dangerous vocation.

"Many," Pheligar answered.

"Too many," Dragon amended the Larentii's statement. "When Kiarra became First, things changed. She carefully measures the Saa Thalarr's talents against the necessary requirements to save the world in question."

"She consults me every time to help determine what is needed," Pheligar said. "It is my job, as Liaison to the Saa Thalarr, to aid as much as I can without interfering. My race does not interfere as a rule, but acting as Liaison is considered a great honor among my peers."

"Wicked," Mack whispered.

"Who was First before—did they die?" I asked.

"Not dead," Pheligar said. "Retired. He did not consult as he should have. He and I had many disagreements."

"Looks like you and Mrs. G have disagreements, too," Mack said.

"These disagreements are different. She will never place a life in jeopardy because we fail to agree on every minute detail," Pheligar said. "We each have our say. We do not dislike one another because we disagree. Not at the core of our relationship, anyway. I cannot say the same about her predecessor. Much of our disagreement stems from the differences in our primary races. Larentii and humans are vastly dissimilar."

"Don't get him started by asking what the differences are," Mom said. "You'll be here all night."

"Are you suggesting that I take too long to express my thoughts?" Pheligar lifted a blond eyebrow at Mom.

"No." She hunched her shoulders. "I feel sick again," she mumbled. "I wish they'd hurry with our food."

"We will not have that," Pheligar declared and pulled her onto his lap. One hand went to her forehead, the other to her stomach. Light formed around both for a few seconds.

"Feel better?" he asked, his voice soft.

"Yeah. Thanks."

"I'm thinking about contacting Merrill," Dad said as Mom settled onto her seat again. Our food was delivered two minutes later while Dad talked about bringing Uncle Merrill to Fresno. When the waiter left, he explained that Merrill, with the help of a werewolf named Daniel Carey, could teach Mack and me about hunting spawn.

"You should know, Son, that Merrill is a modified vampire," Dad said. "He's a vampire who can walk in daylight and eat normal food."

"Seriously?" Mack breathed.

"Seriously."

"Will Grampa Frank come with him?" I asked. I hoped Grampa Franklin would come. "Does he know about all this?"

"He knows. Merrill knows. You can say anything to either," Mom said. "And to Daniel."

"Knowledge of the race protects itself," Pheligar said. "If you attempt to tell anyone who doesn't know already about it, you will be unable to speak. The secret effectively keeps itself."

"That means Gina can't know," Dad said. "I'm sorry, but we don't know her well enough yet. You'll have to keep your other side secret around her until she's approved by your Mother and Pheligar. Even then, she won't be able to talk about it to anyone else, so you see how difficult it could be for some people to know this about us."

I hadn't considered those things before—that someone could be forced to keep a secret and it could cause them harm. What if Gina wanted to tell her mother, and couldn't get the words out? It sounded painful.

"I'll keep the secret," I promised.

"Good," Mom said. "Does anyone have more rice?" Dragon handed her a bowl.

◊

Kent, England

Private files of Charles, Secretary to Wlodek and the Vampire Council

Merrill stalked past me and into Wlodek's private study. He had a right to do so; he was Wlodek's oldest living vampire offspring and a

King Vampire. None in the vampire community could stand against Merrill's strength or compulsion, should he choose to exercise either.

He was dressed casually, which was certainly unusual, therefore, this visit heralded an emergency of some kind.

"Charles!" Wlodek's voice summoned me immediately. It was not unexpected. Gripping my tablet, I followed Merrill through the door.

"Take a seat," Wlodek waved an impatient hand at Merrill and me. We sat. Wlodek's study is richly appointed, from the painting of Napoleon by David on one wall, to the large Monet hanging opposite.

Someone once imagined that everything in his study had a huge, invisible price tag. They were correct. Many collectors would highly prize what Wlodek had ceased to see or consider long ago. Still, vampires sent gifts, in attempts to curry favor or elicit decisions from the Council. Wlodek was never swayed. That was what I admired most about him.

"Tell me," Wlodek leveled a dark gaze upon Merrill, while steepling his fingers. I'd seen the same gesture many times from Merrill, so it was no surprise where he'd gotten it.

"I'd like to borrow the vampires who helped in Corpus Christi all those years ago," Merrill began. "They are familiar with those who need our help, and I think they'd be glad to offer assistance again."

"What will they be doing?" Wlodek's voice was calm. Even. Deadly. Merrill didn't blink; his face remained an impervious mask.

"You've seen the news reports from California, I assume?"

"I have."

"There is something—I cannot say what, exactly—preventing those we know from actively hunting these spawn. They are concerned that spawn are not only being made here, but are also being brought from other worlds to devour the population."

"I cannot imagine why anyone would prevent them from using their full abilities," Wlodek said, revealing a tiny crack in his emotions. There were many reasons for the vampire race to protect humans, the source of blood being chief among them. If spawn were allowed to take over, Earth's vampires would starve.

"They cannot lie—you know this. I heard this directly from Adam."

"Ah. Our former Chief of Enforcers." A multitude of unspoken words lay behind Wlodek's statement. He missed Adam's cool efficiency more than he would ever admit. Russell was a good replacement, but his sense of humor never failed to irritate Wlodek. Oddly enough, Russell was one of those Merrill requested.

Merrill didn't respond, so several minutes ticked by while Wlodek considered Merrill's request. "Very well," he said eventually. "I will allow it. Charles, notify those concerned and have them report immediately to Merrill. I trust you have made arrangements to bring them all to the U.S.?"

"I have," Merrill agreed. "Transport is available and ready the moment I report their locations."

"Good. Keep me apprised; Charles will let you know if we have assignments that cannot be ignored while you chase and destroy these creatures."

I almost breathed a sigh, but held it back. Wlodek had made the correct choice, with no advice or cajoling needed. It was a tremendous relief.

~

Adam's Journal

Kyle will come, Merrill acknowledged. *As will Russell, Will, and Radomir. I hope that will be enough from our side. Who will come for the Grand Master?*

Daniel Carey, I sent. *Martin Walters' son, plus Theodore Williams, Second to Thomas Williams, from the Sacramento Pack. He'll send others if Martin requests it. Martin intends to help if the spawn are in this area—he and his pack are at our disposal.*

Good. I hope this will be enough, Merrill returned.

There's one more, I responded. *My son, Justin. He's a Wyvern and has been deadly against spawn in both battles he's fought. I'd appreciate it if you and the others would assist in his training, and that of Martin's son, Mack. I believe both could be elite fighters with only a bit of tutelage from those most experienced.*

I will see it done, Merrill promised. *I think Russell will be happy to participate in the training of young ones.*

My vampire brother will be a perfect teacher, I agreed. *I'll be glad to see him again.*

Are you planning to tell Justin that Russell is his vampire uncle?

I believe that would be a good start, I said. *Russ is still young enough to engage young ones.*

Precisely my thinking, Merrill agreed. *Will can help—those two work very well together.*

Let me know when you are ready for transport, I said. *Dragon and I will come.*

I will. Kiarra is truly pregnant with your daughter? He asked before ending the mental conversation.

Yes, and this pregnancy is harder on her, for several reasons. I can tell the Larentii is worried—he's hovering, and he never does that. She has become ill several times, and that never happened with Justin.

That concerns me, Merrill said. *How much time does she have before she can no longer employ her abilities?*

Four weeks, I grumbled mentally. *You know she will push it to the limit, too.*

I understand that about her, yes. She despises feeling helpless.

I wish she'd allow us to take care of her, I said. *This will be difficult enough, knowing Justin will be in danger. I don't know whether I can handle all this at once.*

You love them, that's where the difficulty comes in, Merrill said. *Do not fear, many love your wife and will give their lives for her—and for her child.*

I hope it doesn't come to that, I responded, allowing the mental sigh to escape with my words.

∽

Justin's Journal

"This means you'll be homeschooled for as long as it takes, up to the remainder of the year," Dad said. He'd called Mack and me into his study, a place we were seldom allowed. "The Larentii will arrange for all your grades and records to be transferred to the school during the time spent being homeschooled. You will have attended school without having to actually go elsewhere while you're hunting spawn. It is my hope that this situation will be rectified in a month or two, so things will return to normal."

"Seriously?" Mack breathed. He hadn't seen this coming.

Neither had I.

"It also means," Dad continued, "that dates with Gina in the interim will have to be carefully planned around hunting trips. If she has questions, tell her you're working with me. That will be true enough."

"Who'll be teaching us?" Mack asked.

"Joey and Bearcat," Dad grinned. "Be prepared, because Joey will make sure you can graduate from college with the science and math classes he intends to throw at you. Bearcat will teach English and history. Do your assignments or you'll answer to your mother and me."

"Sounds harder than real school," Mack whispered.

"It will be," Dad nodded. "Joey will schedule additional college testing for both of you, and expect you to do well enough to get into just about any school you choose. You're his only students, don't forget. He and Bearcat won't have an entire classroom of pupils, distracting their attention from you two. Mack, we've discussed this with your father and he's happy with the idea that this will prepare you for college—better than what you were getting at Valley High."

"How will we know where to track those things?" I asked. After all, hunting spawn was the reason behind all this.

"Lion is going to teach you how to *Look*, and that's spelled with a capital L. Pheligar says you have the innate ability, you only have to learn to use it properly. You'll be on location duty for the others—just remember that the vampires can only move at night. That means you'll be working nights, too, so you'll have to plan all other activities accordingly."

"When will they get here? The ones who are coming?" Mack asked.

"They'll be here by Tuesday. We'll construct an underground bunker for the vampires, with a door they can lock from the inside.

That's what we'll be doing this afternoon—the Larentii will shield our power signature while we build it."

"It can happen that fast?" I gulped.

"Son, there wasn't anything here when I bought the property two weeks ago. This house went up in a day. We spent a few more days getting it wired, installing the plumbing and placing the furniture."

"Wow," I mumbled. I was too embarrassed to ask how much power Dad and Mom actually had. It ought to be staggering.

"Dad's okay with me staying here?" Mack asked.

"He prefers it, since you were followed by the Pierce boy and attacked outside school. He doesn't want any accidents. Now that you know what you are, you are in a position to do real harm to humans. The Pierce boy is nothing more than a bully; he has no idea what sort of threat you could pose to him and his friends. Besides, we have no desire for any suspicion to fall on you again, should you attack a human. That is the fear that faces both werewolves and vampires— that humans will discover their race and attempt to eradicate it."

"I never thought of that, before," Mack said. "Dad told me to keep my mouth shut, but this sort of explains everything."

"Young Mack, your wolf knew to run from spawn because you were outnumbered. It will always know that. From now on, others will have your back when you fight them—at least that is my intention. I have a feeling that your adoptive mother will give you a gift—as her adopted child. Use your gift wisely. Go, now. She is waiting for you at the indoor pool."

We found Mom right where Dad said she was, lounging on a chair with her feet up beside the pool. The cool water and elevated humidity inside the room made it an oasis compared to the dry heat outside.

"I asked Adam to send you," she smiled at both of us. "Justin, the gifts I'm giving Mack, you already have. This will help keep both of you safe." She beckoned Mack closer.

"I have to put my hands on your head, honey," she said. "This is to give you mindspeech and the ability to *Look*, so you and Justin will be on the same page. Lion will show you how to use both gifts."

Mack knelt beside her chair. At that moment, I was reminded of a painting where a Queen bestowed a knighthood upon a warrior. I wondered if Mack would ever realize that a warrior-knight was what he'd become.

Mom's hands glowed as she touched Mack's head. They'd called her First. I hadn't asked about that before. Uncle Lion would have to tell me, since nobody else explained what that meant.

"There," Mom took her hands away. "You'll be able to *Look* and to mindspeak others with the talent. Don't misuse your *Looking* skills to bypass study and homework. Joey will know and you'll be in trouble with everybody."

"I guess we'll have to be careful," Mack grinned.

"I'm warning you, Martin Everett Walters, Junior," Mom shook a finger at him. He laughed. It was a good sound.

"Aunt Marlianna," I grinned at her when she and Uncle Lion walked into the kitchen ten minutes later. Mom sent us to the kitchen, and said to wait there for Lion. I had no idea that Aunt Marlianna would come, too.

"I wanted to thank your mother," Marlianna beamed at me. "You're going to get a cousin in about nine months."

"Seriously?" Mack said. "That's so cool."

"It is cool," I agreed. "He or she can go to school with my sister."

"That's what we were hoping for," Marlianna hugged one of Lion's huge arms against her. I could tell he didn't mind a bit.

"Baby, go ahead and see Kee," Lion urged. "I'll teach these young ones how to use what they have without getting into trouble."

When Marlianna disappeared down the hallway toward the indoor pool, Lion turned to us. "*Looking*," he began, "is a way to search for needed information. I warn you not to make your search too broad, because the information you get will overwhelm you. Narrow it down and *Look* for specifics. It'll be like looking for Fred on the internet, which will produce thousands of possibilities. You'll have to narrow your Fred search to Fred James from Greenville, Alabama. That will produce a more reasonable response," he said.

"It's like the Internet?" Mack asked.

"The most accurate version you'll ever see," Lion nodded. "You'll only get precise information, and nothing that is wrong or dishonest. It's one of our best abilities."

"How will this help in hunting spawn?" I asked.

"All right, try now. *Look* for spawn," Lion instructed. "I'm prevented by our superior, but you aren't held back by that command."

I'll never forget that first session. Ever. I *Looked*, thinking I might find a few here and there, not far away. After all, we'd killed so many already.

"They're all over," I whispered in alarm when my eyes focused on Uncle Lion again.

CHAPTER 7

*J*ustin's Journal

"Narrow each search to a city, then look for the location within that city," Dad said, spreading a paper map of the U.S. on the kitchen island. When I'd *Looked* the first time, I'd seen red, glowing spots on states across the union. Dad was now asking me to focus on individual states, and cities within those states.

"There's a shitload in Florida," I mumbled, focusing my skills on that state. "In the Everglades. Here." I tapped the map. "A bunch in Texas—maybe more there than in Florida," I confirmed. Mack had seen them, too, just not as easily or as clearly. That meant I'd take point on the *Looking* for spawn thing.

Inside my head, I could see cities. Streets in those cities. Street signs and building numbers in those cities. I was surprised the spawn hadn't made their presence known there already. Were they waiting for something?

"Son, they're building their army," Dad said softly. "They want to hit us and hit us hard in those areas, so they're taking the population a few at a time, probably from the homeless and those whose absence won't be so readily noticed. They do this on other worlds, too. It's their attempt to overwhelm the population and make it ready for the real invasion."

"Real invasion?" I croaked. Images of space ships firing on hapless populations swam through my brain.

"Not like that. Who has need of ships when they can fold in and eat whomever they want?" Dad muttered. "Worlds die within a few months after the Ra'Ak and their spawn arrive to feed."

"And you're the only ones standing between those people and the Ra'Ak?" Mack's voice cracked.

"Yes. Seven of us, against that army," Dad agreed. "There are rules, but there are times when the rules are broken—on their side. This is one of those times. We fought and won this planet twenty years ago. Now they're back."

"How long are they supposed to stay away?"

"A thousand years."

"You think there's something here that they want?" I asked.

"We worry that it could be exactly that," Dad agreed. "That whatever it is may be very important to us in the future, and very bad for them at the same time."

"So we can't give it up," I said, squaring my shoulders. "We can't let them have that."

"And we've had our hands tied in fighting them," he said. "That leaves you, Mack and a handful of vampires and werewolves to fight for us."

"This is so weird," Mack sighed and shook his head. "I have questions, but maybe I'll wait to ask them."

"We'll be going to Texas on Tuesday," Dad said. "There's nothing to prevent us from providing transportation for my son and his friends, so Dragon and I will drop you off in Dallas Tuesday evening. Pay attention to Merrill, Daniel and the others—you'll learn much from their tactics. Between now and then, Dragon and Lion will give you a brief lesson in combat."

∾

"I will teach you bladework someday," Dragon said as we stood before him and Lion in the backyard half an hour later. "The first thing I wish to teach you is this; never let your enemy slip behind you. Always keep him in front of you, or as much in your sight as possible."

"It's better to have at least one or two allies at your back if you are surrounded," Lion said. "Form a triangle. A circle is better if you're surrounded, but take care to keep the circle intact. It cannot be breached, you understand. Close in if one of your comrades falls, but give each other enough room to fight."

"Be prepared," Dragon took over the lesson. "You will see humans in all stages of turning to spawn. Never forget that the human is dead and spawn is what you face. Ignore that you are fighting women or girls. Spawn are asexual. Take them down no matter what."

"They smell nasty. Acidic," Mack confirmed. "All of them."

"Then let your nose be your guide," Lion jerked his head at Mack. "Do not let them live for any reason, no matter what their appearance may be. Any one of them can destroy the population if allowed to attack unchecked."

"What about little kids?" Mack mumbled.

"Most of those you saw the other day would have been completely eaten if we hadn't arrived to interrupt the meal," Lion sighed. "Those are the first choices as a food source goes, because the meat is tender. You understand that the lake areas and Yosemite are now closed after this latest attack. Authorities are saying to proceed with caution at any vacation spot, as a large group of people provides no safety from what is attacking them. The National Guard is looking for these creatures, too, but they have no idea what they are tracking."

"They're showing the footage from the school attack every five minutes on the news," Mack grumped. "We probably won't be the only ones pulled out of school over this."

I blinked at Mack for a moment. "Do you think Gina can have her classes with us? Do you think her mom will allow it?"

"Dude, will *your* mom allow it?" Mack asked.

"We're off topic," Lion cleared his throat.

"What? Oh, yeah," I said, feeling embarrassed.

"You cannot allow anything to distract you when you face the enemy," Dragon's eyes narrowed as he studied me. "Always stay focused. You'll keep your life that way."

"Yes, sir," I nodded.

～

At five-thirty that evening, I was on my way to pick Gina up for our date. That meant I had a ton of stuff shoved aside in my head to make room for her. Her mother answered the door when I arrived, and I knew she wanted to make sure I was a good candidate for dating her daughter.

I was as honest as I could be when she asked questions.

"You've lived in Fresno all your life?" She offered me a seat in the small living room.

"Yes, ma'am—for as long as I can remember."

"I know your father owns a construction company."

"He does." I watched as her fingers twisted together and worried blue eyes wandered to a photograph sitting on a table beside my chair. Shamelessly, I *Looked* to see who it was.

It was Gina's father, who'd died in Afghanistan. His body was never recovered and that probably left a big hole in Mrs. Allen's life. I knew she wasn't married—Gina never referred to a step-dad.

Somebody was taking her daughter out, now, and in Mrs. Allen's mind, threatening to interrupt her close-knit bond with Gina.

"I like Gina," I blurted. "A lot. There's no way I'll interfere with your relationship. I promise."

"Mom, stop with the inquisition," Gina walked into the living room shoving long, dark hair over her shoulder and giving me a lovely smile. "It's just dinner and a movie. I'll be home by eleven, I promise."

"I wish you had another option than going back to Valley High," Mrs. Allen grumbled. "But we don't have the money for private school. I—just don't want you anywhere near those monsters and let's face it, they seem to be stalking Valley High students."

"My parents are arranging to have me home-schooled—at least for a while," I said. "For pretty much the same reason."

"Who's teaching?" Mrs. Allen brightened up immediately.

"My Uncle Joey is teaching science and math—he has a master's from MIT, with honors. Whenever I need help in Calculus, he's the one who explains things for me. My Uncle Bearcat is teaching English, history and everything else. Mom says that when they get done with Mack and me, we'll get into any college we want afterward."

"Is that true?" Mrs. Allen's eyes lit up. "And the Walters boy will be studying with you?"

"Mom doesn't lie," I shrugged. "And she considers Mack to be an extra kid, since he's at the house so much. So, yeah."

"Will you have your mother call me?" she pleaded. "At least she can give me advice, if your uncles don't want to include Gina in their classes. MIT? Really?"

"Oh, yeah," I nodded. "Uncle Joey's kind of a genius at that stuff. If you have any question about computers, he's the one to ask."

"Mom can barely use the Internet," Gina whispered with a smile.

"I heard that," Mrs. Allen said, but she laughed, letting us know it was all right. "Where are you going to eat?" She added.

"I thought maybe Mr. Wong's," I said. "Do you like Chinese?" I turned to Gina.

"I love Mr. Wong's. They have the best wonton soup," she beamed at me.

"I like that, too," I agreed. "And the shrimp fried rice."

"Have a good time, and be back by eleven," Mrs. Allen waved us toward the door. Somehow, I'd passed her test, when I didn't think there'd be one to pass to begin with.

I got Gina home by eleven, with three minutes to spare. I almost didn't kiss her good night because of a sudden onset of awkwardness.

Thank goodness she met me halfway. I drove home after that, with the hardest erection I'd ever experienced. Joey met me at the door leading from the garage into the house.

"Here," he slapped a bottle of lotion in my hand. "I hear cold showers are supposed to work, too."

"What?" I'm glad I couldn't see my stunned expression, because it surely looked as uncomfortable as it felt.

"It was either me or your dad," Joey shrugged.

All right, meeting Dad at the door would have caused me even more embarrassment. "Good call," I mumbled and stalked past Joey toward my bedroom.

"We've already cleared it with the school," Mom said while Mack and I had bacon and eggs for breakfast Monday morning. "They've canceled classes for this week anyway, because of the attacks and deaths last Friday night, but Pheligar made all the necessary changes for you and Mack. I understand we're not the only ones pulling students out of Valley High—the Catholic school in Clovis has been bombarded with requests."

"Gina's mother wants you to call her," I said, attempting to shove aside the fear that threatened to envelope me. I was terrified Mom would say no. After all, we would be hunting spawn between classes and homework. Plus, Gina was human; Mack and I weren't.

"I've already talked to Marie Allen," Mom smiled. "I told her it wouldn't be a problem for Gina to study with you and Mack. Joey and Bearcat convinced me it wouldn't be a bad thing to add another student or two. They've cleared out the two bedrooms behind the garage to make two classrooms, complete with computers at each desk and everything else you may need to do your lessons."

"This, and this," Joey walked in and placed a new tablet in front of each of us. "I have another two for Gina and her friend, Sarah. These have all your textbooks on them, plus access to reference materials and anything else you might need."

"Sarah's coming, too?"

"They'll be here in an hour. Class starts at eight-thirty. Finish your breakfast and clean up," Joey commanded. "You belong to Bearcat and me until three."

"Does Gina have a ride?" I asked.

"Sarah is picking her up. They'll ride together on most days," Mom said. "Eat. You don't get to shirk, just because you're studying at home."

"You're not getting an apple," I teased, pointing a finger at Joey.

"If I depended on you for food, I'd starve," he teased right back.

"I can actually hunt for food," Mack pointed out, grinning.

"I really prefer cow to venison," Joey said.

"Please stop talking," Mom said, slipping off her barstool. She looked green.

"Uh-oh," Joey said. "Come on," he took Mom's hand and they both disappeared. I figured she'd be losing her breakfast in short order. Mack blinked at me. I just shook my head.

"I have already stretched my authority to the limit," Thorsten complained.

"And things are going in the proper direction," his creator offered a cunning smile. "With this forced pregnancy you have manufactured, you have effectively removed the First from combat, making her an easy target. Now, we can take her grown child, too. Then, when we destroy the unborn child with her mother, it will destroy the Former Falchani's will to live and The Saa Thalarr will fall with those two. This has become too easy."

"I can only take this so far," Thorsten whined. "If Belen discovers what I've done, I can't guarantee I'll keep my job."

"Then we'll make sure Belen is occupied elsewhere, shall we?"

"I have to leave that to you," Thorsten countered. "If you expect me to do your will in this, Belen must continue to trust me."

"I will arrange it," came the reply.

Justin's Journal

Joey was an unrelenting taskmaster in the classroom, and he wouldn't let me stare at Gina for more than five seconds before sending mindspeech. I decided right then that mindspeech could become more of a curse than a blessing.

The good thing, I suppose, was that classes with Joey and Bearcat were much more advanced than anything we'd ever gotten at Valley High, and it honestly kept us better engaged. Who knew?

Even Mack enjoyed it, and he'd never particularly liked school before. The assignments, too, weren't dull and dreary retreads on what students had done for the past decade or two. These made you think, asking for research and input. Bearcat asked us plenty of questions, especially on how mass unemployment in Germany, the great depression and ensuing economic failure in Europe were contributing factors in World War II.

Mom was right—this was college level stuff and would help prepare us to score higher on admission tests.

I walked Gina to Sarah's car after classes were over, while she actually gushed about how our classes would help her, especially the math and science classes. She liked Joey so much more than Mr. Draper, because he explained everything in a better, more energetic way.

"I can't wait to tell Mom what a good idea this was," she said, giving me a peck on the cheek. I watched as she and Sarah drove away, wondering whether my future days would all include cold showers.

At breakfast Tuesday morning, I learned that our underground bunker in the backyard was now occupied by vampires, while the third floor was inhabited, not just by Uncle Dragon and Uncle Karzac, but also by Daniel Carey, Second from the Corpus Christi Pack.

"They were all up late, packing, traveling and then holding a meeting," Mom explained while we ate. "The vampires won't be up before nightfall anyway, and Daniel may sleep almost that long. I think you and Mack should take it easy after school today, and nap if you can, since we don't know how late you may be getting back tonight."

"What about Teddy—Beth's boyfriend?" Mack asked.

"He'll arrive before nightfall. We've invited him to dinner," Mom said.

"I thought I'd get to meet him when Beth brought him to the house. This is certainly different," Mack grumped.

I could tell right then that Theodore Williams had his work cut out for him—he'd have to be extra special before Mack would ever approve him as husband material for his sister.

"Honey, keep your mind open," Mom hugged Mack. "Give everybody the benefit of the doubt until you meet them and know for sure what they're made of."

"I'll try."

"Good."

Again, I wondered about Mack's mother, and why she'd never bothered to contact him when he was in the hospital. If she'd called, he would have mentioned it. Mom was standing in—and standing up —for Mack. He was right to call her Mom.

He went to visit his mom for a week every summer, but he seldom talked about it when he got back. I worried that it was stressful and awkward for him, after a year of not seeing and seldom hearing from her.

I'd never asked Beth about it, so I didn't know how she felt about the whole thing, either.

"Don't worry about it, honey," Mom gave me a hug next, as if she'd read my mind. "Finish your breakfast and get ready for school."

After school, I saw Gina and Sarah off again, then went to the kitchen looking for a snack. Grampa Franklin sat at the island, as if he were waiting for me. Mack was already into a glass of juice with peanut butter and crackers.

"Grampa Frank!" I was at his side in three seconds and getting a hug. I didn't want to say it, but he looked so much frailer than when I'd seen him last. "You taking it easy?" I asked, grinning at him when I pulled away.

"Always," he nodded. "I hear you have a girlfriend."

"Yeah," I hung my head to hide the embarrassment.

"That's nothing to be ashamed of," he chuckled. "First one, is it?"

"First serious one." I sat beside Grampa Frank and made myself comfortable. "I think I drooled on some girl in kindergarten, but that's it until now."

"Just don't forget to show her how important she is to you," he said. "Because you never realize how significant that will be in the long run. Now, I hear you and Mr. Mack over there are going to hunt spawn."

"That's the plan," Mack nodded.

"Be careful. While you've dealt with younger spawn up to now, watch out for the older ones."

"Older ones?" Mack stopped eating for a moment.

"They're bigger, faster and more deadly," Uncle Merrill walked in and nodded to Mack and me. "Are you hungry, Franklin?" he asked, placing a hand on Franklin's shoulder.

That was different. Before, it was always Grampa Frank asking that question, and fixing something if anybody wanted to eat.

"I'm fine, stop fussing," Franklin said. That's when I knew that his health really was more fragile than when I'd seen him last. I could have *Looked* to check, but was too afraid to do it.

"Are you prepared for tonight?" Merrill turned the conversation in my direction. "It would be wise to rest an hour or two before night falls. We have plans to be in Dallas, tonight."

"Okay. Ready to go to your room, peanut butter and cracker boy?" I turned to Mack.

"Sure." He slid off his stool, stuffed his plate in the dishwasher and followed me down the hall toward the stairs.

99

~

Adam's Journal

"He doesn't want help, and if he goes, he wants to make sure nobody takes heroic measures. His partner died years ago, and he wants to follow him," Merrill sighed. Franklin had gone to the bedroom we'd prepared for him on the second floor, so I'd joined Merrill in the kitchen. Franklin was the topic of conversation.

"This is going to be hard on everybody," I said. "What did the doctors say?"

"That his heart is giving out on him," Merrill replied simply. "My child doesn't want interference—he wants to enjoy the time he has left and especially doesn't want to linger."

I knew—because I'd *Looked*—that Franklin had steadfastly refused Merrill's offer to make him vampire through the years. I understood that decision, up to a point. I'd been turned early in my life and had never faced the pains and diseases that came with old age.

Merrill had a front-row seat to it, however, as he watched a child he'd adopted at eight grow old and wither before his eyes.

"I don't know what I'll do without him," Merrill muttered. "We've been together so long. At times, I think of ignoring his wishes and making the turn anyway. That will destroy his trust, however, and that would be more painful to me than his death."

"Things have a way of working out," Kiarra walked into the room looking slightly ruffled. She'd been taking a nap in our bedroom and hadn't bothered to look in a mirror before shuffling into the kitchen.

"Hello, my darling," Merrill's face lit in a smile.

"Merrill, how are you?" She leaned in to peck him on the cheek.

"I am more than fine. Franklin's health is failing."

"I'm so sorry." She wrapped her arms around his shoulders and squeezed. "We love Franklin, too."

"How soon?" I asked.

"Unknown. I just don't want him to suffer. We watched his partner, Greg, die of pancreatic cancer, and that was painful enough. To know it's Franklin suffering? I'm not sure I can bear it."

Justin's Journal

I think Mack wanted to growl at Theodore Williams, who asked everybody to call him Teddy when he was introduced. Something was going on, there, that I didn't know. For the first time, I used my ability to *Look* for something personal, and what I found was unsettling.

At the core of it was perhaps the reason Mack's mother remained distant. Werewolf marriages were arranged more often than not, and the rules were that the mother had to birth two children before she could leave the werewolf she'd married.

Mack knew his mother's marriage to his father had been arranged by her father, because Martin Walters, Mack's dad, was a strong and important Packmaster. She'd had little choice in the matter.

She hadn't been mistreated, but the arranged marriage had never been what she'd wanted so when Mack turned eight, she'd left him and his sister, moved away and married someone she chose to love.

He was human.

I understood how awkward that might be for Mack, both in the past and in the future, because now he knew he was werewolf, whereas his two half-human brothers would be considered human.

Human-werewolf children were never werewolf. That's the way it worked. I was almost sorry I'd gone *Looking* for the facts of the matter, but understood better what Mack's grievance with Teddy Williams might be.

Beth's marriage was being arranged by Mack's dad and Thomas Williams, the Sacramento Packmaster and Teddy's twin brother.

Packmasters and Seconds were the top choices in marriage material for any female werewolf, for obvious reasons. I found myself hoping—like Mack—that Beth could have love in her relationship. That her children wouldn't be left behind if she went in search of happiness. That's how things worked in the werewolf community—the children were left with their fathers, who raised them.

All of that information came to me in a matter of seconds. It offered a new perspective on Mack's world, and his struggle to understand his recently altered place in it.

The tension between Mack and Teddy eased considerably when Beth arrived unannounced, went straight to Teddy and wrapped her arms around him. He pulled her close, kissed the top of her head and asked her how her classes went.

I didn't realize how bad it was until I saw Mack visibly relax. I understood, too, that Teddy was in his fifties, while Beth was twenty. He still looked young, and I suppose that if your lifespan might cover two hundred years or more, fifty was still quite young.

"I wish I could go with you," Beth told Teddy later, as the sun was setting over Fresno.

"Baby, it would scare the hell out of me if you were fighting those things," Teddy took her face in his hands. "I know you can do it, I just can't guarantee my reaction if one of them tries to hurt you."

He walked her to her car so she could drive home. Mack and I exchanged glances, but the arrival of Daniel Carey and the vampires distracted us quickly.

"Son, this is Russell Farleigh," Dad introduced a tall, dark-haired vampire first. He smiled and offered his hand. I took it. "Russell and I, well, we're considered vampire siblings," Dad said, shocking me.

"That means the same vampire turned both of us," Russell grinned. "The filthy, conniving bastard."

"Uh, what?" I jerked my head from Russell to Dad and then back again.

"Xavier wasn't the easiest vampire to get along with," Dad growled.

"He was a prick," Russell confirmed. "And he's dead," he shrugged. "We don't care," he added, with a laugh.

Not until then had I considered the fact that as Dad was a vampire, it stood to reason that someone had made him that way. I shivered.

Xavier and another vampire tried to kill your mother and me, Dad sent mindspeech. That explained a lot.

"This is Will," Russell introduced another vampire, who grinned and saluted me. I could tell that Will would be fun, even though he was vampire.

"This is Radomir," Dad introduced him next. He was the one I'd pick as a vampire, because he seemed older and much more reserved than Russell or Will.

Daniel Carey came next. "This is Daniel, the Second for the Corpus Christi Pack and an old friend," Dad said. Daniel gripped my hand firmly and offered a nod. He was tall, straight, dark-haired and had a military bearing about him. Dad said he was Navy, but I didn't ask if he were still an active service member.

"And this is Kyle," Merrill introduced the last vampire. "He is one of my vampire children," Merrill said, causing my eyes to widen in surprise. Kyle was shorter than the others, thin and tough as a whip, with dark hair and eyes. He looked like a lightweight boxer, in my opinion.

"It's funny that you're thinking that," Dad said. "Russell was the boxer, when he was human."

Somehow, Dad pulled the boxer thought right out of my head. *I'll teach you how to block your thoughts*, he sent. *Later*.

Until then, I hadn't realized they needed blocking. Dad grinned. He'd gotten that one, too.

I have to be actively listening, he sent. *I didn't want you to be uncomfortable around Russell and the others, so I opened up to your thoughts. Shutting it down again*, he nodded.

"Awesome," I mumbled. He ruffled my hair in reply.

We trudged into Dad's study after that, and he and Merrill laid out our game plan. "This is the building you targeted," Merrill pointed at the large photo of a satellite image from Dallas. Mostly we saw the roof of an old warehouse on the outskirts of Dallas. I'd selected it as a hiding place for spawn when I'd *Looked* for them.

"These are the entrances," Merrill pointed at the front, the back and one side of the building. "This is a small, side door," he tapped the east side. "The other two are large enough to drive a good-sized van inside."

"Will and I will take the back," Russell volunteered.

"Good," Merrill nodded. "You'll take Justin with you. I warn you, he becomes a Wyvern when he turns, so give him plenty of room to fight."

"Will do," Russell nodded respectfully to me.

"Kyle, Daniel and I will take the side door," Radomir offered.

"Good. That leaves the front for Teddy, Mack and me," Merrill said. "Mr. Walters had an appointment this evening and couldn't be with us," he added.

Pack meeting—they're checking out possible spawn at the lake, Mack sent.

Gotcha. You ready for this? I asked.

Better be, he said.

"Dragon and I will provide transportation," Dad said. "And we'll be back when you send mindspeech," he nodded at Merrill. I understood then that Merrill had mindspeech, too, he just didn't want it known. "If anyone gets hurt," Dad went on, "Let me know immediately. Is everybody ready?"

Mack and I exchanged glances. For us, it was like going to war for the first time. Our first two outings had been unplanned skirmishes— this was planned and for real. When I'd *Looked* for spawn, I'd seen a huge knot of them at this location in Dallas.

I hoped we wouldn't be overrun.

"Ready?" Uncle Dragon stalked into the room. Was it strange that the vampires and werewolves gave him respect? Not at all. Two minutes later, we landed on a street not far from the building in Dallas. A quarter moon hung overhead as we walked as quietly as we could toward the targeted warehouse. Dad and Dragon disappeared behind us.

Mack, Daniel and Teddy hung back—they removed their clothing before becoming wolf. In seconds, three large wolves trotted up beside us, their paws almost silent on the rough concrete—the old road hadn't been resurfaced in a very long time.

The vampires I could barely hear at all, they were so silent. I worked hard to keep from making noise as we approached the building.

It didn't matter how careful we were, or how dark the night was, or how thoroughly we'd planned our assault.

Something spooked the spawn inside the warehouse and before I was ready, they came boiling out of all three entrances by the hundreds.

CHAPTER 8

ustin's Journal
Our game plan was destroyed before we could even implement it. Dragon and Lion's short lesson helped a lot when spawn surrounded us. We formed a circle—as tight as we could make it and still leave fighting room for our neighbors.

After Mack sent mindspeech, I finally remembered to become Wyvern. It was close, too, because Merrill's side, opposite ours, had already been hit by spawn. I learned quickly that the experienced fighters, Merrill, Radomir, Russell and Daniel, had faced the building, leaving the rest of us scattered around the far side of the circle.

Will stood between Mack and me, while Teddy took up the space on my other side. Kyle fought on Mack's other side, and I figured he and Will were assigned to keep an eye on us.

"Watch out," Will shouted beside me as a wave of spawn rolled in our direction. They'd found it impossible to get past Merrill's side, so they pivoted around our circle, looking for a weaker spot to attack.

I knew Merrill and his force were making headway—I could hear the rattle of spawn dust as it burst about them and sprayed eerily across broken concrete. Daniel's growls punctuated his attacks, but the vampires didn't make much noise unless it was to warn those fighting next to them.

"Heads up, Justin!" Teddy snapped as six spawn thought to attack me at once.

Spawn taste nasty—there's no other way to describe it. I took one head that way, while clawing at two others attempting to reach me.

The problem?

Three more climbed over the backs of the three I fought before they dusted, and leapt on me. Will hissed and fought like a maniac, pulling them off me and taking their heads.

Mack yelped—he'd been jumped, too. Kyle helped with that—he was just as efficient a fighter as Will.

Teddy, fortunately, held his own for the most part, but I could see that the spawn were targeting the weakest and more inexperienced among us. More shoved forward, crowding us and forcing our circle to shrink and tighten.

Did I think there were hundreds? Perhaps a thousand or more still waited, and the ones in back were now crawling over the backs of those in front of them, in an attempt to penetrate our circle and attack from the inside.

"They're coming over the top," Will shouted as the mass, like a pitcher of molasses, tipped over and spilled inside our fighting ring.

I will never forget what happened next.

Fifty werewolves appeared behind our attackers, and they growled and fought and tore into spawn as if they'd been doing it all their lives.

The Dallas Pack had come to our rescue.

Two hours later, Mack and I sat in the Dallas FBI office, wondering for the hundredth time how we'd ended up there. That's when Dad walked out of one of the offices with Merrill and Radomir. Someone else strode behind them.

Werewolf, Mack sent after drawing a discreet breath.

"This is Agent Renfro, from the FBI," Merrill introduced us. "He and Agent White, a vampire from the same special division, had information on the warehouse we targeted. Unfortunately, they flushed them out before we were ready, but the Dallas Pack was waiting to be called in if necessary."

"We didn't know there were so many in there," Agent Renfro said, shaking Mack's and my hand. "We've made arrangements to share information—we have resources across the country and we may be in a position to help you."

"I've given them a copy of your map, Justin," Dad said. "They didn't know about Florida or some of the other places, yet."

"Are we finished for now?" A tall, dark-haired man sauntered up to Renfro. He exuded confidence and his clothes and cowboy boots spelled money. Lots of it.

"Thanks, Winkler. We wouldn't have made it without your help," Renfro nodded at him.

Dallas Packmaster, Dad informed me. *Extremely important in the werewolf world.*

When can we go home? I asked.

"You two ready to go home?" Dad asked aloud, to answer my question. Mack and I were exhausted, and all I could think about when I focused on our battle was how close we'd come to being overwhelmed.

"I'm ready," Mack stood stiffly. I rose beside him and nodded at Dad.

"Friday?" Agent Renfro asked.

"That's the plan," Merrill agreed. "We'll meet you at the designated position there."

"What's Friday?" I blurted. Yeah, it was the day before my birthday, and I wanted to take Gina out.

"Florida," Dad said. My shoulders sagged as I nodded my acceptance.

Adam's Journal

"I don't like this," Kiarra said as I pulled covers back to climb in bed beside her. The clock said 4:03 a.m. The boys would have to be up in three hours.

"Don't like what?" I settled in before pulling her against me and laying her head on my shoulder.

"This. All of it. Justin could have gotten killed tonight, Adam," she snapped.

"Dragon and I were prepared to go in. The Dallas Pack beat us to the punch. We're allowed to protect our mates and family; that's within the rules. We've discussed this already."

"You're not hearing me out," she countered. "It's as if we're inside a play that's already been produced once, with a different script. This time, I don't like the roles we've been assigned."

I considered that for a moment. Yes, something felt off, but I really couldn't say why I thought that. "What do you suggest we do about it, then?" I asked.

"I don't know," she mumbled, molding her body against mine. That was my cue—her way of telling me she needed comforting.

"Come to me, my love. All will be well," I murmured against her hair, hoping my words wouldn't become the lie I feared.

"I spoke with Merrill last night when he returned," Dragon informed me as we drank tea on the back deck the following morning. Dragon had Falchani black in a cup, while I settled for my usual English variety. "He says the spawn targeted the weakest of the group—your son, Mack and Theodore Williams."

"That can't be," I said. "Spawn are pretty mindless when they fight."

"He also says they cooperated to pull part of their numbers over the heads of our fighters and into the circle," Dragon went on.

"Are you sure?" I frowned. "That's never happened before."

"It concerns me greatly," he said. I knew he was filling in for my wife—as Second among the Saa Thalarr, that was his job if she became incapacitated. Her pregnancy would ensure that in roughly two weeks. "I've been fighting Ra'Ak and their spawn for more than fifteen thousand years, and this has never happened before. Either we're seeing a new strain of spawn, or a hand of power is interfering in this."

"Why is it happening now?" I asked.

"Why is it happening here?" he countered. "We've had this discussion. It seems the enemy has its eye on this world for some reason, and we cannot guess as to why that is or what it means."

"It is my hope that this is a singularity," Pheligar appeared and fashioned a chair large enough for himself with power.

"Kiarra said last night that it felt as if the play has already been done once, with a different playbook," I said.

"That is why we are ad-libbing for this," the Larentii nodded. "We make waves. Small waves can become larger waves, and eventually have an impact on all," he shrugged.

"A Larentii, ad-libbing? That's outstanding," Lion appeared and took an empty deck chair to join our conversation.

"Are you making light of a serious situation?" Pheligar asked him.

"Oh, no," Lion held up a hand. "I just never expected the term *ad-libbing* to ever leave your mouth."

"I used it because it was simple enough for you to understand."

"Oh, here we go with the insults," Lion grumbled.

"Stating fact should never be perceived as an insult," Pheligar huffed.

"And the logic gun is fired," Lion countered.

"Yet you keep stepping out of the way before it hits you," Pheligar claimed.

"Are you fighting?" Kiarra walked through the French doors at our back and shut them behind her. She patted Lion's shoulder as she passed him, then stopped behind Pheligar and rubbed his back carefully.

I blinked—only my wife was brave enough to put her hands on Pheligar; he might separate the atoms of anyone else who tried. Oddly enough, when she kneaded the back of his neck and the tops of his shoulders, he closed his eyes in pleasure.

That's something you don't see every day, Lion sent.

I had to turn my head so he wouldn't see me smile. It was obvious —the Larentii was worried and cranky as a result. I had no idea until that moment that any Larentii might have tense muscles because he was stressed.

To me, that meant we were in infinitely more trouble than we thought.

~

Justin's Journal

School Wednesday morning turned into torture as Mack and I struggled to stay awake. I realized that Dad faced this same agony— holding down a business and answering calls to fight spawn or the monster Ra'Ak that made spawn.

My job had turned dangerous enough; his—and Mom's —was worse.

I know my fellow students in high school always talked about graduating and finding a job, or going to college and then finding a job, but the word *job* held little meaning to anyone who hadn't really worked one already.

Sure, I worked for Dad during summers and some weekends in the school year, but that had never been serious. This—this was mind-bendingly serious and my life, as well as the lives of others, depended on how well I did that job.

Gina knew what holding a job entailed—she worked as a waitress, a tough job by anybody's standards, so she could go to college. She probably intended to work while going to college, too.

I'd never been faced with that particular dilemma—I had a college fund. My new job, as it turned out, was too important to quit, no matter how I felt about it.

Mack and I—we were saving lives. I almost choked when that realization hit me. A coughing fit ensued.

"Justin, do you need a drink of water?" Joey stopped teaching for a moment to ask.

"Yeah. If you don't mind," I choked out.

"Go ahead," he nodded toward the door. I loped from the room, heading toward the kitchen.

"Justin?" Marlianna stood in our kitchen, pouring a glass of orange juice.

"Glass of water," I held up a hand and walked toward the cabinet. "Got choked," I added after filling a glass with water and downing half of it. "How are you?" I asked.

"Good," she smiled. "We ran out of orange juice, so you mother sent mindspeech, telling me to help myself," she said. "That means we need to make a trip to the grocery store later."

"Yeah. Ran out of crackers yesterday," I agreed. "Mack likes those with a half-ton of peanut butter."

"He's growing, now that the werewolf has made his presence known," she said. "He'll get as tall as his father before it's over."

"Mr. Walters is six-two," I said.

"Mack will need new clothing soon," Marlianna gave me another smile.

"You know, I'm really glad you're here," I said. "You and Uncle Lion both."

"Why, thank you, sweetheart," she said and gave me a hug. "You should go back, now, before Joey comes looking for you."

"Yeah. My head's kinda muddled today," I said.

"Short night," she pushed hair off my forehead with gentle fingers. "Eat a quick lunch and grab a nap in between," she said.

"Will do." I turned and headed back to school.

Adam's Journal

"Justin's birthday is Saturday," Kiarra pointed out later, as she put sandwiches together for the kids. I knew Gina and Sarah's mother had offered to pay for any lunches we provided, but we turned them down. Kiarra told Marie Allen that she was happy to do it, and that was that.

"I know. And he's expected in Florida the night before. I say we let the boys sleep late, then have the party at dinner time."

"I asked Gina about dinner Saturday," she frowned at me. "She has to work. She was really disappointed, too."

"What about the party on Sunday, then, with gifts the day before?"

"Sounds good," she said.

"What am I getting for my birthday?" I draped an arm around her shoulders.

"You put in a request. I'm handling that," she sniffed and moved away.

"Ah. I forgot about that," I said. "*How* are you handling that?"

"I asked Wolf and Tiger to go with me shortly after we got back from the beach house," she said.

"Good," I nodded. "How is Grey House?"

"Fine. Raffian is still snippy, but Glendes is a gentleman."

"That's what you get when you tell the most talented K'Shoufa jeweler to kiss your ass and take his M'Fiyah with him," I pointed out.

"I won't marry an insufferable prick," she muttered and piled fresh-cut tomatoes atop ham and roast beef.

"Then I'm glad I don't fit that category," I said.

"You've come close a time or two."

"Hey, now," I protested.

"Glendes said he'd personally take care of my order," she said. "That means Raffian will probably do the design and spelling, but Glendes will check it afterward. Because he owes me," she added, placing a toasted bread slice on each sandwich to finish it. "Grab the chips," she said. "The soup's ready, I just have to dip it into bowls."

Justin's Journal

"My dad was killed in Afghanistan," Gina told Mom while we ate. "Helicopter crash. His body and three others weren't recovered."

"Honey, that's terrible," Mom said. "Your mother must have been devastated."

"She was. I was too young at the time to realize what was happening. It just seems so long ago," she shrugged. "We have a headstone at a cemetery, but there's nothing else there."

"We saw Randall Pierce on the way home, yesterday," Sarah said.

"Was his Mongol horde with him?" I asked, turning my attention to her.

"Two of them. They honked and gave us the finger when we drove past them."

"His father was fired yesterday," Dad said. "It's not common knowledge yet," he added. "My attorney is working with Mack's dad on a lawsuit—when you willingly break the law, it's generally not a good idea to brag to your coworkers about it."

"He did that?" Gina's soft brown eyes turned to Dad in alarm. "He did it on purpose, then told people?"

"He almost got Mack killed," I growled. It was a decent growl and if I worked on it, I might compete with Mack someday on what he had naturally. "On purpose."

"They're investigating other incidents at the jail," Dad said. "When inmates were attacked or found dead in their cells, just to see whether Raymond Pierce had any involvement in those events. It's not looking good for him at the moment."

"So he's lost his job, and may get jail time?" Mack asked.

"It's possible. He almost committed murder, after all."

"Randall probably knows we're being homeschooled with you and Mack," Sarah pointed out. "Some of the kids at school know, so it makes sense."

"We can make arrangements to pick you up and take you home," Mom offered. "Someone will be with you, in case threats are made. We can notify the police, too, if they harass you further."

"A ride wouldn't be a bad idea," Sarah agreed. "I don't want that to happen again. They were really rude."

"Then Adam will drive you home today, and Lion will follow you in your car," Mom said. "I don't think those boys are stupid enough to toss insults at adults."

"They're not brave enough to toss insults at adults," I said. "They're cowards, and can't stand up to anybody unless they have friends with them."

"That's true," Gina agreed with me. "If they think they have the edge, they'll be as nasty as they want. Threaten them back and they run."

"That's usually how things work. Just watch out for them to come running back with bigger, badder friends," Mack said. I realized he was talking about the night before, as well as Randall Pierce.

Did what we fought last night have bigger, badder friends waiting? Grampa Frank and Uncle Merrill said they existed and to watch out for them. I wanted to shiver. I forced the fear back as best I could and tuned into the conversation again.

"If his dad lost his job, Randall will lose his car," Mack pointed out quietly on our way back to class. "He thinks this is our fault, instead of placing the blame where it belongs. He'll retaliate, just wait and see."

"I hope not," Gina hugged herself beside me. "I know he's a bully, but surely he wouldn't do anything serious."

"I wouldn't put anything past him," Sarah grumped. "We saw what he did to Justin's car."

"Yeah. It still isn't fixed," I said. It sat in one of our garage spaces, a forlorn remnant of its former glory. I'd liked my car, even though it wasn't a sports car like some of the others had, or painted a flashy color.

The Honda was reliable, and never failed to get me where I was going.

Your dad says the property here is warded, whatever that means, Mack sent as we walked into our afternoon classroom and lessons with Bearcat.

I think it means that Randall can't get past the gate, I replied.

School let out early that afternoon. I was glad, because Mack and I were nearly asleep when Bearcat handed out a writing assignment and sent all of us out the door.

Just as Dad promised, he drove Sarah and Gina home and Lion followed in Sarah's car. No sightings of Randall Pierce, but that didn't mean anything. I was suspicious of him, anyway.

Mack and I slept until dinner, worked on our homework assignment for a while afterward and went back to bed. Fighting spawn was tiring work, no matter how you looked at it.

∾

A long grocery list lay on the island when we walked into the kitchen on Thursday morning. Breakfast waited, so Mack and I dug in.

"Extra crackers and peanut butter?" Mom teased Mack as she added things to the list. "Marlianna and I are going to the store after a while."

"Cookies?" I begged. I loved the kind that were crunchy on the outside with frosting on the inside.

"One package, and you have to make it last," Mom pointed a finger at me.

"Will do," I grinned. She didn't buy those cookies often, because of the HFCS and palm oil added. Fresh-baked was always better, but I had a thing for evil sandwich cookies.

Mack and I shuffled away to brush our teeth after breakfast, so we could get to class on time. We'd discovered that Joey liked his students to be punctual.

∾

Adam's Journal

I was on the phone with Martin Walters when Kiarra and Marlianna went out the door. With so many people in the house, we needed more groceries more often. I waved at her as they walked toward the door leading into the garage.

I should have gone with them.

∾

Justin's Journal

About an hour into our afternoon classes, I knew something was wrong. So did Bearcat.

"I'll be back," he stopped in midsentence and practically ran from the room. Gina and Sarah turned to Mack and me, but I felt terrified and ill for some reason.

"I gotta go, I think I'm gonna be sick," I ran out behind Bearcat.

I skidded across the kitchen tiles in time to see Dad carrying Mom into the house. She was covered in blood and I wanted to shout.

Lion followed Dad, and he held Marlianna so tightly against his side they looked like one person.

"Out of the way," Karzac appeared from nowhere with Dragon. Pheligar appeared right behind Karzac and looked like a blue thundercloud.

"Justin, come with us." Uncle Lynx arrived, with Aunt Wolf behind him. Lynx wrapped a strong arm around my shoulders and pulled me back so Dad could get past.

"What happened?" I still felt queasy, but now I wanted to cry, too. Mom wasn't conscious, and that frightened me in ways I couldn't begin to describe.

"Humans, backed by larger spawn," Aunt Wolf growled. I recognized that growl. It belonged to a wolf. "In a parking lot, of all places," she added.

"They attacked in the grocery store parking lot?" I squeaked.

"That's right, in broad daylight," Lynx huffed. "Somebody was watching for them to leave the property."

"What the hell is going on?" Merrill raced into the kitchen and demanded. I could tell he was ready to take somebody apart, too.

"Kiarra and Marlianna were attacked outside the grocery story," Wolf explained. "Kee fought them off, but she was wounded and now she may lose the baby."

Before then, I didn't know Merrill's background. I knew enough, though, to recognize Latin when I heard it. He was cursing and running down the hall toward Mom and Dad's bedroom in a blink.

"What happened?" Mack, Gina and Sarah walked into the kitchen.

"Justin's mother was in an accident," Wolf said. "I think school is over for today. Lynx and I will drive you home."

~

"They attacked her outside the grocery store?" Mack shook his head in disbelief after Lynx and Wolf herded Gina and Sarah into the garage and drove away.

"Yeah. I don't know how many, but Wolf and Lynx said that humans and older spawn attacked."

"This sucks," Mack shivered. "I mean really, really sucks."

"Yeah. I hope Uncle Karzac can do something."

~

Adam's Journal

"Stay with me, Kiarra," Pheligar said. He and Karzac managed to bring her back to consciousness, but she was naked and covered in blood as they struggled to save the babe. She was also crying as she lay on our bed, so I did my best to soothe her with mindspeech while the best physician I knew and a Larentii worked over her.

Dragon was hunched over in a corner, going quietly insane, I think, because his mate, as tiny and inconsequential as she was, was slipping away from us.

Justin and Mack needed information, too, and they'd been left alone in the kitchen while Lynx and Wolf took care of the human girls. Bearcat and Joey waited nearby, in case their healing services might be requested, but there was little for them to do except worry.

Lion had his hands full with Marlianna, and eventually folded her from the room, as she was still terrified after the attack and shaking after seeing what she assumed to be a miscarriage.

"Kiarra, focus on me," Pheligar said. "Connect with me. I will lend you what I can." He began to glow, and eventually Kiarra was bathed in blue light. Karzac pulled his hands away—Pheligar was doing something I'd never seen or heard of before.

We watched as slowly, so slowly, things came back to normal and the blue light disappeared. Karzac placed his hands on Kiarra's abdomen, then dropped to his knees bedside our bed in relief.

"The child lives," he croaked.

"I must feed," Pheligar's voice was little more than a whisper as he disappeared. He'd spent the vast energy he had to save my daughter.

Justin's Journal

"Your Dad and Karzac will stay with her for a while," Joey and Bearcat walked into the kitchen. Joey sat on a barstool, while Bearcat wrapped his arms around Joey. For the first time in my life, I saw Joey shaking while Bearcat did his best to make Joey comfortable and calm him down.

"She's fine; they saved the baby," Bearcat laid a kiss on top of Joey's head. "They're letting her sleep, now."

She's all right, Son, filtered into my head. *The baby, too. Karzac's keeping her in a healing sleep, that's all.*

Thanks, Dad, I returned.

Wolf and Lynx didn't come back until an hour and a half later, but they had Dad's SUV filled with groceries. They'd gotten what was on Mom's list and then some. Mack and I, still feeling as if the ground had shifted beneath our feet, helped them unload everything and put it away.

I never knew Wolf had a healer until then, but he arrived and she introduced him. Antiani wasn't human. Oh, he looked mostly human, but he only had three fingers and a thumb, instead of the usual four. His skin was the color of pale coffee, his eyes were green and he smiled a lot.

He fixed dinner for us—beef stir-fry, with help from Wolf and Lynx. Dinner that night was a somber meeting with everybody in the house. Daniel, who'd been out most of the night before with the Fresno Pack, wandered downstairs and stopped dead still when Wolf turned to hand him a plate.

Lynx caught the plate before it fell, because Wolf had done the same as Daniel, forgetting she held a plate to start with. Mack blinked at me before we both turned back to stare.

Daniel moved first, raising his hand slowly, as if he were afraid he'd spook Wolf and make her disappear.

I heard her intake of breath, then, because for a few moments, she'd forgotten to breathe.

It's the M'Fiyah, Lynx sent as he stepped back quietly. *Mate recognition,* he translated, after realizing I didn't understand what M'Fiyah meant.

I think I released a breath I didn't realize I'd been holding when Daniel's hand touched Wolf's face, then held my breath again as Wolf turned her cheek into Daniel's cupped hand and closed her eyes in ecstasy.

We were watching love at first sight, six-point-oh.

"Holy, freaking cow," Mack mumbled beside me.

They heard, Daniel dropped his hand, Wolf turned pink and both laughed. Then, all during dinner, Daniel had his hands on Wolf as often as possible and both disappeared the moment it was polite to do so.

Mack and I did the dishes, so everybody else went to the back deck to talk. Half of them carried drinks. Dragon, who'd come in at the last, didn't speak, ate quickly and poured bourbon from Dad's private stash into a glass before going with the others.

He'd had a hard day, too.

"Think we can sneak in to see Mom?" Mack whispered as he shut the dishwasher door and turned it on.

"I hope so," I nodded. "Let's go."

Karzac and Dad were with her; she was still asleep when we walked in as softly as we could.

I was surprised that the blood had disappeared. Actually, it shouldn't be a surprise. If somebody can build a mansion in a day using power, I guess cleanup is nothing after that.

She's fine—we'll wake her in a few minutes, she needs to eat, Dad sent.

So do you, I pointed out. *Leftovers are on the stove, and Antiani made noodles with mushrooms and tofu for Mom.*

Antiani is a good cook, Dad replied. *That's your mother's favorite dish that he makes. When he and Raheela cook together, your mother always asks for a plate.*

Raheela?

Lynx's healer. She's an elf. They're together, they just like to keep that fact secret. Antiani doesn't want to aggravate the Elf King.

There's an Elf King? My head was reeling as *The Lord of the Rings* swept through my mind.

It's nothing like that, Dad offered a mental chuckle. *I hear the Elf King can use profanity better than anyone, and that includes your mother. He was angry that Lynx stole one of his citizens away to become his healer. That's where the secrecy comes in.*

I wish I understood that better, I shook my head.

That's when Mom moved on the bed and opened her eyes. "Honey?" she spoke to me, first. "Have you and Mack had dinner?"

Mack relaxed visibly and laughed.

CHAPTER 9

*J*ustin's Journal

Friday morning, things were almost back to normal. Or as normal as they could be, under the circumstances. Pheligar appeared, though, during breakfast, which was served by a smiling Antiani.

Dad herded Mom to the kitchen, and I guess that's what Pheligar was waiting for. "I know you will not like this, but you must stay on the grounds or ask someone else with sufficient power to be with you if you leave," he said as Mom sat at the island with Dad's help. "This child is draining you in some way, so it is advisable to stop using your power immediately."

"I've already figured that out," Mom frowned at Pheligar. She didn't want to be reminded, I think, of what she'd already discovered for herself.

"I see that," Pheligar said softly. "I wish it could be otherwise, but I cannot change this for you, as much as I'd prefer to do so."

"This is so fucked up," Mom dropped her face in her hands.

Dad rubbed her shoulders carefully while Antiani set plates of food in front of them.

"Are you prepared for this night?" Pheligar turned to Mack and me, then. Mack, who'd been busy shoving scrambled eggs in his mouth, blinked at Pheligar.

"Yeah," I rolled my shoulders uncomfortably. We'd had time, Mack and I, to repeatedly consider the events of Tuesday night and what that had almost cost us, then the events of Thursday morning added to that worry, when Mom had been hurt while fighting off two huge spawn and three humans.

"What happened to the humans?" I thought to ask. I figured the spawn were dead—nobody said they weren't.

"In jail," Dad growled. I went still. "Your mother got injured attempting to save their lives," he added. I could tell that angered him.

"One of them was Randall Pierce's dad, wasn't it?" Mack asked after swallowing a mouthful of egg.

"You guessed correctly," Dad nodded, his eyes showing a flash of red. I knew then that if Dad had been there, all three humans might be dead for attacking Mom.

"Who else, then?" Mack dropped his eyes and picked at a piece of bacon on his plate.

"Friends of Raymond Pierce," Mom said. "Older bullies, just like him, who thought they'd have an easy time of it, getting back at people who had nothing to do with his getting fired."

"It's a no-brainer to see where Randall's habits come from," Mack muttered.

"They had no idea that the spawn intended to bite them after they took me down," Mom explained. "When I fought back against the spawn, they turned on those men, instead. It was all I could do to fend off the humans and still fight the spawn, who wanted to attack all of us at that point."

"Lion and I got there as fast as we could," Dad said. "Your mother was forced to use the last bit of strength she had to protect Marlianna and keep us from killing the humans after the spawn dusted. The dusting hit her—she couldn't shield herself and Marlianna, too."

"Pheligar sent Tiger to deal with the police," Mom sighed. "She took care of all that while your father brought me home. It was inconvenient for her, because she was on assignment."

"Wow," I shook my head. "Have you ever done that?" I stared curiously at my parents.

"Kiarra, as First, is usually the one I rely on, if she is available. Lion is also good at that sort of thing. Dragon generally intimidates everyone, so I hesitate to send him into a situation such as that," Pheligar answered my question. "Your father has gone a few times," he said, "Although his first instinct is to place compulsion to ensure cooperation."

Mom snickered and rubbed Dad's back at Pheligar's admission.

"Kee?" Wolf walked into the kitchen, closely followed by Daniel, who looked as if he wanted to warn every other male on the planet away from Wolf. She hugged Mom while Daniel waited patiently.

"That jealousy will be terminated immediately, it has no place here," Pheligar waved a hand in a dismissive gesture. Daniel stepped back and blinked, confused for a moment.

Dad turned his head to hide a grin. I added another question to the huge backlog accumulating in my head.

"You okay?" Wolf asked Mom as she pulled away, ignoring completely whatever Pheligar had done and the effect it had on Daniel.

"I'm okay, thanks to Pheligar and Karzac," she sighed. "The baby, too. I just can't use any power from here on out. It's too dangerous."

"It is," Dragon appeared and nodded to Daniel and Wolf. "How is my little one?" he patted Mom's stomach.

"Your little one is fine," Mom said. "I intend to keep it that way."

"I worry that you'll not keep that promise, if things go awry," Pheligar said.

"What?" Mom and Dad said in unison.

"Kiarra, I am asking your permission to suppress your power, so you will not be tempted," Pheligar said. "I will leave your shields intact, but everything else I can suppress until the baby is born."

"But that will mean," she said, slipping off her barstool and blinking at Pheligar.

"It means that you will have to rely on others for the next six months, just as it would normally be," he said. "The only difference is that you can't be tempted to use what you do not possess at the moment."

"You're really worried about this, aren't you?"

"Yes." Pheligar's eyes were half closed as he offered a small nod. "I fear that too many things might go wrong. You were targeted yesterday. I do not wish to see a repeat of that. You cannot go anywhere alone from now on, and you must depend on others to fight the battle. You will still provide input, as you usually do, but the war will be waged by those around you."

"I feel bad enough that we're shoving Justin and Mack into this mess, along with Mack's dad and his sister's fiancé," she complained while Dad helped her onto the barstool again.

"Mom, stop worrying," I said. "We'll find a way."

"Then fine," Mom flopped a hand in the air. "Suppress my power or whatever it is you have to do."

"Kiarra, I know this troubles you," Pheligar rose and placed his hands on her shoulders. "This is to prevent worse things, I assure you."

"I know."

Mack and I watched, openmouthed, as light formed about Mom. When it was gone, Pheligar sighed. "It is suppressed," he said.

"Boys, it's almost time for school," Mom reminded us. Mack and I left the kitchen to brush our teeth.

~

Larentii Archives

"You know what I think of this," Nefrigar placed an extinct grouse from Serendaan in stasis, so it could be examined by future Larentii students.

"I know." Pheligar watched his brother work while attempting to hide his discomfort.

"If you had made your feelings known long ago instead of muting them, you would not be faced with this dilemma now and she would be welcome on the Larentii homeworld."

"As it is, I cannot interfere in an attack upon her, because she is not my mate," Pheligar muttered.

"Yes, many things should be different," Nefrigar nodded, turning the grouse this way and that to search for its most pleasing angle in the display. "I understand you suppressed her power so the child would live, in order to preserve the Second's emotional balance."

"He has served past the required term—it is my fear he would retire and ask me to separate his particles, as is his right, should the child perish."

"Too many things weigh in the balance," Nefrigar agreed. "He is needed. She is needed and crippled at the moment. She is also in danger, due to her position and condition. Her oldest child's life is in danger. Her unborn child's life is in danger. If one or more of those things is destroyed, the race could die and the Ra'Ak may reign."

"Many times I wish it were within our power to approach the High Demons and remind them of their duties," Pheligar complained. "Yet there is nothing we can do and they remain on their world unless it pleases them to skip away for entertainment on other planets. They have become too full of themselves and too sure of their supremacy. Someday, that could prove false and create their downfall."

"The Wise Ones concur," Nefrigar agreed. "They also believe that this will be tied to the God Wars but I, as do they, hope those will be long in coming."

"There is no evidence as yet that any of the Three have appeared."

"That may be by design," Nefrigar pointed out. "There. Would you study this grouse if it were presented thus?" He stepped back from the display, which included plants and soil from its natural habitat.

"I would rather study the passenger pigeon from Earth," Pheligar sighed. "Extinct because it was tasty and easy to hunt," he shook his head. "But the grouse is quite fine, brother. Had I not known of the passenger pigeon, I would certainly study this one."

"Do you believe that humans may become the passenger pigeons to the Ra'Ak if the Saa Thalarr fall?" Nefrigar asked, turning his attention to his younger brother.

"I am afraid it would be so," Pheligar conceded.

～

Justin's Journal

"I have to work tonight; you have to work tomorrow," I said, holding Gina's hand as I walked her toward Dad's SUV. He was taking her and Sarah home, but Lynx had brought them in earlier. I think Sarah had a crush on Lynx already, because she'd stared at him after he dropped them off.

"We can go out after the party on Sunday, though," I pointed out before swooping in for a quick peck.

"That sounds great," Gina brightened. "How about a movie?"

"That's good," I said. "Anything you want."

"There's a comedy I want to see," she said, her voice turning shy.

"I like comedies," I shrugged. If it got me alone with her in a dark place, then I'd settle for watching anything.

"Good. Call me tomorrow before six," she said and waved before climbing into Dad's truck.

"Will do," I said and waved back.

"Get a snack and take a nap," Joey's hand dropped on my shoulder as Mack and I watched the truck pull out of the garage. "You have Florida to look forward to, tonight."

"I've never been to Florida," Mack said as we walked inside the house.

"Neither have I," I said.

"It's usually humid," Joey said. "And where you're going, it's filled with mosquitos. Not that they'll bother either of you," he held up a hand. "We repel them naturally."

"We're headed for the everglades and swampy area," I said. "Those FBI guys gonna be there waiting for us?"

"Your dad heard from them this afternoon. They want you to meet them at an office in Miami, then go on from there."

"Is that safe?" Mack asked.

"Yeah. Already checked out," Joey grinned. "Come on, snack time then nap time."

~

Adam's Journal

Pheligar was correct—something about this pregnancy was sapping my wife's strength. That shouldn't be. She was as feisty as ever during her pregnancy with Justin.

Karzac already informed me that every pregnancy could be different, but I still didn't understand this much difference. Martin had been a godsend, taking over the business for me so I could handle this. I still felt guilty about not driving her to the grocery store.

She wouldn't go alone next time, that's for sure.

"Adam, what are you fretting about?" she called from the bathroom. She'd gone to brush her hair after taking an afternoon nap.

"Not much," I said. "Want a snack?"

"I probably should so I won't get sick," she walked out, showing me that she'd braided her hair. "How many shields are around the strawberry farm?" she asked.

We'd started referring to our new home as the strawberry farm, and the name looked as if it would stick. "Mine," I said. "Dragon's, Lion's and Pheligar's. Is that enough?" I pulled her into my arms and held her tightly.

"It'll have to be," she nodded against my chest. That's when I knew how frightened she really was after the attack in a grocery store parking lot. She was terrified to leave home, now that she was effectively helpless.

I didn't tell her what I'd noticed on the way home. Four blocks from our house, on a street lined on both sides with tall oleanders, a car was parked on the side of the road. Randall Pierce and three of his friends sat inside it.

Waiting.

Raymond Pierce had bonded out of jail; I'd learned that the evening before. He and the others had assault charges filed, but as he hadn't committed murder and had bail money, there was no choice except to let him go until the case came to court.

I'd considered a protective order, but those were less effective than what I could level at the bastard if he didn't step back. It concerned me, too, that he could go looking for more friends of the scaled variety, or that they might go looking for him, for the same reasons.

He had no idea that when they got what they wanted from the transaction, he'd be on the menu, the same as any other human.

His son appeared to be following in his father's footprints, and watching whenever we came or went. That meant Justin and Gina would have to be shadowed on their date Sunday evening, but that could be accomplished easily and he'd never realize someone was there.

Joey and Bearcat would be ideal candidates—they could defend themselves easily and help Justin do the same if it proved necessary. Joey still held compulsion as a weapon, and I'd make sure he used it if required.

The Pierce family had become a nuisance to us, and I didn't want that to continue.

~

Justin's Journal

Joey got us up at seven, in time for dinner. Mom, Marlianna and Wolf cooked, with help from Lion and Bearcat. Steaks were on the menu, and that's what Lion and Bearcat were tending when we walked to the deck outside.

Dinner would be served on several picnic tables that had magically appeared from somewhere. It was a nice night for it, actually—the heat in the evenings was dissipating better, making it pleasant to eat outside.

"Smells good," Mack's stomach rumbled when we took seats at a picnic table. Trees and a patch of grass outlined the raised deck, and I wondered again at the talent and power it took to place trees that appeared as if they'd been there for decades amid grass that looked tended for nearly the same amount of time.

The guesthouse, a two-story rectangle that matched the main house, stood past that, trimmed with flowers, shrubs and plants that would survive in the Fresno sun. I recalled that I hadn't been inside it yet—that was Uncle Lion's and Aunt Marlianna's private residence, so I needed an invitation.

"Look," Mack nodded toward the wall beside us. A tiny lizard, with rapid stop-and-go movements, made his way up the stone blocks.

"Cool," I said. He was a pale, grayish color, and against the color of the stones, almost impossible to see.

"You know, that gives me an idea," I said.

"What?"

"Camouflage," I said. "Is that possible for us, or are we gonna stick out like a sore thumb in the Everglades?"

"Did I hear you say camouflage?" Dad sat on the bench opposite ours and studied us across the thick-planked picnic table.

"Yeah. Is that possible?" I asked.

"Spawn eyesight is weaker than their scenting ability," Dad said. "But your idea is a sound one. Especially if you're camouflaged for sight, sound and scent."

"Can you do that for us?"

"I think that might be considered interference, but we haven't explored your talents, yet," he said. His brow furrowed for a moment, as if he were considering something. "The rest of us," he said after a few seconds, "got our talents when we were added to the Saa Thalarr. You, on the other hand, were born into it. That means we have no idea what you're able to do."

"You think I might be able to do some of the stuff you and Mom do?"

"I sure hope so. Without your mother's power, we're down a man, so to speak."

"Try this," The bench beside me creaked as Dragon settled his weight on it. He dropped a saltshaker in front of me. "Change it to look like pepper," he said. "Leave it salt on the inside; you'll be changing the superficial outside. That's important, because you don't want to get confused and turn Mack into a stand of cattails." I think he was kidding, because he grinned when he said it.

"I don't want to be cattails," Mack scooted away from me in mock terror.

"You won't be cattails," Dad chuckled. "That's not the way this works."

"Think of the shape in front of you," Dragon instructed. "See it in your mind, and then see it becoming a pepper shaker."

I tried. Really. It just wouldn't work for me. The saltshaker remained a saltshaker, no matter how hard I concentrated. My disappointment was palpable afterward—I felt as if I'd failed a test and I hated that.

"We'll try again in a month or two—this is still new for you and you haven't gotten comfortable with it," Dragon said, dropping a hand on my shoulder and standing up to stretch.

It worried me—what if I couldn't protect myself or those around me, because I just wasn't talented enough? There had to be levels of talent, after all. What if all I was able to do was turn to Wyvern and fight off spawn?

"I'll teach you to fly soon," Dragon said as he walked away.

"Fly?" I turned to Dad, my eyes wide with shock.

"You have wings," Dad shrugged. "It makes sense."

I blinked a time or two before shifting uncomfortably on the bench.

Flying.

Way up in the air.

What if I forgot how, suddenly, and dropped like a rock?

"Spawn don't fly," Dad pointed out. "Learning to fly would give you a definite advantage, as well as an avenue of escape."

"That would be useful," Mack said. "Can you give me a lift, dude?"

"I'd sure try if we needed to get the hell away," I said. "I just need to know how, first."

"It's this way," Mack said philosophically, "You spread your wings, I hop on your back and you take off. Easy."

"That werewolf of yours gonna hang on?" I teased right back.

"I got claws, man. Not as impressive as your dad's or Mr. Merrill's, but I got some."

"Sounds painful," I shook my head at him.

"Dude, you need to look at that wyvern in the mirror. I don't think much is gonna go through those scales."

"Let's take pictures," Joey arrived with his phone and a grin.

"Joseph," Mom warned as she walked onto the patio.

"It'll be encrypted. Nobody on this planet can get past that because they don't understand the language," he said.

That's when I knew that Joey's ordinary-looking cell phone contained alien technology.

The sneak.

"Turn, Justin. I'll take pictures," Joey grinned.

I did, because Mack had made me curious. I'd never thought much about it before. Jumping off the deck, I walked to the middle of our grassy area and became wyvern.

"Great," Joey said. "Spread your wings."

I only realized then that I'd never done that, either. Taking a deep breath, I did as he asked.

They were larger than I thought they'd be.

"They have to carry your weight, you know," Dragon stood beside Joey and studied my wings carefully. "The hand and claws attached are quite useful; I've watched you fight."

"I want a picture with my son," Mom said and walked up to join me.

"Say cheese," Joey said. I opened my mouth in what I hoped was a wyvernly grin.

"Dude, that's kinda scary," Mack made a face at me, making me laugh. Except it didn't sound like a laugh. More like a coughing growl, actually.

"Is he laughing or threatening us?" Bearcat carried a bowl of salad to the deck and set it down.

"I think it's a laugh," Mack said. "Dude, can you eat like that?"

"I'd suggest not doing it," Dad offered. "Salad just gets stuck in your teeth, and it's not easy brushing afterward."

That made me snort, and flames shot from my nose. "That's

different," Mom said stepping away from me. "Dragon, you'll have to teach him to control fire-breathing."

"I see that. Anybody singed?" Dragon came to stand right in front of me.

"Nobody singed," Mack said. "He had it pointed away from us."

"Good." Dragon studied me, his arms, covered in tattoos below a short-sleeved polo, shoved firmly across his chest while he contemplated me. That was uncomfortable; I blinked first.

"Fire, if hot enough, will destroy spawn," he said. "But it must be hot enough to burn them to cinders, you understand? Normal fire will not harm them enough to stop an attack. I normally don't use it, because I have to add power for my fire to become hot enough. The Ra'Ak, if they are contesting a world, will destroy that world if they realize Saa Thalarr walk upon it."

"They hold that much power?" I was back to myself in a blink and struggling to understand Dragon's words.

"As do some of us," Dragon nodded. "It is not something to employ lightly."

"Here," Joey held his cell phone up and scrolled through the photographs he'd taken. Sure enough, I was a red-gold wyvern, looking similar to a dragon but on a smaller scale. After all, I'd seen Uncle Dragon's dragon. He was huge. I wasn't even half that size.

Dragon patted my shoulder and chuckled. "It's not the size, it's the courage," he said.

"Time to eat," Mom announced, stopping the conversation. I was grateful—worry gnawed at me more than hunger did, and I had no idea what to do about it.

Merrill and Radomir looked grim as we prepared to leave for Florida shortly after sunset. Mack and I stood together in the kitchen while Dad and Dragon prepared to transport us to Miami.

Dude, I'm getting a weird feeling about all this, Mack used mindspeech.

You and me, both, I agreed. *I'm starting to feel like we don't know what's going on—not really, anyway, and I think Dad, Dragon and the others are beginning to think the same.*

You think it's a trap? Mack asked.

I don't know what to think anymore, I forced myself not to shiver.

Dad's still working with his Pack and part of the Sacramento Pack, Mack said. *They've found a few spawn here and there, and they've managed to kill them, but he says it's like somebody just dropped them from above, because there's no trail to follow until they're right on top of those things.*

What? I blinked at Mack is surprise.

"Ready?" Dad asked, peering around Merrill.

"Yeah." I wasn't, but how could I tell Dad that?

Sure, the outside of the FBI building in Miami was different from the one in Dallas, but inside, it was much the same. Agents White and Renfro waited for us in a large meeting room that held a huge table in the center. Agent White explained that they'd done research on the area after we'd informed them of the spawn there.

"We have water if you want it," Agent Renfro offered as we took seats around the table. A large screen was lowered at the end of the table, and I figured we'd get to see slides or a video.

I wasn't wrong. Once those of us who wanted it had a bottle of water, the room darkened and the show started. The everglades looked much like the television footage I'd seen before—swampy areas with high trees and shallow waterways that looked like fields of tall grasses. Airboats could be employed to navigate the narrow, open waters lying between.

Photographs of alligators came next; Mack yawned.

However, when the large footprints of an unusual creature appeared on the screen, we sat up and paid attention.

"We don't know what made these tracks," Agent White said. "We have two missing rangers and several fishermen whose cars were parked in the same spot for a week. Missing persons reports have been filed on three of those, but we don't have specific numbers as yet to understand how many are really missing."

"This isn't good," Dragon said quietly.

"You know what that is?" White pointed at the print left in soft mud. A ruler had been set beside the print, and the indentation was more than twice as long as the ruler's standard twelve inches.

"I've seen one before, and this one shouldn't be here, just as the other one shouldn't have been." Dragon's half frown would have frightened Chihuahuas and small children.

"What's that supposed to mean?" Agent White asked.

"That isn't local," Dad offered. "It had to be transported here. If there are spawn in the area, it's a toss-up whether they attacked the rangers and fishermen, or whether the kapirus got them instead."

"Spawn can transport something that big?" Agent White asked in disbelief.

"Spawn can't transport anything—they have to be transported or shoved through a gate," Dad offered cryptically.

"You called it a kapirus?" Agent Renfro asked. "What is that, exactly?"

"Something that finds human blood a delicacy," Dragon answered. "They're water demons; scaled amphibians that prefer fresh water, but they'll swim in saltwater if forced to do so. The Everglades has both, posing no problem for these creatures; they normally drink the blood of wild mammals. To them, the blood of a humanoid is preferable to anything else, but they'll take whatever they can get if humans aren't available."

I could see that my mounting questions would have to be asked soon; Mack and I were ill-equipped to handle all of this. Teddy Williams, too, was shaking his head in confusion. The others—they looked as if nothing Dragon said surprised them at all.

He said they had to be imported, Mack's voice whispered in my head. *Who is importing them, and why?*

I don't know, but he also mentioned gates. What are those? I replied. *This is too much sci-fi for me, man.*

There's no fi in that—it's reality, dude, Mack pointed out.

Yeah. That's what scares me.

Our attention was turned back to the screen when Agent White showed us a map of the Everglades, and the point at which the footprint was found. The muddy ground was surrounded by a swampy area where bald cypress trees crowded in.

"Could it be a trap?" Merrill turned to Dad and asked.

"No idea. I can't see anything by *Looking*," Dad said.

"Not good," Merrill said and leaned back in his chair. His fingers steepled and his eyes narrowed, as if he were considering the problems facing us.

Adam's Journal

Lion had to bring the kapirus down before, Merrill sent mindspeech. *While Dragon fought the Ra'Ak that appeared in Corpus Christi. We have vampires and werewolves to fight this one. What do you suggest we do?*

I have to wait until my son's life is in danger to intervene, I sent back, my anger boiling at a dangerous point. While it didn't surprise me that Ra'Ak were releasing spawn on earth in alarming numbers and sending them to make others of their kind in equally alarming numbers, it surprised and aggravated me that a second kapirus now inhabited the swamps of Florida.

It concerned me, too, that if a kapirus were released on Earth, what else might the enemy have collared and released on an unsuspecting population? After all, the events of twenty years earlier had been isolated and quickly resolved with Kiarra's hard work and the assistance of Dragon, Lion and the handful of vampires with us now.

Placing your son's life in danger is the last thing I wish to do, Merrill responded to my last sending, breaking me away from my train of thought. *He fights well and with proper training and patience, will become an elite warrior. We are placing a new recruit into the midst of an overwhelming battle—the werewolf boy, too.*

I worry that this is a bigger trap than I originally imagined, I returned.

While we can find no evidence of Ra'Ak upon the planet by Looking, *we may not have sufficient information to* Look *for other forms of attack.*

I hear that the number of dangerous creatures throughout the universes is many and diverse, Merrill sent back. I understood he had that information from Griffin. I didn't want to bring that topic up, so I left it alone.

You're right, I agreed. *And until now, the only worry about the importation of illegal, nonindigenous creatures belonged to those worlds with space travel capability. It is illegal on all of those worlds to import anything dangerous without proper documentation and a cage strong enough to hold it.*

Do you believe these creatures are being sent through gates, then?

It makes sense, although gates, for that sort of transport have to be held open at both ends.

Who might accomplish that? Merrill asked.

Elemaiya, I grumbled mentally. *They're here, but as they're mostly content to kill their own, we cannot interfere. They're not sending creatures through, they're merely holding gates open, for whatever reason. At the moment, we can't prove an alliance with the Ra'Ak, even if we suspect it. Thorsten hasn't been forthcoming about that, and it's his job to watch for those things.*

"Are we ready?" Agent White interrupted our mental conversation. It was time to go; I worried for my son and those with him.

"Son, send mindspeech if you find that thing," I said, dropping a hand on his shoulder. We stood in tall grass not far from the swamp where the footprint was found. Dragon and I intended to find a coffee shop in Miami, close enough to fold to the Everglades in a blink should it become necessary.

I could tell Justin was uneasy and Mack stood nearby, trepidation vibrating off him in waves. I hadn't informed Martin of the dangers they faced—I hoped it wouldn't prove necessary.

"We're going now," I sighed, nodding to both boys. "Be safe." Dragon and I folded back to Miami.

~

Justin's Journal

A feeling washed over me, like the ones I used to experience while watching a horror movie late at night and then being too frightened to sleep afterward. "Dude, I don't like this," Mack whispered as we waded through tall grass in Merrill's wake. The swish of tall, thick-bladed grasses against our jeans and the squish of damp ground beneath our feet almost drowned out his words.

Mindspeech, Merrill cautioned both of us. Mack nodded his silent assent.

Radomir moved closer to Merrill when the sound of something slithered through the grass ahead. Faster than the eye could follow, both vampires disappeared from view, only to reappear, holding a huge snake between them.

What came next was terrifying—the snake became a man, who struggled in their grip.

CHAPTER 10

ustin's Journal
Mack growled and began shucking his clothes beside me. Something about the snake bothered him, that was easy enough to see, but the man the snake became? That was worse.

In moments, Mack's wolf stood beside me, and I noticed in a distracted way that he was taller, now. The werewolf really was growing and Mom was right—he'd need new clothes soon.

Lion snake shapeshifter, Merrill sent back to us, referring to the snake-man. *Confirmed by Dragon and your father. He's more dangerous than the kapirus, according to them.*

"You kill, I not help," the lion snake shapeshifter wriggled again.

"What the hell?" Radomir blinked at the man he and Merrill held.

"I say I here to help. What wrong with you?"

"He speaks English?" Will waded through grass to get to Radomir's side. Russell wasn't far behind as they studied the man. He wasn't more than five-six or so, I noticed, when they set him on his feet.

"Who are you?" Merrill demanded.

"I Darzi. You Merrill. I know this. Let go. Claws hurt."

Merrill cursed softly in Latin, but he released Darzi. Mack and I watched, as if we were witnessing the most bizarre plot twist ever.

"Why are you here?" Merrill wasn't done with the questions. I figured Will and Russell stood nearby, just in case the snake got out of hand.

"Asked to come. Help," he shrugged.

"Wait, I'm getting mindspeech from Dragon," Merrill held out a hand as he listened to the mental sending. Merrill never let you know how he was feeling—he kept that bottled up, somehow. I watched as his shoulders sagged in relief after the mindspeech was over.

"They heard from a superior," Merrill said quietly. "This one is coming home with us afterward—he's extra manpower who volunteered to help."

Wow, Mack mouthed at me.

"I change. Go with," Darzi nodded to Merrill and Radomir.

"All right," Merrill conceded. We watched as the man became a snake again, disappearing below the tall grass.

Dude, Mack shook his head. *There's something you don't see every day.*

Adam's Journal

Belen sent word? Kiarra was just as surprised as I'd been.

He did. He says the Saa Thalarr boat is sinking, so he's providing a patch. Somehow, I get the idea that Thorsten knows nothing of this. Belen also said he is engaged in settling other abnormalities, but he's still keeping an eye on us, I added.

If that's the case, then Thorsten isn't supposed to know about this, she pointed out. *Just as well, I'm so pissed at that bastard, I can't think straight. Thank goodness Belen is still concerned about us.*

We'll have another houseguest when we get back, I said. *Somebody Belen approved.* I wasn't sure how Kiarra felt about snakes, but Belen said he could help and I wasn't about to turn that away.

Who?

A lion snake shapeshifter.

Seriously? We have one on our side? Do you know how cool that is? Kiarra was excited, suddenly.

I hear we have one, I haven't met him yet. He crawled right up to Merrill and Radomir to introduce himself and almost got killed.

Wow. I'm glad they waited, Kiarra sounded breathless. *What's his name?*

Darzi, or so I hear, my sending was dry.

I'll make sure he has a room, she replied.

Do we have bedrooms left? I asked.

A couple of small ones.

Good. I've lost track of everybody. I suppose we could build another guesthouse in the back—we have enough room.

I'll let you worry about that. I can't build anything at the moment.

You're building our daughter. I think that's enough.

Yeah. I hope you're right.

~

Justin's Journal

They were out there—we just didn't know exactly where. We were nearly to the swamp, too, and that wasn't a good thing. Merrill asked me to *Look* for spawn, and there was a hotspot in our area, but it faded in and out, as if somebody were taunting us with it.

How was that possible? I gave him the information and watched him square his shoulders. Darzi dropped back to crawl between Mack and me. Now and then, he'd lift his head and sniff by allowing his tongue to slide out.

I guess it was a good thing I'd studied all that in biology. Therefore, when Darzi veered to the left, crossing in front of me, I followed him. He'd found something. I became Wyvern almost immediately.

It was a good thing, too.

That meant Mack and I were facing the kapirus instead of letting it blindside us, as it did the others.

~

Merrill—Report to Wlodek

The monster—a kapirus as suspected, rose from the swamp to our left. The creature was ten feet tall, larger than the one we'd faced in Texas. Justin Griffin, already shifted to his Wyvern state, went on the offensive.

The rest of us had no warning of the creature, so I cannot say how he and the young werewolf knew to go in that direction.

It failed to matter as a ring of spawn, some of them much older than the initial wave of young ones that attacked first, hemmed us in and prevented immediate escape. Somehow, with the wavering visions the boy offered and a shield provided by something we could not find or identify, the spawn had driven us into a trap.

As you know, that is more than improbable, as spawn have no method of communication and far less skill at devising such complicated maneuvers. Nevertheless, we formed a loose circle and fought off hundreds of them, hoping that the boy at our back held the proficiency to defeat a kapirus.

～

Justin's Journal

Mack's werewolf stood at my back, protecting that side from the spawn that popped up and down from the tall grass around us like a terrible game of whack-a-mole.

The kapirus lunged while Mack snarled and fought at my back and I was distracted for a moment. If it hadn't been for Darzi's snake, I might have gone down in two feet of marshy water.

As it was, the kapirus leapt toward my throat, locking its teeth onto it and stealing my breath when I heard Mack yelp in pain and Kyle shout a warning behind me. My attempt to shake off the kapirus met with too much resistance and my vision began to dim—until the grip of his teeth loosened unexpectedly.

When I dropped with a splash, a wave of dark, stinking water washed over me while I struggled to draw a breath. The kapirus grasped at Darzi's lion snake, which tenaciously held onto his throat. Within seconds, the light left the kapirus' muddy-gray eyes and he fell, while Darzi's snake let go and swam in my direction.

I struggled to rise before the wave created by the kapirus' fall overwhelmed me, only achieving it halfway when two more monsters rose from deeper water farther into the swamp. I had no idea what was happening behind me; all I could do was rise on trembling legs and attempt to stand upright, facing this newest attack.

Bubbles began to form around my legs and something brushed past me with a sickening swoosh and a burst of bubbles—alligators had arrived to take the spoils of the fight. I had no idea if a snake could take on alligators, or whether Darzi would provide a good meal to larger predators. Some of the alligators were longer than ten feet and had to weigh a thousand pounds.

Dad, I sent, *I think we're in trouble.* My mindspeech echoed in my own head—it hadn't gone anywhere.

How was that possible? What was preventing it from traveling away from us? It was as if someone blocked the waves of it before it could leave my head. We were alone in our battle, and that lifted my fear to a different level.

Adam's Journal

Karzac sent mindspeech. Of all the times for things to go awry, this was the worst, I think.

Franklin's health was deteriorating and he was now refusing Karzac's help. Karzac, as a favor to Kiarra, had been tending Franklin all along. Justin assumed that Franklin was all right, although he'd only seen him for a short time after his arrival.

Kiarra asked me to return to Fresno, and then to fold her to Franklin's bedside, upstairs. Did Franklin realize that Justin and Merrill were both gone? Did he want to slip away quietly so there would be no painful good-byes?

Mindspeech to Merrill would be crippling, even in the best of circumstances. I couldn't send it.

"Franklin?" Kiarra approached his bed. A dim, bedside lamp illuminated the room while Franklin drew uncomfortable, rasping breaths. His hands, thin and withered with age, lay on the comforter that covered him. His eyes were closed, as if he were hoping the end might come soon.

"Let me go," he gasped. "Want to."

"But Merrill?" Kiarra took his hand in one of hers and brushed tears away with the other.

"Best father. Tell him," Franklin whispered.

"How can I tell him?" Kiarra held back a sob. "How?"

"Love. Forever," Franklin said. "You. Mean it." His eyes were glassy as he made the effort to open them. "Honey, no," Kiarra dropped her head on the comforter and wept.

"This will be hard for him to accept, you know that," I said softly, taking the chair next to the bed.

"Know. Someday, understand."

I hoped so, because those were the last words he spoke. Twenty minutes later, he exhaled his last breath and left us, grieving at his bedside.

Justin's Journal

The two monsters I faced casually stalked in my direction. I'm sure they knew how easily I'd fallen prey to the first one. Darzi couldn't bite two at once, and I still wondered at how he'd killed something that large so fast. He hadn't reappeared, either, so the gators could have already gotten him.

It didn't matter—I was bleeding, I knew that—blood dropped into the water around me, sending the alligators into a near-frenzy.

Dude, I think my arm is broken, Mack sent, as sounds of fighting behind me pervaded my senses. I'd almost blocked it out, facing what I knew could be my end. At least mindspeech from close range worked —I'd attempted to reach Dad again, with the results still echoing inside my head.

The swamp pulled at the feet of both monsters as they took another step toward me, the muddy waters reluctantly releasing their feet with strong, sucking noises. I forced myself to ignore the pain in my neck and stand upright, stretching my wings out to their widest.

Making myself look larger didn't fool them for a minute. Another sucking step. Then another.

They were close enough to jump.

Frantically I studied them—they were armored with scales, I knew that much, as Darzi had a difficult time finding a place to bite the first one.

Once more, I attempted mindspeech with Dad. Again, it echoed inside my head, the desperate notes mocking me and my fear as death approached.

Somewhere behind me, Mack was injured. Perhaps dying. This time, the Dallas Pack couldn't come to our rescue.

This time, the enemy was going to win.

~

Adam's Journal

I knew before Gina called. The Fire Department was on the way but her mother was trapped in a burning house and the firefighters wouldn't arrive in time.

Yelling at Lion to come with me, I folded to the small, frame house two miles away. Gina stood outside the house while flames roared and shot high into the air—this was no ordinary fire. Part of the roof collapsed while fire sucked at the new source of fuel and sparks popped high into the night sky. Neighbors watched from their yards, many of them dressed for bed but outside, curious but unwilling to help.

"Mom's trapped in her bedroom," Gina shouted, tears streaking her soot-smudged face.

"We'll handle it," I said, allowing Lion to pull her away from the blaze while I formed a bubble shield about me and stalked through the front door.

The bedroom was at the back of the house; fire surrounded the door. Sadly, iron bars covered the only outside window, keeping burglars out and Gina's mother in. She'd die if I didn't pull her away.

Heat surrounded me and flames licked at the bubble shield; fire has no thought as to prey—it only consumes as it goes in its attempt to stay alive. I had to kick the bedroom door down—Marie Allen huddled in the farthest corner of the bedroom, her tears dried by the heat almost before they formed.

A rush of fire bloomed and followed me into the room but it found no victim—I'd already included the terrified woman inside my shield. Striding carefully across a sagging wood floor, I lifted Marie Allen, kicked out the bedroom window and the iron bars beyond it and slid out.

She fainted on the way and I was grateful.

~

Justin's Journal

They were close enough to leap, like the last one had. Backing up in muddy water, I searched for solid footing in a swamp, bracing myself with my tail and hoping to withstand the onslaught.

The first one leapt at me. I shouted, which became a roar, while flames poured from my mouth.

The kapirus screamed, its eyes singed by my weak fire. I had no idea what to do past that point—even blinded, the monster prepared to strike again. It jumped toward me just as a huge, black-scaled hand appeared from nowhere and caught the monster by the throat in mid-leap.

I almost fell at the vision that appeared before me. If I'd been frightened before by a ten-foot kapirus, this increased that fear a hundredfold. If I could imagine a demon from hell, this just blew those images away and replaced them with reality.

Smoke poured from wide nostrils as the demon studied the kapirus before burning it to cinders in his grip. While I'd been busy watching that, Darzi had bitten the second kapirus, which was now sagging into the swamp as it died.

I did fall, then, blinking up at the monster to end all monsters. Black wings unfurled as the scent of burning kapirus stung my nostrils. Eyes as black as obsidian blinked back at me while stars fell through their depths. Fleetingly, I wondered if I were next to die.

A low, growling *hmmph* escaped the demon as more smoke poured from his nostrils. Turning his head, he nodded to the lion snake that swam in my direction. Darzi appeared unconcerned that a giant, curved-horn, black-scaled creature stood over him as he wriggled through the water.

"All right?" Darzi asked, becoming human once he reached my side. I did the same, finding myself sitting in two feet of water. I struggled to my feet,

"Mack?" I croaked, my throat dry and blood soaking the wet shirt I wore. "Merrill?"

"Behind. Need help. Still live," Darzi nodded as he took my elbow to steady me.

"What?" I jerked my head as inconspicuously as possible toward the demon standing over both of us.

"High Demon, that all. You need—he help. Come. Shield gone. Send mindspeech now."

I almost didn't get the mental words out as I turned to survey the damage and the condition of the others. Mack and Teddy Williams were bleeding. I could see that Mack's right arm was broken, too, but spawn dust swirled in the water around him—he'd kept fighting and protecting my back while I faced the bigger monsters. I just wish I'd had as much success with them as he'd had with spawn.

Every vampire's clothing, with the exception of Merrill's, was shredded where spawn had gotten their hits in. They were injured too, and all of us needed attention.

Dad? My mental voice quavered as shock began to set in. Before Dad could answer, I turned to see that the High Demon had disappeared.

147

Son? Dad replied.

We've had some trouble here, I sent. *I think everybody is hurt. I tried to contact you before, but something kept that from happening.*

We'll be right there, Dad returned. If Darzi hadn't held me up, I'd have fallen again.

~

Adam's Journal

Lion stayed with Gina and Marie Allen, to see to them while the fire department worked to extinguish the fire.

Dragon and I brought our small army home.

We were lucky we hadn't lost any of them. All of them, with the exception of Merrill and the lion snake shapeshifter, Darzi, needed medical assistance. Joey and Bearcat arrived to assist Karzac.

Mack had a broken arm, while the bite on Justin's neck bled profusely, soaking an already wet and dirty shirt with fresh blood. The kapirus had attempted to make a meal of my child.

Teddy Williams was covered in slashes and claw marks, but no spawn had gotten close enough to bite. I was grateful—if they had, he'd be dead already. Instead, he sat at the kitchen island, answering questions while Bearcat worked to heal the worst of his wounds.

Karzac handled Mack's injuries while Joey dealt with Justin's problems. Marlianna arrived to do what she could for the vampires. Mostly that involved cleaning wounds with power so their skin wouldn't heal over debris, trapping it inside. Daniel had the least number of wounds compared to the other two werewolves—he had the most experience fighting spawn.

Merrill still didn't know about Franklin. He was exhausted but refusing to show it as he watched Marli heal Radomir's cuts and slices.

That's when Kiarra arrived in the kitchen. I knew she wanted to fuss over Mack and Justin. Instead, she took Merrill's hand and led him toward the stairs. No matter how gently he was told, Merrill would be devastated by the news.

So many things had happened, I was numb with the thought of it. I did know who set the fire at Gina's house, however.

Randall Pierce and two of his friends had done it. The scent of gasoline was everywhere outside the home when Lion and I arrived to help. I'm sure the investigation would reveal the accelerant used to set the fire, but Gina and her mother now had no place to stay.

We're done here, Lion sent mindspeech, as if reading my mind to begin with. *Do you mind if I take the Allens to your old house on Hornet?*

Not at all, I returned. *That's the best idea I've heard all night,* I added. *We can let them live there while they wait for the insurance company to settle up.*

Good idea. I'll let them know. How's everybody? Marli isn't overdoing it, is she?

She's tending the vamps—their injuries are the lightest. Karzac, Bearcat and Joey are doing the heavy lifting this time.

What the hell happened? he asked.

I don't know the whole story yet, I said. *I'll let you know when I do.*

Good. At least we didn't lose any. Except Franklin.

Yeah. Kiarra is telling Merrill now. This will devastate him.

I know.

Justin's Journal

Somehow, Joey and Karzac cleaned Mack and me with power, because we were too exhausted and shaky to take a shower after they did their healing magic. Both of us sat side by side at the kitchen island, shirtless and shivering in the air-conditioned air after our fight in a hot, humid swamp.

"I thought they'd never stop coming," Mack's voice cracked as he explained the fight with spawn. "Will there be a cast?" he asked as Karzac worked on his right arm.

"No, young one. The bones are knitted together. No heavy lifting for a day or two, and things will be just as they were."

"You, on the other hand, had a close call," Joey informed me. "A kapirus spreads infection with a bite if it doesn't kill you. You had a good infection going already when we got you back here. That's neutralized, now. If you'd been Saa Thalarr, your blood would have killed anything attempting to drink it. Immediately."

"Huh?"

"Don't worry about it—I'll explain later. I know this isn't the best time or ideal circumstances, but it's after midnight. Happy Birthday."

"Fuck," I said. As my first official word upon hearing I was eighteen, I guess it was appropriate.

Adam's Journal

"Justin, Mack, Teddy and Merrill, all in a healing sleep," Joey sighed as he settled on the sofa beside me. He held a glass filled with bourbon and Coke and sipped it while the leather creaked softly beneath him.

"What about the shifter?" I asked.

"Seems to be fine—Bearcat took him to his bedroom and told him we'd find clothes and anything else he needed in the morning. He was okay with that."

"We'll have to wait until then to get the full story out of them," I nodded, lifting my glass of straight Scotch and emptying it. "What a fucked up night," I sighed.

"Lion says Gina and Marie Allen were more than grateful for a place to sleep. It's a good thing you left most of the old furniture there."

"That house is shielded. I'd like to see that filthy brat try to burn it down."

"Randall Pierce, right?"

"Right. He and two friends who have fewer brain cells than he does. He leads, they follow."

"I can place compulsion," Joey offered.

"I think we're past that. I hope the local authorities do their jobs. This was in retaliation against Justin and Mack," I said. "There was no reason for this."

"How is Martin Walters' lawsuit coming along?" Joey changed tactics.

"Very well, but any proceeds will come from the city, instead of Raymond Pierce."

"Getting arrested for assault won't be good for the lawsuit—it'll just make it look like the vendetta it is," Joey muttered and drank more of his concoction. He seldom drank, so this was and wasn't a surprise—we'd all been hit in one way or another, and he needed to relax after our multiple scares and Franklin's passing.

"Did Merrill say anything before Karzac placed a healing sleep?"

"He asked Karzac for verification that Franklin was in a better place."

"Fuck."

"I feel the same."

I let my arm drape around Joey's shoulders—he sighed and sagged against me. While Merrill had made him vampire, I still felt as if he were mine in some way. Franklin's death hit him hard, too, because he'd lived with Franklin and Merrill for a few years before going to work for the Council. He'd had healing to do, however, so he'd shoved his grief aside to deal with that.

He'd come to me for comfort now. I was willing to give it. "You know we love you," I leaned in to kiss his forehead.

"Yeah. I know," he mumbled and closed his eyes.

Justin's Journal

I'll never forget my eighteenth birthday, for all the wrong reasons. Not only had Mack and I come close to getting creamed, Grampa Franklin died while I was facing monsters in a swamp and Gina's house was burned down by stupid asshole Randall Pierce.

It was all over the news the next day—that Randall had been arrested after one of Gina's neighbors reported a suspicious car driving slowly through the neighborhood before the fire started.

Randall was found; his car still had gas cans in the trunk and his friends confessed to everything. I had a feeling they were angling for deals with the DA in exchange for lighter sentences, but Randall, the ringleader, might spend a few years in jail. He was already eighteen and considered an adult, so there wouldn't be any juvenile court in his future.

I didn't get up until nearly noon, discovering that I was up before Mack. Feeling numb at best, I shuffled into the kitchen and poured juice into a glass, downing the whole thing and refilling it before noticing my surroundings.

Sacks and boxes filled the floor space between the island and the back door, which was quite a large area. "That's stuff for Gina and her mother," Joey yawned as he walked up and patted my shoulder. "How are you feeling?"

"Neck's a little stiff, that's all," I shrugged. "Not too bad, considering."

"Considering," Joey nodded agreement. "I was hoping you'd feel up to helping me haul this to your old house. That's where Gina and her mother are—your parents said they could stay there until the insurance company settled on their house. It's a total loss."

"It makes sense, and our old house was just sitting there empty, anyway. Where did all the stuff come from?" I nodded toward the boxes on the floor.

"Marlianna called local churches and charities and asked for donations. She only kept what they could use and sent the rest back, so there's clothing, dishes and a few small appliances, that sort of thing."

"They don't have anything right now, do they?" I asked.

"Nope. Their car was in the garage, so it's toast, too. Your dad had to pull Mrs. Allen out—she was trapped inside."

"That's terrible. I'll bet she's heartbroken that she didn't get the picture of Gina's dad out—it was in the living room on an end table."

"This is just tragedy on top of tragedy," Joey squared his shoulders. "We'll have to plan a funeral for Franklin, too—Merrill has all the information on what he requested."

"This is so sad," I mumbled. "I'll never forget this birthday, that's for sure. I hope the party is canceled. I don't feel like celebrating today."

"Maybe next week?" Joey asked.

"Maybe."

"I doubt that Gina will have to work tonight, considering the circumstances," Joey pointed out. "She might need your company, instead."

"Yeah. We can be walking wounded together."

"True. What happened last night? Mack says he didn't see you take down the kapirus."

"I didn't. I only managed to blind one of the three. Darzi got two, and the High Demon killed the one I blinded. That's all I could do—blow fire in his eyes."

"Did you say High Demon?" Dad appeared beside Joey and both now stared at me.

"That's what Darzi said. I thought he was something bigger and badder that wanted to have me for dinner. That turned out to be wrong."

"Son, sit down," Dad instructed, pointing me toward a barstool at the island. "Then, tell me what happened last night. From your point of view."

"The first kapirus was the one that bit me," I said, sliding onto a barstool and preparing myself for the inquisition. "When Darzi bit him and he died, I hoped that was the end of it. Two more, just as big, came out of the swamp."

Before the questioning was over, I had a glass of milk, eggs and bacon in front of me. People stood all around me, including Darzi, who'd somehow managed to find jeans and a shirt that fit.

"That right—he tell truth," Darzi nodded when I described the High Demon. "Not in Full Thifilathi. Smaller one."

"What?" I didn't understand what Darzi meant.

"They have two sizes, depending on the situation," Dragon explained. "It's not common knowledge. Be thankful you only saw the smaller one last night. The large one would be terrifying."

"Hey, he was big enough that I'd have messed up my underwear if that was possible," I huffed.

It wasn't—I'd never had to use the bathroom. I sort of knew why now, but that was beside the point.

"Others not see," Darzi explained. "They keep fighting grz-gitch spawn. Have to."

"Honey, thank you for saving Justin's life," Mom hugged Darzi. He blinked in surprise for a moment before giving her a shy smile.

"It nothing," he shrugged. "How Merrill? He lose child."

"He's trying to make arrangements. It hasn't been easy," Mom said. I knew she'd spent most of the morning with him, after he'd gotten out of bed.

"So your poison can kill one of those things?" Dad shook his head. "That's wonderful."

"Have to bite throat—scales thin there. Can pierce," he gestured with a hand. "Closer to vein. Kill fast." Darzi's face was animated as he described how his snake could take down something that large.

"I can't tell you how glad I am that you were there," I said. If he hadn't been, I wouldn't be sitting where I was, casually eating breakfast and talking about it. "Glad you found clothes, dude," I nodded at him. He'd come home with us the night before, completely naked. It didn't seem to bother him much, either.

"We've already ordered a few things for him—he likes the jeans," Joey said, offering a wry grin.

"Like jeans. T-shirts. Not much shoes, but have to wear."

I liked his speech shorthand. He could make himself understood perfectly and still cut corners.

"As far as I'm concerned, you can have anything you want. If you hadn't been there last night, we'd have been in terrible trouble," I shrugged.

"Maybe he'd like Nikes," Mack said. "They're my favorites."

"I say take him to the athletic shoe store," Mom said. "In your new car." She held up keys and rattled them at me.

"What?" I blinked stupidly at her.

"It's your birthday, dude. I think you got a new car," Mack grinned.

"It's in the garage, and Lynx said he'd go with you to the mall," Mom said. "Take Darzi and get whatever he needs, and get Mack clothes too, while you're at it—his pants are too short. He's two inches taller than he used to be and his feet are bigger."

"Seriously?" Mack stared at his feet. His pants no longer reached the Nikes he was so fond of. "The toes of my shoes pinched now and then, but I didn't realize," he shrugged at Mom.

"It'll be our gift, for what you did last night, baby." She gave him a hug. Mack went pink, but he hugged her back.

"I'll make sure we get plenty of stuff," Lynx appeared with a sly grin. "I have your dad's credit card," he added, holding up the item in question. That meant a video game or two might be added to the pile.

"Can I take Gina and her mom?" I asked. "They'll need stuff, too."

"Yes. Lynx, give Mrs. Allen a call, haul these boxes over there and then take all of them shopping. I'll pay for the Allens' things," Mom handed Lynx a second credit card.

I started to ask how he was going to work around signing for my Mom, then let it go. They'd work it out.

"Power," Lynx said, reading my thoughts. "I just changed the name on the card to mine." He turned the card so I could see it. "I'm an authorized signer on your mom's account, did you know? So are your Aunt Wolf and your Aunt Tiger."

"It's in case of an emergency, like this one," Mom shuffled over and rubbed my back. "But Lynx had to use his power to change the name —I can't do that again until after the baby comes. Honey, Gina lost the laptop she worked so hard to get when her house burned down. Buy another one at the electronics store for her." She patted my shoulder and moved away.

"That's a lot of money," I croaked, staring at her for a moment.

"Don't worry, your mother seems to have more of that than previously imagined," Dad offered dryly.

"You're no pauper," Mom accused, poking Dad in the chest with a finger. I could tell this had been a point of contention sometime in the past. I sure didn't want to get in the middle of it, though, and the thought of buying Gina a new laptop?

155

Score.

"Let's go before the fur flies," Lynx herded Darzi, Mack and me toward the door. I was more than ready to get out of the house, and Lynx would make sure we were covered if anything tried to jump us. I'd already *Looked* and didn't find spawn or a kapirus anywhere in Fresno, but I did see a few in Tennessee. After the oddness of the night before, that was a good thing.

CHAPTER 11

ustin's Journal

Gina couldn't believe it when we invited her and her mother to the mall, and explained that we were prepared to buy whatever they needed, including a new laptop for her. That's when she cried.

I'd never been faced with that dilemma before. Of course, I'd never gotten mindspeech from Lynx before, either—telling me to hold her and tell her that everything would be fine.

I did that. It went a long way toward clearing up the waterworks and got me a tighter hug and a kiss. Who knew? Besides, it made my birthday better to know that I could help someone else instead of just getting stuff for myself.

We drove to the mall in my new Jeep Rubicon, which was red and awesome, complete with the smell that new cars have. I let Lynx drive while I wedged myself in the back seat between Gina and her mother. There was a light in Gina's face that hadn't been there earlier, and I was grateful to be part of it.

Halfway through our shopping trip, I sent mindspeech to Mom, telling her the cost was mounting. She told me to keep going. Lynx grinned—he'd been included in her return mindspeech.

"Don't worry, kiddo," he crooked an arm around my neck. "It's for a really good cause and she can afford it."

Mom called my cell phone before we left the mall, telling us that Dad was on his way to haul packages, and to bring Gina and her mother to the house.

Dad had to haul most of the stuff in his SUV; there wasn't room for much in my Jeep. When we got back to the house, my old Honda, which had been miraculously restored, waited on the circular drive.

Mom and Joey came out of the house. Joey handed the Honda keys to Mrs. Allen and told her the car was hers to drive until her insurance paid, and then she could give it to Gina.

"We have to stick together," Mom told Mrs. Allen. "That Pierce boy and his father have done damage to all of us."

"I heard he attacked you at the grocery store," Mrs. Allen offered a watery smile. "I'm glad you're all right."

"She almost had a miscarriage," Joey grumped.

"You're pregnant?" Mrs. Allen breathed, her eyes widening in surprise.

"Unplanned," Mom nodded. "We thought we were past that."

"Do you know if you're getting a brother or sister?" Gina asked shyly.

"Sister," I said.

"That's so sweet," Gina hugged me. I hugged back. Hell, I'd take the affection any day.

"Would you like to come inside?" Mom invited them in. "Joey and I are making dinner."

"I'd love to," Mrs. Allen said.

"I'll transfer your bags to the Honda," Dad offered as Mom led the way to the front door.

Mrs. Allen went to the kitchen with Mom and Joey; Gina, Mack and I ended up in my bedroom playing Joey's video game until the food was ready. We had to leave the door open, but I got to sit on the floor with Gina curled against me while we played. Mack didn't say anything when I kissed Gina's hair or her temple now and then.

All three of us had close calls to deal with, so it was nice to get some comfort that way. Gina wouldn't ever know what Mack and I had done, but that didn't lessen her terrifying experience the night before. If Dad and Lion hadn't helped, Mrs. Allen would probably be dead.

At least one other life had been saved, besides mine.

Darzi showed up after a few minutes to join the game, making it two against two. I have no idea where lion snakes originate, but he got the hang of it quickly and was wicked fast at it. Gina and I lost to Mack and Darzi twice before Mom and Mrs. Allen, who'd offered to help with dinner, called us to the kitchen to eat.

Everybody showed up to eat smothered chicken, mashed potatoes, fresh green beans and salad. Mrs. Allen, who'd stared at Lynx earlier, now stared at Uncle Dragon. I guess it was a girl thing. Or a woman thing.

It didn't matter, because Gina only stared at me, and I liked that just fine.

Later, when Gina and her mother walked to the Honda to drive to the old house, I pulled Gina close to give her a quick kiss before she got into the car. Randall Pierce was still in jail, but I knew his dad had to be putting bail money together. This was a new experience for me— worrying about the safety of my girl. That's what she was to me, now —my girl.

I was glad, too, that she felt comfortable calling Dad for help. She couldn't have picked a better person to ask. I owed him thanks and a big hug for what he'd done.

Waving as they drove through the arched wrought-iron gates, I realized something else—that behind those gates lay a sanctuary that Randall Pierce and his father couldn't breach. I felt just fine with that, too.

Adam's Journal

Sunday morning, I transported Franklin's body—and Merrill—to his brownstone in New York, where he called the coroner. Merrill wanted the service to take place there, because Franklin had friends in the city.

A few vampires planned to attend, too, so an unusual evening service was arranged. Merrill had already given a generous donation to a local church, organizing Franklin's funeral in advance. He'd also hired musicians from the symphony, but he had a very odd request past that—he'd asked Kiarra to sing at Franklin's funeral.

I blinked at him in surprise. "What did she say?" I blurted. My wife sang? That was an enormous shock.

"She said yes when I told her it was at Franklin's request," Merrill shrugged. "Griffin said long ago that the angels listen when Kiarra sings."

"I intend to have a conversation with my wife," I growled.

"I didn't bring this up to create tension," Merrill held out a hand. We stood inside the kitchen at his brownstone while he held a cup of coffee in his hands. I realized then that this was my first memory of Franklin, bustling about in Merrill's kitchen, finding food for Kiarra. Somehow, even then, he'd been prepared for a vegetarian's needs and had plenty of fruit and vegetables on hand.

"This is a terrible loss," I turned my head and stared at the multimillion-dollar view through Merrill's wide kitchen windows.

"That was my true child—the child of my heart," Merrill's façade cracked as he wiped moisture off his cheeks. "I don't know what I'll do without him." Using a vampire's speed, he fled the kitchen. Only a blink later, I heard his bedroom door closing. He had grieving to do, and only reappeared when the attendants arrived to collect Franklin's body.

Justin's Journal

"Will you and Mack be all right while I'm gone?" Mom asked,

poking her head in my bedroom door. "Your father and your uncle need me right now."

"We're fine, Mom," I said, giving her a nod. "Darzi and Uncle Lion will be here, and I don't intend to go out."

Uncle Dragon was taking Mom to New York—that's where Merrill wanted Franklin's funeral to be held and lots of other things had to be taken care of. It didn't make sense to haul Grampa Franklin's body from one end of the country to the other by conventional means—it was just undignified.

Mack and I had watched, too, as Merrill carried Grampa Frank from his bedroom early that morning, holding his shrunken body so carefully in his arms, so Dad could fold them to New York.

I had to wipe tears away when they were gone.

"I'm going," Mom said as Dragon appeared behind her and laid a hand on her shoulder. That brought me back to reality with a jolt.

"Okay. We're going to Grampa Frank's funeral, aren't we?" I asked.

"Of course. Honey, he was a good grandfather for you. The best." She nodded to Dragon and they were gone.

Merrill's Private Journal

Griffin appeared during what I'd hoped to be my private grieving time for Franklin. "Things are going strange and working in your favor at the same time," he pointed out.

"I'd like to be left alone," I said, my voice gruff and my sudden impatience clear.

"Don't you want to know that Kiarra is softening toward you? That the hold on your M'Fiyah is unraveling?"

"I don't give a damn about any of that at the moment. My child is dead, Brother. Leave me alone to come to terms with that terrible reality. I have no idea why he kept refusing to allow the turn. I would have him with me forever if he'd consented. First Greg, and now this." I no longer cared that he might see my tears—they streamed unchecked down my face and I stubbornly refused to wipe them away.

"I've said that things will come around," he began.

"I care not," I growled. "Leave me in my grief."

"Fine. I will return when things are better."

"You truly were a vampire," I snorted. "At times, I wonder if you ever feel."

"I'll leave on that note," he snapped and disappeared. For once, I was grateful for his hasty exit.

Adam's Journal

I didn't wish to pick a fight with Kiarra. Truly. What was I supposed to do, however, when she spoke to the musicians who'd be playing at Franklin's funeral as if she were used to giving directions?

Merrill requested two songs for her to sing—*Time To Say Good-bye* and *Nessun Dorma*. A rehearsal time was set; she arranged to meet the musicians at the church in the morning, before the funeral that evening.

"I think only once or twice through the songs will be enough," she said before offering coffee and snacks to the twelve musicians who'd arrived at Merrill's apartment. He was a huge donor for the symphony, so they'd given him anything he wanted for the service. These twelve were those Kiarra selected.

Were you intending to tell me sometime? I attempted to keep my mental voice civil as she placed sandwich croissants, deli meats and condiments in front of the musicians.

Adam, now is not the time. I thought this chapter of my life was closed. Griffin chose to revive it, and I won't refuse Merrill this last request on Franklin's behalf.

When will be the time, then? I persisted.

I'll tell you after the funeral. I promise.

I hope so, I grumbled. Yes, I should have backed off; I was ashamed of my belligerence later, but there were things she'd kept secret and that upset me. Justin—my brother Justin, anyway—always called me a controlling bastard. His words had only been partially in jest.

In addition, I should have recognized this for what it was—an attempt by Griffin to drive a wedge between Kiarra and me. I hadn't traveled that path, yet, and had no suspicions as such. Then, I had no idea how any M'Fiyah might be broken, without interference by one much more powerful.

I had many things to learn.

~

Justin's Journal

I got mindspeech from Uncle Lion, telling me to get clothes together for a quick trip to New York. Mack wanted to go, too, so after a short phone call with his dad, he packed a small bag and was ready to go with me.

Uncle Lion looked worried when he showed up at my bedroom door, ready to take us to Uncle Merrill's place in New York. I'd never been to New York before—not that I could remember, anyway.

Mack sure hadn't been there, so he was looking forward to seeing it, although it was for such a somber occasion.

Yeah, I probably should have asked Uncle Lion what he was worried about.

I didn't. Hindsight is always clear and pristine when you're examining it—once you've passed the point where it's too late to do anything about it, anyway.

~

Adam's Journal

Lion brought Mack and Justin to New York; the funeral would be held Monday evening at nine so the vamps could attend. Radomir would be one of those, as he was Merrill's vampire sibling and cared for Franklin.

Wlodek also cared for Merrill's human child, but you'd never catch the old bastard admitting it. I knew, whether anyone else did or not, that Franklin had Wlodek's private number and could have asked for anything. He never did—not for himself, anyway.

My wife would sing at his funeral. That still irritated me and although I refused to admit it, waited to hear how good she was or whether she'd fall on her face and embarrass all of us.

I should have paid better attention, too, as she wasn't eating much. It hurt her more than I realized I think, that I slept on my side of the bed as far from her as I could get. She was pregnant and facing an ordeal I had no knowledge of, and I chose to behave like the proverbial American asshole.

Joey folded in by himself on Tuesday morning, looking as if he'd been crying. As Kiarra's and my healer, he was connected to us. He felt the upset from the current rift between us, and that added to the burden of his grief over Franklin. I attempted to hug him when he arrived, but he moved deftly away and headed toward his old bedroom without a word.

Kiarra made breakfast for Merrill and the boys when they shuffled into the kitchen; I'd gone to a nearby restaurant to eat after rising early.

Yes, I'd already taken things too far.

Merrill drove us to the chapel for the rehearsal at ten, so I took a seat with Justin and Mack at the back of the church while the musicians warmed up. Kiarra was somewhere in the back, warming up too, I suppose. I knew little about music, other than what I liked.

When she walked to the front of the church, I crossed arms over my chest, waiting. The musicians played the introduction to *Time to Say Good-Bye*.

My arms dropped, as did my jaw, when Kiarra began to sing. I understood then why the angels would listen when she sang. Somehow, I knew that voice—had recordings of it in the past. I wanted to knock my head against a nearby wall for being so obstinately obtuse.

Renée Mendenhall, the diva from Mississippi, sang in church that morning. I'd even read her biography shortly after her death.

Her reported death, anyway.

Five years into her career, she'd been attacked by a deranged fan, who'd flung acid in her face. Back in the 1920s, plastic surgery wasn't as viable an option as it is now. She'd been disfigured throughout her career, but it hadn't affected her voice. On records and on the radio, her voice was just as lovely as she'd once been. She'd refused public appearances afterward, and hid from the press and photographers.

She'd died of a sudden heart attack in the fifties.

Or so we thought.

I was married to Renée Mendenhall. My anger began to rise because she hadn't told me.

Jealousy was no longer a part of me, but when Merrill kissed her cheek after an incredible performance of *Nessun Dorma*, I realized that he'd known, somehow. Griffin likely was behind Merrill's knowledge of her former life, and I had no trouble including those two in my increasing temper.

I walked out of the church without a word to Kiarra or the boys. Let her *Look* for me if she wanted; I intended to stalk the streets of New York for a while.

～

Justin's Journal

Mack and I usually listen to rock music. Rap once in a while. Mom blew us away, and we didn't even listen to the kind of music she sang.

The thing was—both those songs would have made Grampa Frank happy. Somewhere, wherever he was, I hoped he could hear them.

Dad, though, stormed out of the church with an angry look on his face and that worried me. Mack noticed too, but didn't say anything, although he did call his dad after we got back to Merrill's apartment.

I gave him privacy and didn't listen in, although Mom sent mindspeech, telling me that Mack's dad was working during the day and hunting spawn with the Fresno pack at night, so he wasn't getting much sleep.

She didn't say anything about Dad's defection, probably because she didn't want me to worry. I could tell she was worried though, even when she tried to hide it. I should have mentioned it or said something. Hindsight—again.

~

Grampa Frank's funeral was a celebration of his life. During the memorial video, I saw photographs of him when he was little; some of them showing him holding an adult's hand, but the adult was never included in the picture.

I knew it was Merrill.

When Mom sang, though, people wept and I got chills, it was so beautiful and haunting.

Dad had shown up at the last minute, wearing a really expensive suit and shoes I'd never seen before. He looked different. I couldn't define how he was different, but something had changed.

Mom, for her performance, wore a black evening dress that made her platinum hair shine. I was so proud of her then—as if what she was doing required more courage than it took to fight spawn or the Ra'Ak that made them.

Sometime soon, she would show everybody that she was pregnant, but for now, nobody knew unless they'd been told.

"Mom looks amazing," Mack whispered beside me, so I nodded in agreement.

Merrill and Joey seem so alone up there, he added in mindspeech.

They were, sitting on the front row together, shoulder to shoulder, as Grampa Franklin's only family. *We should be sitting with them,* I sent back.

Once Mom finished singing, she stepped off the stage at the front and exited through a side door. I assumed she'd join Mack and me at the back of the church where we sat.

She never came. I wish I'd worried about it then. I didn't. I'd never make that mistake again.

~

Adam's Journal

Kiarra didn't come to sit with me after she sang the second song. I couldn't blame her for that, as I'd refused to speak to her since early morning and didn't let her know where I was all day.

Yes, part of the day I'd spent in London at the apartment I kept there, still, and chose to wear one of the custom suits hanging in that closet, paired with Italian-made shoes. I'd been allowed to keep my assets when I was made Saa Thalarr. Kiarra's, or Renée Mendenhall's —had been carefully portioned out to charities according to her will.

What she had now, she'd earned as a member of the Saa Thalarr. I had no idea why I was so upset about it, but I was. I should have been more upset that she didn't come to sit with Justin and Mack after her performance, but I wasn't.

More the fool, I.

~

It wasn't until the service was over that I understood how much damage I'd done. Merrill and Joey sat at the front, accepting condolences from those who passed Franklin's coffin, but Joey had the presence of mind, at least to let me know.

Kiarra has disappeared from my healer's radar, he informed me. *What did you do, Adam? She's on the run.*

~

Merrill's Private Journal

My heart couldn't take another blow; therefore, Kiarra's disappearance almost destroyed me.

Whatever rift Adam created had hurt her greatly. If Franklin hadn't requested that she sing at his funeral, I would never have asked. When I did, she'd turned pale, making me realize how much it would cost her to perform in public.

I'd read her biography, after all, and several musicians and sound technicians all described how she'd hide her face whenever she was forced to go out, and how they'd cringe at the first sight of her when she removed the scarf to sing in the studio.

My heart wept for her. And for me.

Kiarra did not resemble the vibrant young diva she'd been when she was young—then she'd had dark hair, gray eyes and a heart-shaped face. I believe she'd asked those who'd brought her to the Saa Thalarr to make her different so none could recognize her.

Her refusal to sing was for the same reason—to keep anyone from knowing who she was before. She'd reportedly passed from this world alone, unmarried and still virgin.

Griffin told me once, when he'd been drinking, that her first experience with sex was when Saxom raped her. I cursed him again, for perhaps the thousandth time.

More than grateful when the last of the mourners had come and gone, I turned to Joey, who'd gone pale.

"Where do you suppose she is?" I asked. Yes, I knew she was gone, I just had no idea where.

"I don't know," he wiped tears away with trembling fingers. "I just sent mindspeech to Adam, giving him the news. He caused this."

I cursed—fluently—in Latin. It was my native language, after all, and as a former centurion for the Roman Legion, I could do it with unparalleled vehemence.

Franklin—my child, lay in a coffin feet away, the love of my life had disappeared and I wanted—more than anything—to strangle Adam Chessman at that moment.

"She is draining her shields to keep us from knowing where she is, and that is a very dangerous thing," Pheligar appeared beside us. I wondered that he'd come to Joey and me instead of to Adam, but he answered my mental question quickly.

"Do not think for a moment that you can hide your feelings for her from a Larentii," he huffed. I noticed, then, that his skin appeared more gray than blue. He was terrified for some reason, and I had no explanation for it.

Any color left in Joey's face drained away at that moment—my secret had been revealed to him at last. How could he not have known? How?

Franklin knew, but I'd confided in him long ago. He knew I drank more heavily after seeing her—whenever I was invited for a visit. I'd spent twenty Christmases with her and Adam, always receiving lovely gifts and warm kisses on my cheek.

That was nice but never what I truly wanted.

"Fuck," I breathed in irritation.

Franklin had requested cremation after the funeral, therefore no graveside service was scheduled. He wanted his ashes scattered on the garden behind the manor house in Kent, and that would take place soon.

It could be put on hold, however, while I went in search of Kiarra.

"We will begin our search now," Pheligar declared. "Use every bit of knowledge you have. She is alone, virtually powerless and in more danger than she realizes."

He disappeared after that, while Joey wrapped his arms about my waist and wept.

"Child, it will be all right," I soothed, cradling his head against my chest. I only hoped that my words would prove to be truth instead of the hollow promise they seemed.

Adam's Journal

I stood on the sidewalk while Justin and Mack looked to me for comfort and support. At that moment, I began to realize what Kiarra was to all of us. A rock. A comfort. Someone who watched over all of us like a guardian angel.

I was a fool.

Stop behaving like a fool and look for her! Pheligar's voice echoed in my mind. *She is not responding to my mindspeech. We will have words, vampire, if any harm comes to her.*

It wasn't the first time he'd threatened me, but it hadn't happened in a very long time. He hadn't called me vampire in a long time, either. I learned early on that from him, it was a derogatory remark.

It hit me then—because my heart squeezed in my chest. She had no power, was alone and pregnant and running from my temper. I'd allowed my foolishness to shove aside my love for her, thinking that it was my right to know everything, no matter how painful it might be for her to reveal those things.

If I'd just waited for her to tell me—she said she would—I could have held and comforted her through the terrible memories. I hadn't acted as a husband and a mate, I'd been a belligerent, overbearing fool.

"Son, we have to look for your mother," I said to Justin, but I included Mack as I pulled both of them close.

"Where would she go?" Mack's voice wobbled. Yes, he'd been abandoned by one mother already. With everything else that had happened to him, this could destroy the young werewolf.

As it would destroy me.

"Let's go back to Merrill's," I said, my voice nearly as unsteady as Mack's. "She doesn't have the power to fold space, so she can only travel by normal means. I hope she hasn't gone far."

I folded the three of us back to Merrill's brownstone and found Merrill and Joey there ahead of us. I will never forget the look he leveled against me as he held Joey close—Joey wept openly and refused to look at me.

Lion and Dragon appeared quickly—Lion was more worried than I'd ever seen and Dragon looked ready to kill.

Yes, that look was directed at me and I imagined he'd have taken me by the throat and unleashed his wrath if Mack and Justin hadn't been with me.

"Where do we look first?" Lynx appeared and brought all of us back to the present. I was grateful for his interruption, as things had gone decidedly tense in Merrill's kitchen. I was Fourth and a former vampire, but I couldn't fight the Second and Third among the Saa Thalarr and hope to come away alive and whole afterward.

"She needs transportation if she wants to leave us this badly," Merrill looked pale as he made that announcement. "I suggest we begin by checking cab companies, rental car agencies and her credit-card usage."

Joey nodded and pulled away from Merrill, wiping tears as he moved aside. "I'll get my laptop," he said. "We can make the kitchen our command center. Justin, you and Mack can help. Get your tablets and we'll find out what we can. The rest of you—start folding to likely places. Figure out where she could have walked by now and go there, first."

"I'll go out in the Range Rover," Merrill said and strode toward the front door. "Joseph, send mindspeech if you get any information."

"I will," he agreed. "Immediately."

He didn't include me in his brief nod. I wanted to curse, but I deserved what I was getting. Justin and Mack raced toward their shared bedroom to bring their tablets and I was grateful Joey included them in the search. Being busy was so much better than sitting and worrying.

~

Justin's Journal

"Has this ever happened before?" Mack whispered as we trotted down the hallway toward our bedroom.

"No," I said. I wanted to shiver—Mom and Dad had a few disagreements in the past, but those usually blew over pretty quick and they'd never seemed serious anyway. Things were now deadly serious—we'd seen the looks on Dragon's and Lion's faces, Uncle Merrill was ready to throttle somebody, Joey had been crying and Dad suddenly looked lost.

~

Larentii Archives

"Can you tell me anything?" Pheligar begged Somagar, eldest of the Wise Ones as Nefrigar stood by, listening.

"I ask you this—why did you wait so long to come to me?"

Somagar, so ancient he appeared more light than physical body, answered with a question of his own. "You made a mistake in waiting. Find her quickly, Liaison, as the continuation of the Wise Ones depends upon this."

"Are you telling me that my child will," Pheligar began, a hope in his eyes that Nefrigar had never seen before.

"I tell you nothing—find the woman first, then I may tell you what you wish to know," Somagar rumbled, his hand held aloft to stave off Pheligar's question. "You were foolish to mute the M'Fiyah. Now the future dangles by a fragile strand. Find her before the enemy does."

Grey House

"What is this?" Glendes Grey looked up from the paperwork on his desk as several small boxes were laid before him. He blinked—he never expected to see the one standing in his study. It had been so long, after all, since anyone had seen Kalenegar of the Larentii. He was almost a myth, even to many of his own race.

"This is the order you will fill for Kiarra of the Saa Thalarr," Kalenegar rumbled. "These are gifts, made by your own wizards—in the future. See that they are delivered to her mate, Adam Chessman, very soon. Names are inscribed on the bottom of each box. Do not forget, or you will face the wrath of the Larentii."

"I will send someone now," Glendes said.

"Do so. The continued survival of Grey House depends upon it."

"Are you threatening me?" Glendes rose from his seat.

"Only a wizard would interpret his salvation as a threat," Kalenegar snapped. "In the future, Grey House will be saved from its own foolishness, if you deliver those boxes as requested."

"Who is behind this request?" Glendes demanded.

"The Mighty. Ask no more questions, I have already answered too many." Kalenegar disappeared, leaving Glendes to sag onto his chair in surprise.

CHAPTER 12

*J*ustin's Journal

Mack and I learned that night how to check bank accounts for charges. Joey had Mom's account information but so far, nothing had shown up on any of them. Dad, Lion, Lynx and Dragon disappeared two hours earlier and hadn't reported anything yet.

Joey had information on three of Mom's bank accounts that he checked, so Mack and I stared at the amounts she'd given in the past to charities. Sure, that money would have bought fancy cars and huge houses, but I realized how foolish that might seem to those who were starving or fighting for their lives.

I realized, too, that we'd never wanted for anything. Joey began to talk, then, as he navigated from one account to another. "She earned this by putting her life in danger. I don't think she's gone to save a single world classified as *Not Worth Saving* since she got pregnant with you. Something worries me about the fact that she got pregnant again now, but it's not my place to make conjectures."

Mack and I occupied the barstools on either side of Joey's, scanning charges just as he was, but we kept finding the same thing—

nothing new had been recorded. "Did she have any cash with her?" Mack thought to ask. "Or a cell phone?"

"I have her cell phone, because Fresno PD still has mine," I pulled it from my pocket and dumped it on the island. "She never bothered to get another one."

"I don't know about cash," Joey shrugged. "Probably, but who knows how much? Fuck. It's late and she's out there by herself. I've sent mindspeech several times and she won't reply. I'm guessing the others are doing the same, but she's not talking to us."

"I hope she can take care of herself," Mack said.

"Before her power was muted, I'd have said she was more than capable of protecting herself and anybody with her. She's been in terrible situations with the Ra'Ak and always won. Now, she may as well be human."

Joey's words chilled me to the marrow of my bones. "I wish I knew how to fly already," I said. "I could fly over the city and look for her."

"You can't shield yourself," Joey pointed out. "It would be too dangerous. People would see you and you could be killed, since they wouldn't know you had no intention of harming them. That won't keep Dragon from doing fly-bys, though. He can shield himself and you can bet he'll try everything he can think of, because he'll be married to your sister someday."

He didn't add what he was thinking—*if she and Mom survived.* I knew it anyway, without his verbal confirmation.

"If she could fold space, I'd look for her at her beach offworld," Joey mumbled as he navigated the bank accounts another time.

"Wait, what's that?" I pointed to his laptop screen—something new had popped up.

"Fuck," Joey breathed. "That charge was made three hours ago and it's just now showing up." It was a charge from a rental car agency, more than ten miles from the church. Joey sent mindspeech to everybody right then, and I figured there would be a convergence at the business where Mom had rented an SUV.

"Three hours," Mack shook his head. "She could have driven out of the state by now."

"This late at night, it's more than possible, since the traffic wouldn't be as bad as it is during the day," Joey acknowledged. "And New Jersey is just across the river."

"Why would she go to New Jersey?" I asked.

"She could have gone somewhere else," Joey pointed out, "but New Jersey is the quickest way to get out of New York from here."

"Maybe she went in another direction," I said.

"Anything is possible—she's not that fond of the Northeast," Joey confirmed.

Adam's Journal

My fears were rising. Yes, I'd sent mental apologies. Many times, in fact, in the three plus hours I spent searching for her. Joey sent mindspeech, closely followed by a message from Justin, giving me the location of the car rental agency Kiarra found.

I folded there immediately. Dragon and Lion arrived seconds after I did, and Merrill drove up minutes later. Shamelessly, I placed compulsion on the clerk behind the desk, ordering him to provide as much information as possible. That's how we discovered that Kiarra's rental had GPS tracking.

Once we'd done a search, however, we learned the locating device had been disabled rather quickly. The last known location on the car she'd rented was in Newark. The device hadn't functioned past that.

"Do you think she's heading south?" Merrill asked.

"Possibly. You know how much she loves the beach," Lion replied. I noticed they'd spoken to each other, leaving me out of the conversation. I forced myself to swallow my anger—and my pride. I had twenty years with her. Lion had known her for several thousand years.

"There's beach all the way down the Eastern Seaboard," Merrill pointed out. "I'll head toward Newark and the last place she was seen. It's my guess she didn't disable the tracking device by herself. Someone did that for her, I think."

It was time to suck up my pride even further. "I'll take you there faster than you can drive," I offered. "After dropping off your vehicle."

"Good," Merrill nodded. "I appreciate that."

Five minutes later, after a hasty trip to Merrill's parking garage, we were in Newark, outside an independently owned auto repair shop.

Ancient, peeling blue paint spelled out "Mel's Auto and Body" in script on a rusting metal sign, which hung precariously over a building dating back to the sixties. The structure had never been aesthetically pleasing, even when it was new.

We discovered that Mel's grandson ran the business now, and looked more than capable of disabling the tracking system on a rental vehicle for the proper amount of cash.

"You will tell me everything I wish to know," Merrill growled, gripping the young man's shirt collar in a tight fist and leveling the intensity of compulsion only a King Vampire could deliver.

He wet himself—Merrill and I smelled it, although it wasn't immediately apparent through dark jeans covered in grease and oil. "Y-yes, sir," he quavered, attempting to nod, although Merrill's grip was too strong for him to achieve any sort of head movement.

"A woman, blonde, asked you to disable the on-board tracking system on a rental vehicle, didn't she?" Merrill demanded.

"Yes. Pretty woman. Offered me six hundred. I did it for five."

"Did you put your hands on her?" Merrill hissed.

"N-no. Wanted to, she moved away."

"I want to kill you for that," Merrill grinned nastily. "Shall I kill you?"

"Please, no," he whispered.

"If you had touched her without her consent, I would have."

I think I realized then how big a fool I'd been. Merrill loved Kiarra. Likely had known of her for years uncounted, through Griffin. It made me wonder why Griffin had never introduced them—surely he knew of Merrill's feelings.

Merrill knew, just as I did, of Saxom's rape. Saxom had been warped—twisted in some way, and he'd brought irreparable harm to my wife.

Another thought hit me—what if she didn't want me anymore?

Merrill could step into my position and I'd have to abide by her decision—she was First and could ask Pheligar to mute or destroy our M'Fiyah.

That terrified me.

My cell phone rang, pulling me away from my morbid thoughts. It was Martin Walters, telling me that the east side of Fresno was on fire —Randall Pierce had made bail and this was his first act after his release.

The strawberry farm was safe, as was the old house on Hornet.

I couldn't think of a better way, however, of telling anyone who might be interested just where the power lay inside the city. That alone would signal any powerful enemy as to where we lived and how well our property was shielded.

On it, Lion sent to me, allowing me to sag in relief.

"Someone is on the way," I informed Martin over the phone.

"Thank you," Martin sounded just as relieved. "The shapeshifter went with me last night—a couple of my wolves would have bought it without Darzi," Martin reported.

"We have trouble here, too," I said, without going into detail. I figured Mack would fill his father in soon, if he hadn't done it already.

"Mack needs to be home in two days for the full moon," Martin said, jolting me back to reality. Mack was werewolf, and since his wolf had manifested, he'd be forced to change. It would also mark the first run with his father's pack, and that was always a rite of passage for any werewolf.

"I'll make sure he's there," I promised. "One way or another."

"Thank you," Martin said. "It's an important night for him—he'll run with me and his sister for the first time. I figure it was easier for the wolf to manifest the first time, as that blasted party was near the full moon. His wolf answered when it was necessary."

"I wasn't even thinking of that," I sighed. "I was more worried about the boy and the fact he almost died at the hands of humans."

"I'm grateful he didn't turn at the jail, or things could have gone quite badly for all of us," Martin agreed. "While that human criminal would have deserved what he got, I think Mack was too traumatized by that point, and the wolf couldn't fight both of them."

"I understand. At least he's dealing with it now."

"Karzac helped a great deal, as did Kiarra. He felt the loss more than Beth did, when his mother left."

"I'm afraid I have a confession to make," I admitted. "I've really upset Kiarra, and she's gone. I know this is upsetting both boys, as well as the others and me. It's imperative we find her, however, because she can't use her abilities and she's defenseless and pregnant. Things could go badly if the enemy finds her."

"That's not good," Martin mumbled. "Is there a search ongoing? I can probably contact the Grand Master if you need wolves to help track her. He knows he owes you—and her—for past favors."

"I'll let you know," I said. "We're checking her credit-card charges and the like, but she's so upset with me she's foiling our search at every turn."

"You must have really pissed her off," Martin pointed out.

"I did. Look, we can discuss my many failings another time. I need to get back to our search."

"Let me know if there's anything I or a good pack of wolves can do to help," Martin said.

"I will."

Ending the call with a troubled sigh, I turned to Merrill. "Now what?" I asked.

"Fold us back to New York. Let's have a talk with Joey, Mack and your son. They know her well, and it's time to put our heads together."

"I say we look for a beach somewhere—she loves the ocean," Joey said.

I already knew that and Justin and Mack merely nodded—she and I had taken them on trips to Morro Bay, Pismo and San Francisco too many times to count. Kiarra always found a hotel with a view of the water, no matter what.

"Look, Dad." Justin passed the cell phone that had been Kiarra's to me—a news alert showed that the fire raging in Fresno had been pushed back by strong winds, and as it was blown toward already-burned ground, it died from lack of fuel.

Trust Lion to come up with a good way to avert a crisis—Fresno lay in a bowl, almost, surrounded by higher elevations. The winds didn't hit often, but when they did, they could be fierce.

The alert also showed that Randall Pierce had been arrested and held without bond—three people died in the fire he'd set. I shook my head—arson appeared to be his preferred method of destruction, and the authorities should have kept him in jail after the incident with Gina and her mother.

"Creep," Mack mumbled as he stood beside me and read the screen.

"Worse than that," Justin pointed out. "A murdering creep and he's not even out of high school."

"It makes me wonder if these recent incidents aren't his first," Merrill reflected. "His father may have gotten him out of other troubles in the past."

"I'll *Look* later," I said, handing the phone back to my son. "We have other things to attend to, first."

"Here's my question," Joey said. "How far could Kiarra have gotten by now? We know when she was at the repair shop. Let's do some estimates and draw a circle on the map."

Merrill found a map in a drawer, shook his head because it had belonged to Franklin and spread it across the island in his kitchen. The repair shop was at the center of the circle, so Joey estimated an average speed for main roads and back roads. A large portion of the circle he drew encompassed ocean, so Mack and Justin began mapping possible destinations on land.

"I don't think she'd stop there," I shook my head. "Atlantic City isn't her thing, and I think she wants to get as far away from me as she can."

You really fucked this up, didn't you? Merrill sent.

Yes. Feeling guilty and apologetic now gets me nowhere, as you've likely noticed, I responded dryly.

Merrill and I had become very good friends after the events in

Corpus Christi, so I made an effort to be as honest with him as I could, given the circumstances. *Why didn't you tell me you loved her? I* added. *You know there is no jealousy now.*

Griffin, Merrill responded enigmatically. *You know he sees things. He told me that it was important that she find you, first.*

Griffin muted Kiarra's M'Fiyah with Merrill, Pheligar appeared and joined our mental conversation.

I wasn't aware that you knew about his involvement. It was Merrill's turn to send a dry comment, only he intended it for the Larentii.

I knew quickly, but as it hadn't anything to do with me, I let it go. I thought perhaps you asked to have her part of it muted, Pheligar replied, his bright blue eyes turning thoughtful. *What happens outside the Saa Thalarr is generally none of my business, and it was my guess that you didn't wish to hurt her with a rejection.*

Reject her? Merrill's snort was audible. *I would never do that.*

If we find her, I can arrange to have the M'Fiyah gradually dissipate, Pheligar offered. *That way, she will think it natural. Otherwise, she will know it was muted and may become angry again. We don't need a repeat of the day's events—I doubt I could handle another disappearance without showing a great deal of temper.*

What about Justin? Our daughter? I moaned mentally. *How do we explain plural mates to them?*

Frankly, I was having difficulty with it myself. I'd had her all to myself for twenty years. What would I do when she didn't sleep in my bed every night?

Many races do this easily—you have seen it already, Pheligar huffed. *Why should it make a difference? You are measuring everything in terms of your home planet, when you know that many cultures upon that planet encourage multiple mates.*

Yes, but it's mostly one man and more than one woman, I pointed out, *in cultures where the woman is not considered an equal to the man.*

Why should it be that way? Pheligar responded. *You are giving credence to the idea that one gender has supremacy over another, and that thinking is wrong.*

All of this is irrelevant, Merrill broke in. *She may refuse me, and I worry that she'll learn that Griffin tampered with our M'Fiyah. I know her well enough to realize she won't like that and may refuse me because of it.*

You didn't have anything to do with that, if my knowledge of Griffin is correct—and it is, Pheligar said. *When the M'Fiyah unravels, feel free to talk with her about it. Make her understand. I believe she wouldn't be running now if she'd had you to come to—to offer comfort and support in this misery left over from her former life.*

I wish I could offer comfort and support—as a mate and lover, Merrill sighed. *Alas, I cannot, because she has no idea how I feel, and as her portion of the M'Fiyah is muted, she cannot feel it in return.*

Let us return to the task at hand, Pheligar redirected our conversation.

Yes, I agreed. *We have to find her.*

The sooner, the better, Merrill nodded.

~

Justin's Journal

It wasn't hard to figure out that Dad, Uncle Merrill and Pheligar were having a mental conversation the minute Pheligar appeared. Merrill nodded and sighed a time or two, letting me know they were having a private discussion.

I wished I knew what they were talking about.

Mack and I had been searching the map for likely places for Mom to stop and spend the night, but everything we looked up on the 'net wasn't appropriate—at least down the New Jersey coast. Sure, there were lots of places available, but they just didn't seem to suit *her.*

I didn't think she'd turn around and go back to New York, either, so we continued to look southward, down the East Coast.

"I worry that she may have gone westward," Joey said, breaking up the mental conversation around us and pulling Dad's focus to the map again. "It also concerns me that these three bank accounts I have may not be all she has."

~

Adam's Journal

"A secret bank account?" My words came out in a growl. Merrill placed a hand on my arm, forcing me to recall why we were in this mess to begin with.

"You have several," Pheligar huffed, making me blink.

I did. The double standard I was placing on my wife hit me, then. Yes, I had two hidden bank accounts—mostly savings and investments I'd made so Kiarra and Justin would never have to worry about money. Call it a life-insurance policy or some such. I couldn't buy a traditional life-insurance policy—if I died on another world while fighting Ra'Ak, Kiarra couldn't explain that to any insurance company.

It was an effort to protect my family.

She, likely, was doing the same. I hadn't thought all this through from the beginning, as I should have.

"You're not pregnant, either," Pheligar observed. He'd read my thoughts, or at least my expression. I'd have to be more vigilant in the future and place stronger shields.

~

Kiarra's Notes

I've never spoken to anyone about my past. Pheligar likely knows; he has never brought it up. In fact, he didn't have time to collect me when I was chosen for the Saa Thalarr. He sent Dragon and Lion instead. I've worried since then that he just didn't want to see my scarred features.

So many others didn't.

I know the tale of my collection is one of Lion's favorite stories. It only makes me cringe when he talks about it. Seldom did I ever go out in public, but I'd driven to a small inn in Vermont one summer, and found myself the only patron for three days.

The proprietor knew who I was. I was aging by that time and it didn't matter that I kept my face behind a scarf all the time. I'd come down from my room for a drink before dinner, choosing to sit on the small porch behind the house and watch the scenery while I had my wine.

Dragon and Lion appeared from nowhere. I understood later why I never heard their footsteps, although both wore heavy boots. They drew chairs up to my small table while I set my wineglass down with trembling fingers and adjusted my scarf.

Lion, tall, broad-shouldered and grinning, his teeth gleaming white against black skin, scooted his chair close to mine, scraping it across the bare boards of the small porch.

Dragon, who was undoubtedly Asian to my untutored sensibilities, quirked a smile as he settled onto the other wooden chair and crossed heavily tattooed arms over his chest.

Always, it was my habit to attempt to diffuse any situation with humor. I did that then.

"I'm sorry," I said, looking from Dragon to Lion, only my eyes showing through the narrow space left after pulling my scarf tighter against my face. "I completely lost track of time. I thought the mob hit was tomorrow night."

Lion guffawed while Dragon tucked his chin against his chest and attempted to hold back a snicker. He was unsuccessful.

Lion took my hand after that and kissed it gently. "You don't have to be afraid," he said. "We're here to offer a gift."

It had been a gift.

Most of the time.

I will say that during the times I faced a Ra'Ak larger than I ever imagined, I still considered their offer a gift beyond price.

The times I didn't?

Those times orbited around Saxom.

I'd always felt ill at ease around him.

That wasn't why I was running now. I was pregnant. Perhaps my hormones were out of balance as so many say. My past had come calling—the past I'd run away from when I'd said yes to the offer made by Lion and Dragon.

I have no idea where the body came from that was left in my place, but everyone thought it was mine—found lifeless, sitting on the back porch of a tiny Vermont inn. The estate and life-insurance policy I left behind were designed to help those in need, and all proceeds from record sales after my death would go to the same charity.

My brother fought to get all that for himself. For years he petitioned the courts, telling them I wasn't in my right mind when I made my will.

I was grateful he was never able to prove that.

That story, however, started long before that.

Our mother died in the influenza epidemic in 1918; Joshua's father died sixteen years earlier. My father only stayed long enough to get my mother pregnant; my Aunt always said he was an itinerant salesman, as well as a scoundrel. I never knew who he was.

Joshua and I survived our bouts of the flu after our mother passed. He was seventeen at the time; I was fifteen.

Our Aunt Fiona, who was living in Pittsburgh, took us in, but Josh only stayed with her for a year before taking his inheritance and disappearing. I didn't see him again for ten years.

Aunt Fiona made sure that I received an education, then sent me to music school in New York. After our mother died, music was all I cared about. Soon, I was singing solos at a local church on Sundays.

Until my singing teacher arranged for an audition with a radio producer.

Everything after that is a matter of history. They called me The Diva from Mississippi, after the state of my birth. It was also where my mother died, and I never went back there again.

For five years, I did radio shows, live performances, private performances and even sang with a few orchestras. I had no idea what my life would become when I agreed to sign that first contract.

When the first written notes came from what people would now call a stalker, the police ignored it. He alternated between confessions of undying love to threats against my life because I refused to reply.

One police sergeant called him a crackpot, and me a fainting female for taking it seriously. Nevertheless, I kept away from the streets, having no desire to meet up with him.

I hired a bodyguard, who went with me to any performances and saw me home again. He was gay, in a time when that knowledge was kept mostly secret. I didn't care then and never have. Francis knew I knew and trusted me with that information.

I couldn't have asked for a better bodyguard, either—Francis served in World War I and was more than effective in his chosen profession afterward.

Then, Josh arrived one night at my dressing room backstage after a performance, penniless and asking for money. Francis didn't like it, but I gave my brother what I had with me. I know now that he spent it on alcohol and gambling.

Josh never told me where he'd been for ten years.

The second time he showed up, again I gave him money. It lasted two days and he was back, only this time, he asked for a great deal of money, telling me he'd go to the papers and give them a sob story about how I was refusing to take care of my family.

I *was* taking care of my family, actually. Aunt Fiona had a live-in caretaker that I paid, who cooked, cleaned and helped her get up and down because she refused to leave her house.

I ended up giving Josh five thousand—a fortune at that time—after which he promised to disappear and not bother me again.

He did disappear, but not before he accepted a second five thousand from my stalker, in exchange for information on where I'd be and when, without Francis coming with me.

I made the mistake of telling Josh that I intended to visit Fiona in three days, in between performances. The stalker waited outside my apartment building until I came down to the street to climb into a cab.

He threw acid in my face.

I remember that pain even now. Nearly fifteen thousand years and that memory remains undimmed.

The courts sentenced him to five years in prison, where he died. Apparently, someone there took a dislike to him and broke his neck six months before his release.

Perhaps that encounter with a stalker colored my later experiences with Saxom—he had the same feeling about him—a stalker waiting to destroy me.

In a way, they both had.

Adam, in a fit of male ego, had shown his temper and thrown all this back in my face.

While it wasn't as corrosive as the acid that melted and burned my skin, it was nearly as painful, because I loved him. He was the first man who'd offered me real love and sex without pain. I wanted to weep for this rift between us, but I wanted to weep more for his turning away from me when I needed him most.

I wanted to weep for my daughter, too.

I had a terrible feeling that if she weren't protected, she could fall. I worried that she might take the rest of us with her if she did.

I could never say that to her father—I had no evidence of such, after all. Only a feeling gnawed at my gut and made me nauseated.

At first, I had no idea where I was headed; I just wanted to get away from the pain. I'd been powerful for nearly fifteen thousand years. While pregnant with Justin, I'd been on my private world and hadn't needed any power.

Here, danger surrounded me at every turn. I felt as though I needed my scarves back—to hide my face from the world.

What I needed most, however, was time alone and a place where I could think. There was a need for me to finally lay my past to rest—obviously that hadn't happened yet.

Adam would likely never understand that. I worried about Justin and Mack, but they were almost grown, now. Surely they could live without me for a few days.

I needed the space, too, to consider the recent spawn attacks. My second unexpected pregnancy. The revival of my past and the revelation that those wounds were still unhealed.

My brother died in 1972, still attempting to collect money from my estate. He is buried next to our mother in Mississippi.

My plot is in a prestigious cemetery in New York, with a tall, elaborately carved headstone. Humorously enough, mythical creatures—dragons, lions, unicorns and gryphons—twine about it. I still have no idea who made that decision; I only arranged for a headstone, after all, and hadn't given any particulars as to decoration.

Sleep threatened, so I pulled off the highway in Columbus, Ohio. I'd driven more than nine hours; I was exhausted and needed to eat something unless I wanted to be sick when I woke. A nice motel stood next to an all-night diner.

That would work.

~

Darzi's Journal

I write. I speak. Eliminate useless words. Not many understand language shared with brothers.

Nenzi smile at me when I say I love. He say I have long wait. I know this. I say he redundant. He say *you know what that word mean?*

I call him grz-gitch. He laugh.

She missing. I try following with mind talent. I know if she in danger. Vampire act stupid. He need to fix.

~

Adam's Journal

At least the fire was out in Fresno, but Randall Pierce had broken out of jail—with help, according to the news, and was now on the run. I wondered how many other fires he planned to set before he was captured again.

His father was also missing. Probably in on planning the escape, since he had intimate knowledge of the county jail, both in and out of it. Still, we had no hits on Kiarra.

That's where Glendes Grey found me—searching for clues on my wife's location at Merrill's brownstone in New York. Glendes is ancient and looks thirty. Griffin and the Larentii are the only ones I know who are older.

His son, Raffian, looks very much like him, too, with dark hair and strong features. Although Glendes is married, Raffian could attract almost any woman, if he weren't so impatient with nearly everyone.

Raffian is also considered Grey House's best K'Shoufa jewelry designer. I figured the Tiralian crystal cufflinks that Glendes delivered to me had been designed by Raffian—they were beautiful.

And spelled.

"These are for the ones whose names are marked on the boxes," Glendes handed more boxes to me.

Kiarra's name was on one, and it contained a pair of earrings. Another box had Justin's name written on it, with a wristwatch inside. Spelled Grey House jewels decorated the band.

Mack's watch matched Justin's.

Merrill, surprisingly, also had a box. I handed it to him. A ring lay inside—a spelled ring in gold and platinum, with the traditional dark-gray jewel set in it. At that point, I was sorry I'd asked for cufflinks—the ring could be worn anytime, while the cufflinks could only be worn with my nicest dress shirts.

Merrill, understandably, placed the ring on a finger immediately—on his left hand. I wasn't sure that was the way it was meant, but he was taking it as such. I wasn't surprised that the ring fit—another spell placed upon it to do just that, and it would only fit and protect the designated owner.

As would the other items. I nodded to Glendes, who, having the talent to do so, folded away quickly. "Don't take these watches off," I instructed as I handed the proper ones to Justin and Mack. "They're built to protect you. I hope we won't need that protection, but you never know. I imagine it will accommodate your change to wolf," I added as I watched Mack place it on his wrist.

"It's really spelled?" Mack blinked at me curiously.

"By the best wizards anywhere," I agreed. "What's on your wrist would cost anyone else a fortune."

"Can somebody steal it?" Justin asked as he admired the timepiece on his wrist.

"It won't allow it," I said. "I figure any would-be thief will get a nasty surprise if he makes the attempt."

"Too bad we can't get the earrings to Mom, then," Justin tapped her box. "I'd feel better if she had these right now."

"Adam, I'm getting mindspeech from Lion," Dragon interrupted.

"What is it?" I asked.

"A small town in Arizona was just attacked by spawn. Everyone there is either dead or missing. We have to go."

I cursed.

CHAPTER 13

*J*ustin's Journal

Coppertown, Arizona is tiny. Not even a speck on most maps. Dragon shielded us as we watched emergency workers move through the short, main street of town, attempting to identify remains.

Mack shook his head and barely muffled an angry growl. His scenting ability was quite keen—much better than what it had been before the wolf manifested. He smelled spawn and death everywhere. If he were wolf, his hackles would be raised and his ears laid back.

I touched the new wristwatch I wore, stroking the dark jewels lining the band. Merrill, his new ring unfamiliar on his finger, did almost the same thing as he surveyed the blood, gore and mess left behind by ravaging spawn.

"Had to be at least a hundred, to leave this kind of destruction behind in such a short period of time," Dragon mumbled.

It had been a short period of time. A cell-phone conversation with a resident had been cut off and less than five minutes later, the carnage was discovered by a delivery driver.

"They blew through here like a tornado," Dad growled. He was angry that this was taking us away from our search for Mom. Joey stayed behind in New York and was joined there by Uncle Bearcat, who offered to help while we took care of spawn.

If we could find them.

Police and National Guard helicopters were flying over the desert surrounding Coppertown, but the spawn had disappeared like rabbits down a hole.

Only there wasn't any hole. Not that was obvious, anyway. Uncle Dragon couldn't get a fix on them, either, and that was strange. I'd thought my inability to see them by *Looking* in Florida may have been my newness with the talent, but the fact that mindspeech had been held behind a barrier there was still unexplained.

That was coming back to haunt us, now.

"Ten people are missing and likely turning to spawn while we stand here talking about it," Dragon's voice rumbled as he grimaced at the grisly scene before us. "Whatever prevents us from tracking them has moved far enough from this area that my *Looking* skills are currently accurate through the town."

"We are still crippled by Thorsten's command," Dad huffed. "That means Merrill and the others will be forced to place their lives on the line again if we can get a position on this horde."

"I would like to bring my brother in," Dragon sighed. "He is almost as skilled as I with his blades. Spawn will be sorry if they attack him."

"I wasn't aware you had a brother," Dad said.

What he wasn't saying was that at Dragon's age, his brother should have died long ago.

"It was part of the deal offered to me to join the Saa Thalarr," Dragon replied, his face falling into the familiar scowl. "My twin brother would be given immortality if I agreed to fight with the Saa Thalarr. At the time I joined, the mortality rate among our current race was much higher, you understand. Crane was suffering from a terminal disease. I did this for him—and for me."

"Identical twins?" Merrill queried.

"Yes. Except in our tattoos. Crane's tats are of cranes, naturally. I became Warlord. He was my General on Falchan."

"Cool," Mack breathed beside me, his anger at spawn forgotten for a moment. His hero-worship of Dragon just ramped up several notches.

"You may be risking his life," Merrill pointed out.

"I know. What else can I do? My hands—and the hands of every other Saa Thalarr—are tied at the moment. We must use what we have to destroy this threat."

"I understand what might happen if you disobey a direct order," Merrill shook his head. "Expulsion from the Saa Thalarr and the removal of your power and immortality is a terrifying prospect."

"That is why we must do what we can behind the scenes," Dragon nodded. "We were never told we couldn't provide support to those doing the actual fighting."

"Then let's go to Fresno," Dad said, his shoulders sagging. "Joey promised to keep me updated on the search for Kiarra, but he can search just as well from Fresno as he can from New York. We need the vampires when they wake to help track these spawn. They're trained to do research while hunting a target. We'll put them to work."

Dad called our new friends at the FBI, too. They had vampires and werewolves on the payroll, and had even better informational resources than we did. They were now looking for Mom and the missing spawn. I asked Dad afterward why we couldn't find Mom by *Looking.*

"She's an unreadable," he explained. "Those are so rare they almost don't exist. It's good for her—and bad for us. We can't find her by *Looking.* Neither can the enemy, but without the power she normally has, if they find her using traditional means, then she's more than vulnerable. If they take her, they'll either kill her or demand a ransom of some sort. Who knows what they might ask in exchange?"

I'd been scared before by Mom's disappearance. This terrified me. "Will they let her die?" I quavered. Mack, who'd been listening in, went completely still and his face went pale. After all, we'd both heard the phrase *we don't negotiate with terrorists.* Wouldn't this be the same thing?

"Son, let's concentrate on finding her, all right? We have the best we can get working on that right now, including the FBI Paranormal Division. We have to focus on the spawn that are now attacking entire towns."

"She has to be all right," Mack mumbled, stuffing his hands in his pockets in an uncomfortable gesture. "Dad says I have to go on the Pack run tomorrow night. I'd rather stay here and help Joey."

"Son, you won't be able to stop the change—it's in your blood," Dad dropped a hand on Mack's shoulder. "We're all worried about Kiarra, but none of this is your fault. It's mine. We'll find her. We have to."

A weariness came over Dad and lines appeared around his mouth that I'd never seen before. This was taking a greater toll on him than I thought and I was only beginning to realize what the stakes were in all this. Yes, Mack and I had a narrow escape with spawn and three kapiri, but this one thing could bring all of us down.

"Perhaps you should have left her power intact." Nefrigar studied Pheligar, who'd uncharacteristically *Pulled* in a chair to sit while they spoke. He didn't mention that Pheligar's blue skin was tinged with gray, or that worry clouded normally bright-blue eyes.

"I see that now. At the time, I imagined it to be the prudent thing to do. I had no idea she would choose to disappear like this. I had to deliver Wolf to her new assignment on Grelx, else I might have been more aware of the situation."

"Have you attempted bending time?"

"Yes. I encountered a maelstrom when I did."

"The time is in flux, then, intersecting with imaginary time in another juncture of the multiverse."

"Imaginary time," Pheligar huffed angrily. "There is nothing imaginary about it. Why would it be named thus, when it can result in a chance intersection of one timeline with another, at which the same events occur in both timelines at the same moment, at an extremely critical point?"

"You know that in some exceptionally unusual circumstances, the timelines can spin away in different directions as a result?"

"I have read the books and studied the phenomenon," Pheligar grumbled. "It does me no good, as there is no way I can prevent any of this, and, as Kiarra is unreadable, I cannot find her."

"Have you attempted mindspeech?"

"You think she will listen to me?" Pheligar seldom employed sarcasm, but he did so now, tapping his chest and shaking his head at Nefrigar.

"Any attempt is worth the effort to get her back," Nefrigar replied, turning back to the ancient book he'd been repairing with power when Pheligar appeared. A fragile page, ravaged by time and almost eaten away, became whole in his hand. Carefully placing it atop the other pages he'd already repaired, he turned to the next page in the text.

"You are correct, of course," Pheligar admitted with a weary sigh. "I should have listened to your advice early on, when you said to remove the mute on our M'Fiyah. She has two muted M'Fiyahs upon her, and that cannot be a good thing. Do you suppose that lent to her confusion now?"

"It will not help it in any way," Nefrigar responded, making another page whole with power. The parchment rustled softly as he smoothed it in place atop the other repaired pages.

"You already know that her life would have been better had you not muted your M'Fiyah with her," he continued. "You likely realize that Kiarra's M'Fiyah with the King Vampire, had it not been muted, might have kept her from running away. She could have relied on his strength and his desire to comfort and console. That is a beneficial aspect of multiple mates that is often overlooked."

"I understand that—if you recall, we did research on that subject centuries ago."

"I remember. All I can tell you is this—it is imperative that she be found. If she is lost, many events will rupture and the future may be lost."

"You do not reassure me, brother." Pheligar turned his head.

"I cannot—too many things have become critical, and this may be at the center of it. If she dies, your child will not be the same. It matters not that you carry the complete and healthy embryo in your body. A mother can have a great deal of influence on a Larentii child, even if he does not carry her genes or DNA. It is usually the reason Larentii young name themselves after their mothers, ever since the rift."

"I know. Most Larentii do not remember the times before the rift, when female Larentii numbers were much the same as the males."

"Ferrigar's fault," Nefrigar repaired another page. "And yes, brother, I know not to speak that aloud outside the archives. Somewhere inside him, he knows he erred, but he may never admit it. His second mistake was making the race forget the times before. I recall them perfectly, as I am archivist and the Archives are protected against any power that might tamper with history. Nevertheless, Ferrigar ordered those records sealed and none may read them now. The Wise Ones, you and I may be the only ones, besides Ferrigar, who know the truth."

"The Vhirilaszh knows," Pheligar whispered.

"And he disappeared long ago. None have seen Kalenegar for millennia, and even the Wise Ones cannot find him, as he is also an unreadable."

"I worry that he may have separated his particles, leaving us without that added level of protection."

"I believe he still is," Nefrigar repaired the back cover of the book and closed it carefully with a sigh. "That, of course, cannot be proven, no matter how much I'd like to try."

"The Vhirilaszh is neither here nor there, as humans often say," Pheligar pointed out. "We must find Kiarra before the enemy does. Everything hinges on that."

Adam's Journal

Lion and Marlianna cooked breakfast for us the following morning—we'd snacked the night before while we studied and pondered the problem of disappearing spawn and a missing member of our family.

Hardly any of us slept. Karzac looked like a thundercloud and snapped at any adult in the house, with the exception of Mack, Justin, Darzi and Marlianna. We'd heard from Pheligar, early on, warning us not to attempt to bend time in our search for Kiarra. It was one of those instances when we could lose ourselves in an inescapable vortex.

I had no idea what that meant, but knew enough to heed the warning. I was too worried that Thorsten might become aware of the situation and order us to cease our search for Kiarra, writing her off as a lost cause.

Could he—would he—do that to the First among us?

In my few direct dealings with him, I came away with the feeling that he had no care what happened to any of us, and was prepared to find a replacement if any of us fell. Only Kiarra had worried about that—more than anyone else, at least.

With Pheligar's input and Dragon's and Lion's help for the past fourteen thousand plus years, she'd managed to keep the tiny race of Saa Thalarr intact, and that included Griffin, who'd never appeared to care whether any of his charges fell while he served as First.

Worlds had been lost when Saa Thalarr died. Kiarra had never lost one, and had saved many considered *Not Worth Saving*, including Earth twenty years past.

They all owed her a debt—those many worlds attacked by the Ra'Ak. Countless souls had been saved by her perseverance and the tireless support she offered her charges. Those in her care included me, as well as the others.

Only the feeble-minded would fail to see that she'd stopped rescuing worlds classified as *Not Worth Saving* since the birth of our son. For those, she'd risked her life more than she normally might. I imagined that she had no desire to leave Justin without his mother while he was young. Now that he was grown or nearly so, she was pregnant again. Once more, I wondered at the timing of everything.

"Adam?" Dragon's voice broke into my thoughts.

"What?" I turned sharply in his direction.

"Another small town has been hit—this time in Arkansas," he said.

~

Kiarra's Notes

A television was on and breaking news was announced when I stopped for a late lunch in Nashville. I'd loaded the car with snacks, juice and water before leaving Columbus behind, so I wouldn't be hungry and begin to feel sick while driving.

The small truck stop had a diner and I could fill the gas tank while I was there. Instead of eating my grilled cheese sandwich at first, however, I stared at the carnage depicted on the screen above the counter.

Remains were scattered throughout the small community in Arkansas, covered by sheets, tarps and anything else emergency workers could find to hide the bodies from curious onlookers and the swarming media.

The National Guard was on the scene, securing the perimeter, just as they were doing in a small town in Arizona.

Were there now two hordes of spawn on the loose? Were Adam and the others planning their searches? Was this the work of one horde of spawn that had somehow managed to appear and disappear with the help of something more powerful?

I'd asked Pheligar, the last time I'd seen him, whether any Ra'Ak could be detected on the planet. He'd already *Looked* for them and said he'd found no evidence. If they were here and could hide from a Larentii, the future of the Saa Thalarr was in serious jeopardy.

It was all we had—Pheligar always knew of their presence. No, he couldn't interfere in our search for them after we reached a world, but he always knew they were there.

197

I felt ill anyway, and belatedly lifted my sandwich, taking a determined bite while I watched the rest of the broadcast.

~

Justin's Journal

Mack had to go home with his dad before most of the rest of us were folded to Green Bluff, Arkansas. Darzi and Karzac stayed in Fresno with Marlianna, Joey and Bearcat.

For the second time, I stared at covered bodies while emergency crews searched buildings and houses for more remains.

Nobody was left alive.

Nine missing here, Dragon sent mindspeech to all of us.

They're gathering allies while they have a snack, Dad's mindspeech was little more than a snarl. *This town is slightly larger than the one in Arizona. It's my guess they'll select larger and larger targets as they go along.*

By now, on any other world, we'd have found and killed them, Lion said. *I have no idea what is hampering us from Looking for them here.*

People are beginning to panic everywhere, Merrill broke in. *I've heard from Wlodek in the UK. While Europe hasn't been attacked yet, everybody is afraid and passengers are refusing to get on planes headed to the States. The President is attempting to calm everyone by calling these isolated incidents, but that won't last much longer. We could have rioting soon, if something isn't done. The military is worse than helpless in this situation—because they could become the spawn horde's next target.*

Agreed, Dragon responded. *That is my worry, too, as those trained for the military will make deadlier spawn if they are turned.*

All it will take is a spark in the proper place to start a conflagration, Lion nodded slightly. *After that, nobody will be safe here, and the Ra'Ak will have won the world without a challenge.*

There is no trail to follow, here—it disappears just as the one in Arizona did. Shall we return to Fresno, or somewhere nearby so we may plan our next move? Dragon asked.

Fresno, Dad said.

Everybody agreed. We were there in less than a minute.

"Where's Darzi?" I asked Karzac, who moped at the kitchen island over a cup of tea.

"With Martin and young Mack Walters," Karzac sighed. "He worried that he might be needed, so I didn't argue. At least he feels useful, watching the Pack while they run."

"I like him—a lot," I said, opening the fridge and pulling out the orange juice. "We need groceries again," I sighed, pouring the last of the juice into a glass and drinking it in three swallows.

"Your mother does so much that goes unnoticed, until she is gone," Karzac observed.

"Yeah." I took a seat nearby and studied the orange juice carton, turning it this way and that in my hands. That's when Gina called.

"Hi, baby," I strode away from the kitchen while answering her call. "You okay?"

"I was calling to ask you the same thing," she said.

"We're still in a funk after the funeral," I said, not mentioning the full reason why.

"I'm so sorry," Gina said. "I don't suppose you could come over for dinner tonight? Mom's making pot roast and there's plenty to go around."

"I might be able to," I hedged. "Let me check with Dad and I'll call you back."

"Okay," she said brightly. "I hope you can come."

⁓

"Go ahead. I doubt we'll arrive at any sort of solution for a few hours, so there's no reason not to," Dad said when I asked if I could visit Gina. "Just be careful," he added.

"I will. The old house isn't far away; I should be fine. Oh," I said, remembering something, "What are we going to do about lessons, now that we're officially back?"

"We'll have to continue them," Dad sighed. "I don't see how we can do otherwise at this point."

"I'll let Gina know," I nodded. "Thanks, Dad."

~

An hour later, I was in my Jeep and driving toward the old house. I'd phoned Gina before I left, letting her know I was on the way. She sounded happy—excited. That made me feel good. Honestly, I needed some happy around me, after everything else that had gone down recently.

Mom's absence still worried me, but I shoved it aside for now, determined to have a good time with Gina and her mother. After all, they'd gone through trauma, too, and who knows what they needed to make them feel secure?

Security—it was a thing I'd never been concerned about, before. Mom and Dad always made sure I was safe. Half that team was now missing and in need of protection herself.

Still, it hadn't sunk in completely how vulnerable she was. I'd seen Joey close to tears several times as he frantically switched from one website to another, searching for any activity on her bank accounts and such.

Maybe teaching our lessons would pull him out of his funk—at least for a while.

It wasn't long before I was parking in the driveway of the old house. It's funny how things change once you leave something so familiar behind, replacing it with something new.

The strawberry farm was home, now. That's when it hit me—home wasn't a place—home was the people. Mom, Dad, Mack, Joey. They made home what it was. It was never about the structure, although I had fond memories of it—of us, rather—inside it.

This house was home for Gina, now, because that's where she and her mother were. Opening the door and climbing out of my truck before more nostalgia set in, I strode over the familiar walkway, my shoes crunching on the concrete walk as I walked toward the front door and rang the doorbell.

Gina met me at the door and lifted her face to me, inviting a kiss. I gave it to her willingly.

It felt good.

~

Darzi's Journal

Nefrigar come to me before I go to Earth. He say to write, for Larentii Archives. He say it important.

I agree. I write often. Did not before. Nefrigar make sense.

I watch from hill as Pack run by. They in danger. I here to make safe. Was told to keep alive.

All important.

I do.

~

Adam's Journal

"This is where the footprints and other evidence disappears in Arizona," Lion tapped a map spread across the kitchen island as we had sandwiches for dinner. "Here, they disappear in Arkansas." He tapped the second map. "Both times, they travel less than half a mile from the town before vanishing. Something powerful is behind this, but I'll be damned if I know what it is."

"It has to be more powerful than the Larentii, or something that the Larentii may not be able to detect. Has there ever been such a thing?" Dragon asked. His eyes, narrowed and questioning, turned toward Lion and me.

"Do you want to call Pheligar and ask?" I said. Dragon was currently in charge of the Saa Thalarr, and Pheligar should heed his call anyway. Dragon seldom asked the Larentii for anything.

"I'll ask, just be prepared for a refusal to answer, or an answer cloaked in even more mystery," Dragon sighed, leaning back in his chair and lifting the glass of Scotch he'd poured for himself.

Radomir, Russell, Will and the other vampires sat around the island with us, but were more than content to listen. They were completely trustworthy and we talked freely in front of them.

If they hadn't seen Pheligar yet, they were about to be surprised.

"I know what you're asking," Pheligar appeared—he'd employed nexus echo and heard his name mentioned. "The Larentii seldom speak of it, but yes, there was something we could not detect. We thought it extinct. That may no longer be true."

Frowning, he enlarged a barstool with power and sat between Lion and Dragon while Radomir schooled his face to hide the surprise. "Can you elaborate?" Dragon asked politely.

"I do not wish to, but yes, I will." He sat for a moment, as if considering how he might tell us what he knew. The information was painful to him, unless I missed my guess.

"There was a world," he began, "called Sirena. Its inhabitants were called Sirenali, and they could place obsession. As terrible as that seems, it wasn't the most dangerous thing about them. The race was created—as a whole—as unreadables to all. Even the very powerful cannot see their presence. That, in itself, made them very, very dangerous."

"What happened to them?" Will blurted, staring wide-eyed at Pheligar. After all, Pheligar said they were supposedly extinct. The question was valid and one I wanted to ask myself.

"The Larentii destroyed their world, after they attacked the Larentii homeworld," Pheligar said simply. "If a few escaped, or any enemy capable of bending time rescued some before their world was destroyed, we could be in terrible trouble."

I learned something by listening to Pheligar that evening. Obsession was stronger and more volatile than compulsion placed by any vampire. It was a frightening truth that we heard from our Liaison, and I was glad I never knew of it until now.

Of course, if Pheligar's suspicions were correct and a Sirenali was involved, then we could be waging a war we couldn't win. If there were more than one involved, that was too terrifying to contemplate.

I longed for the days when Ra'Ak were deemed the worst enemies we might face. Those days could be gone with the sweep of a hand. The Ra'Ak could bend time. And, although the knowledge of Sirenali had been removed from every other race, the Ra'Ak may have obtained it in some way.

It was inevitable that they'd use whatever they had to destroy the Saa Thalarr. I'd never felt that my new race might feel like a tiny island under siege, but that's how I saw things, now.

We needed help. We needed more Saa Thalarr. We needed so many things.

I needed Kiarra. To talk to. To discuss this new turn of events. I had no doubt that Pheligar would never have given us information on the Sirenali if he didn't suspect their presence.

I shuddered. *Kiarra*, I sent, *we are in terrible trouble. Be safe. I'd beg you to return to me, but I know I haven't apologized properly, yet. Nevertheless, I miss you terribly and love you more than you know.*

Justin's Journal

Gina's mom was a good cook. The pot roast was great and we ate and talked at the table. I felt comfortable with them, too. After listening to some of my old friends at high school tell about their experiences with girl or boyfriends' parents, I figured it would be the inquisition all over again.

It wasn't. Mrs. Allen treated me like a member of the family and I appreciated that. We talked about Grampa Frank; how he wasn't related by blood but had been just as close and just as loved.

What surprised me, though, was Gina's best friend, Sarah, had been invited, too. Perhaps she was hoping Mack would come, because she asked about him.

"He had a family function he couldn't get out of," I shrugged without elaborating. Sarah accepted that and I was relieved. After all, how can you explain to humans that your best friend is out running through fields, hunting deer or bear with his dad and sister, and that on full moons, he can't help turning to wolf?

For the first time in a while, I felt almost normal—as if I were still in high school instead of worrying about monsters. The fact that others might consider me a monster wasn't a concern.

At least not then.

We laughed, joked, teased, played Monopoly after dinner and I went home at eleven, because the following day was a school day, as it turned out. The drive home was peaceful, with no unexpected surprises.

Kiarra's Notes

(Deleted from her personal files by her father.)

I'd stopped at another motel next to a restaurant in Little Rock, Arkansas. Somehow, somewhere along the road, I realized I was driving toward Corpus Christi and ultimately, Port Aransas. Yes, that's where Adam and I met, and our M'Fiyah manifested. I'd driven more than eleven hours and was exhausted for the second day in a row. I only wanted to crawl in bed after my meal and huddle there, feeling lost, alone and sorry for myself.

Everybody has days when they want to crumble. This was one in a string of several, all in a very short period of time, beginning with Mack's near-death in a Fresno jail cell.

Slumping on the side of my hotel bed, I tossed the key card onto the nightstand with a plastic, ticking noise. I wanted to cry, but the tears refused to fall. I knew they would eventually, but for now, I was just too tired.

That's when he came. I hadn't seen him since I'd become Saa

Thalarr. It's funny that I never recall him until he appears again, and then I remember.

My father.

Yes, I tell everybody I never knew who he was.

That's true. I still don't know who he is—he's never told me. I can tell now, however, that power vibrates off him like snow sweeps off a tall mountain in a strong, winter wind.

He's tall. Dark-haired. Gray-eyed. More handsome than Adam, even, though their coloring is much the same. Perhaps some part of me saw that in Adam when we met the first time. I didn't consciously recognize it, however.

"What's wrong with my darling girl?" The comforter rustled beneath his weight as he sat beside me and pulled me into his embrace.

"Daddy, everything is wrong," I sniffled against his shoulder.

CHAPTER 14

iarra's Notes
(Deleted from her personal files by her father.)

When I stopped crying—eventually—he tipped my chin up with a gentle finger. I stared through tear-blurred eyes at him. At his earnest, loving gaze. "Why is all this happening?" I croaked. My voice had deteriorated after sobbing for a good twenty minutes.

"Sweetheart, so many things are happening wrongly at the moment. We must remain vigilant. You," he tapped my nose with a finger, "must go back to your family. You will be safer there, and they will be safer with your advice added to the mix. I know what you want in Port Aransas, you were unconsciously driving there—to the beach house you bought years ago. Isn't that right?"

"Yes." I hung my head.

"I'm going to take you home, instead—both you and your rental vehicle," he grinned. "All you'll have to do is pull into the driveway and punch in the code. At any other time, I'd have let you stay away as long as you wanted, but you have no power now. That presents a very big problem. If you don't want to sleep with Adam when you get back, then tell him to sleep on the patio or while hanging upside down from a tree. It's one thing to have your pride wounded. It's another to be a total prick about it."

"That's the truth," I nodded, hoping he'd hug me close again. He did. "I don't know what to think about this baby," I sighed.

"I know. Raise her properly. I'll see that the decisions will be hers, when the time comes."

I wondered briefly what he meant by that before letting it go.

"One more thing before we go," he kissed my hair.

"What's that?" I mumbled against a crisp, white shirt.

"Wear the earrings. You'll know when to stop wearing them."

Justin's Journal

I'd pulled up to the keypad outside the gate. Rolling down the window, I reached out to punch in the number. A car I didn't recognize immediately pulled up behind me. I froze.

Cautiously poking my head out the window, I looked back to see who it might be.

"Justin, it's me," Mom said, sticking her head out the car window to look at me. She sounded exhausted. "Will you let me in?"

Adam's Journal

"I don't remember driving here," Kiarra mumbled as she shuffled past me. Joey stood in the foyer, wringing his hands. He knew, as did I, that Kiarra was ready to drop. Had she driven all the way from New Jersey in the space of two days?

"The last thing I remember is Little Rock," she said as Joey lifted her and carried her toward our bedroom.

I should have done that. Feeling like a callous dolt, I followed Joey and watched as he laid her carefully on the bed before checking her vitals. Karzac appeared immediately, as did Dragon, and both checked the baby. Merrill stood behind me, afraid to push in any farther.

"Just let me sleep," Kiarra mumbled, attempting to fend off the many hands touching her.

"Back away, I will deal with this," Pheligar appeared. After he lifted Kiarra and began the soothing, trilling noise only he was capable of making, she fell asleep quickly. The others stole away. I took a chair in the corner of the room and fell asleep while watching Pheligar hold my wife.

∽

Justin's Journal

Nothing seemed amiss when classes started on time the following morning. Bearcat went with me to pick up Gina and Sarah; Mack showed up looking only slightly worse for wear.

He offered me a tired smile, though, so I figured the night had gone well enough.

Darzi had come in for breakfast before school, ate two bowls of wheat shreds with four strips of bacon and then went to the backyard, where Uncle Lion reported that he was sunning himself (as a snake) on a big rock that was part of the landscaping around the house.

Lion warned me, in case the girls wanted to go into the backyard. I wasn't sure how I'd explain that the huge, unidentifiable snake meant them no harm. Mack snickered—he was included in Lion's mindspeech.

Mom was still asleep at noon, but the Internet had been busy since we'd left New York. No idea which attendee at Grampa Franklin's funeral had done the deed, but Merrill was furious when Joey showed the YouTube video to all of us at lunchtime.

Mom had been recorded, singing both songs at the funeral and the video had already gotten half a million hits.

Comments were piled atop each other, ranging from *why isn't she on America's Best Talent?* to someone offering to act as her agent and sign her to a record deal.

Everybody wanted to know who she was and nobody could find any information. The only good thing—in my opinion—was that the image was grainy and you couldn't make out much of Mom's face in the dim interior of the church. Her voice, though, sounded like an angel's.

"Look at this—they're already comparing her to Renée Mendenhall," Joey pointed at a comment.

"Fuck," Dad shook his head. "What are we going to tell her? How are we going to tell her?"

"Tell me what?" Mom shuffled into the kitchen, dressed in a robe and pajamas. Gina and Sarah, who'd sat quietly by while the rest of us went batshit over the unexpected video, turned toward Mom.

"I never knew that about you," Gina said. "You sound incredible."

"You think so?" Mom offered Gina a smile.

"A bunch of other people do, too," Sarah breathed. "I couldn't tell it was you, until Justin and Mack said so."

"At least my face isn't in the light," Mom said as she studied the video over Joey's shoulder.

"You sound better about this," Dad said.

"You should stay out of it," Mom retorted, pointing a finger at Dad's chest. He shut up immediately.

"At least the fees were paid to the rights holders," Merrill grumbled. "Those were the songs Franklin requested, and that had already been taken care of before the funeral, since the symphony was involved."

"You know, this gives me an idea," Mom said.

"What idea?" Dad asked. Mom did her best to ignore him, but answered the question anyway.

"Gina, I know your mother has never gotten closure on your father, because his remains were never found. What if I sell both those songs as a limited release to raise money for that—I know someone will take money to turn over what they have to a neutral party—it's not widely known, but they do accept bribes."

"Would you do that?" Gina breathed before wiping tears away. That was my cue—I moved to her side and put my arms around her. She leaned against me and that felt right and proper.

"I'll do it this once, just to get the right thing done," Mom said, determination showing in her blue eyes. "We'll make this work. Adam, will you contact those people you know in the FBI? I think we can offer suggestions on who to contact."

That's when I realized that Mom had gone *Looking* for Mr. Allen's remains. It might take some finesse, but I couldn't help but think that the deal might be as good as done.

"What about the—you know," Dad protested.

"I'm not directly involved," Mom pointed out. She sounded huffy, too. "All I can offer is advice. I'll sing two songs into a microphone, and hire local musicians to give them some extra money. Works for everybody, right?"

"If you say so," Dad grumped.

"And we need groceries," Mom said.

"I'll make sure we have people ready to go to the store," Dad agreed.

"So we do have our priorities, don't we?" Mom said sweetly and flounced out of the kitchen.

"You didn't eat," Joey yelled at her.

"Then bring me something," she yelled back. "I have plans to make."

"I'll take something to her," Merrill offered. Joey didn't argue, so Uncle Merrill filled a plate with scrambled eggs, fruit and cheese, placed that and a glass of milk on a tray and hauled it toward Mom and Dad's bedroom.

Dad hesitated for a barely a second before following.

Adam's Journal

I think Merrill would have been happy to feed Kiarra by hand if she'd allowed it and I hadn't shown up steps behind him. As it was, he set the tray on the bedside table, offered her a smile and the glass of milk.

Yes, I should have realized that he'd been watching her carefully for years. She loved cold milk and drank half the glass before giving him a smile in return. He offered her a napkin, which she gratefully accepted and wiped the milk moustache off her upper lip. The smile turned into an all-out grin.

"These came while you were away," I interrupted the breakfast interlude.

"What?" Kiarra leaned forward, peering around Merrill's broad shoulders to see what I meant. I held up the box containing her Grey House earrings.

"Are those earrings?" she asked eagerly.

"Yes. I already have my cufflinks—they're very nice. As is Merrill's ring and the boys' watches."

"Gimme," she held out her hand. Stepping forward, I placed the small box in her hand with a mock bow.

"I'm wearing them," she announced, fumbling with the lid on the box for a moment. Merrill took the box gently from her hands, opened it and revealed the earrings nested inside.

"Pretty," Kiarra breathed and lifted one up to examine it.

"Here." Merrill took the earring and slipped the wire into her ear.

"Does it look nice?" she asked.

"It is lovely," he smiled. "Let me do the other one."

He did. She now wore both earrings, which dangled delicately from her ears. The gray jewels were designed carefully and would reflect anything she wore, effectively matching all her clothing.

If Raffian Grey designed them, he'd done a magnificent job.

"Thank you for this," Merrill held up his hand, displaying the ring he wore.

"I asked for something for you, but left it up to them," she blinked at him. "It suits you."

"Good. Now finish your breakfast, before the eggs go completely cold," he coaxed.

Those words should have been mine. I should be sitting there, convincing her to eat. Warming the eggs for her with power. Telling her how much I loved her.

Merrill held words of love back, although they were in his eyes as he watched her eat.

～

Justin's Journal

"Why don't we clean the kitchen?" Gina asked when school was over for the day and we sat at the kitchen island having peanut butter and crackers as a snack. It was practically all we had left in the house.

"Huh?" I said, confused for a moment.

"Your mother isn't feeling well, so somebody has to do it," Sarah laughed. "Come on, you and Mack can help." With all four of us working, the dishes in the sink were placed in the dishwasher, counters were wiped clean and a grocery list began to take shape.

I wasn't sure what meats to place on the list, but Gina and Sarah offered suggestions and Mack took it from there. "Chicken—for sure, either for fried chicken or chicken and dumplings," he said. "Maybe something to make meat loaf or burgers? What about grilling fajitas?" Mack was still hungry—and still growing, looked like.

"Maybe Uncle Lion will go with us to the grocery store," I said.

"Maybe Uncle Bearcat and Uncle Joey will go with you, in your dad's SUV," Joey and Bearcat walked into the kitchen. "We have orders from your mom, and she gave us a list." Joey pulled a folded paper from his pocket. "Let's coordinate and go. We can drop the girls off while we're out."

"Sounds great," Gina giggled. "Can we go to the store with you?"

"Sure," Joey shrugged. "I'll let you be in charge of fruits and vegetables."

～

Adam's Journal

Karzac pronounced Kiarra run-down and suggested she take it easy for several days. It hadn't been very long, after all, since the attack and near-miscarriage. "Take it easy around the house, too," he ordered. "No heavy housework. No lifting more than ten pounds. Do I need to go on?" His green-gold eyes informed her—and me—that there would be no argument over this.

"But," Kiarra began.

"No. The answer will be no," Karzac held up a hand. "This pregnancy has already proven itself fragile enough. Do I have to find someone to babysit you?"

"No." She turned away before he could see evidence of her pout.

"Good. Kiarra," he turned her toward him, "Please do this. For me. For Dragon. For all of us. Things are so critical, now. You understand that, don't you?"

"Yes." She hung her head and nodded her agreement.

"Good. I hear supplies are being bought. Do not skimp on protein, and eat regularly, even if you do not feel hungry. You have lost weight the past few days. I do not wish to see that continue."

"I know."

"Good. Let Adam care for you. That is his duty after all, to you and his child."

"Karzac Halivar, I hope you've noticed by now that we're having a spat. I trust your doctorly duties do not include interfering with that?" Kiarra lifted an eyebrow.

"While doctorly may not be an actual word, I will bow out of the tiff for now. However, that will not stop me from shouting at both of you, if your disagreement becomes detrimental to all involved." Karzac displayed his stubbornness, which could rival Kiarra's any day.

"Great. Out. Out—the both of you," Kiarra pointed toward the door.

"Sweetheart, I want to talk to you about disappearing spawn," I reasoned. "I can't do that very well if we're in separate parts of the house."

That brought on a string of curse words—in Refizani. I'm sure she did it on purpose; I saw Karzac cringe at least twice.

"Dearest," Merrill interrupted, "I'd appreciate your words in a language I might understand. That way, I can agree with confidence, rather than relying on instinct."

Kiarra stopped in mid-sentence, blinked at Merrill and burst out laughing.

Thank you, I sent to Merrill later as he, Kiarra, Dragon, Lion, Joey,

Bearcat and I sat on comfortable chairs around the indoor pool, discussing missing spawn, the little we knew about Sirenali and what —if anything—we might do about all of it.

You're welcome, Merrill replied, his face never revealing the fact that we were having a mental conversation. Somehow, in all this mess, there had to be an answer, we just hadn't arrived at it, yet.

"Invite me?" Darzi walked in, dropping cross-legged onto the tiled floor surrounding the pool.

"Hi. Sorry we didn't think to send for you," Kiarra smiled at him. He smiled back. "We're trying to think of a way to find the spawn that are disappearing. So far, we haven't come up with anything. I've tried *Looking* into the future for towns or cities that get hit, but nothing is showing up."

At the time, I didn't think a shapeshifting lion snake with limited English could come up with anything, or know what *Looking* actually meant. He nodded at Kiarra anyway and appeared to be considering her words.

The rest of us had reached a standstill.

"Maybe they use random selection," Darzi said after a moment. "Like casino. Random number generator."

"You mean they might not be targeting these things—that they're relying on a machine to do it for them?" Kiarra stared at Darzi.

"Possible," he shrugged. "You not find by *Looking*, because there nothing to find—yet."

"This is impossible," I rubbed my forehead. "The first town was small. They took ten away. The second was somewhat larger and they took nine from there. All of those were men, tall and strong. That's what they're looking for. Didn't you say that the military could end up being a target?" I turned to Dragon.

"That would make sense to me," he said. "As a military leader at one time, if I were recruiting, I'd carefully select my candidates. The problem, as we all know, is that until now, spawn haven't discriminated as to their turns—after they sate themselves on the more tender victims, generally consisting of women and children, they only bite what they can't consume afterward. With them, it's instinctual."

"Unless something interferes with that instinct," Kiarra pointed out. "Tell me again how an obsession works? Doesn't it stay in effect until the victim dies? Does that mean completely dead, or does it carry over to the spawn made from the victim?"

"Holy, fucking hell," I snorted. "Spawn with an obsession? That could make them a hundred times more dangerous."

"Darzi agree," Darzi said, jerking his head in a nod.

"While hell may be a topic best left to philosophers, I agree with the gist of your comment," Pheligar appeared. Lifting Kiarra from her chair while she squawked and slapped at his hands, he enlarged the seat with power and sat, Kiarra held carefully on his lap.

"That doesn't help us at all," Joey tossed up a hand in resignation. "Anybody with a laptop or a tablet can do a random selection of small towns. Maybe they're building up to grabbing the National Guard troops when they arrive at the scene, or maybe they're planning to take an entire base somewhere. We don't know the answer to that."

"What did you say?" Kiarra struggled in Pheligar's arms. He pulled her closer and soothed her with gentle hands.

"Which part? The National Guard part or the military base part?" Joey asked.

"The military base part," she said, making another attempt to escape Pheligar's embrace. He didn't allow it. After a brief tussle, which lasted barely three seconds, she gave in and relaxed against him.

"It's possible," Dragon replied. "But which one? What would they want from there? The most men? Technology? Equipment? All three?"

"At this point, it's still conjecture," Lion observed.

"Very good conjecture, from my point of view," Kiarra said. I watched as Pheligar tucked pale blonde hair behind her ear. "It could be impossible to figure out where they're going to strike next. We may have to gamble on the military base thing and work from that end."

"So they're looking to produce superspawn that have an obsession to achieve an unknown goal?" Bearcat asked. "But why? Regular spawn have no trouble taking any world in very little time if they're not stopped."

"We know that we're targets, but what if there are others we don't know about?" I asked. The idea had concerned me for a while, but it was now at the forefront of my thoughts and I wasn't sure why.

"Who else would the Ra'Ak target?" Bearcat asked. "Aren't we the ones they're worried about the most?"

Nobody had an answer, but I could tell that Kiarra, Dragon and Lion were concerned about it, too.

"Adam, we bent time and moved to Fresno two years before Corpus Christi happened, when Justin turned four years old," Kiarra told me later. The others had finally left us alone, going somewhere else to ponder the conundrum for a while. Pheligar had gone too, and I'd had to approach Kiarra carefully.

She allowed me to sit with her and then pull her against me.

Always, she feels good in my arms. I wrapped her up as much as she'd allow and rested my cheek against her hair.

"I remember," I said. "It was a better time and fit, and we knew to stay away from Corpus during that time. We bought the beach house afterward, for our anniversary."

"Something about all this bothers me," she shivered in my arms.

"I know. It bothers me, too, but I have no idea why."

Justin's Journal

Mack got his wish on dinner—we had steak and chicken fajitas with tortillas, grilled onions and peppers, rice, beans, salsa, sour cream—the works.

I had no idea Darzi could cook. He said he learned from the best, but didn't elaborate. Actually, his exact words were, "I learn from best cook. I not as good, but do fine enough."

He was the one who grilled the vegetables separately so Mom could have veggie fajitas. The beans were vegetarian, as was the rice he seasoned and served. She was very happy with what she got and offered Darzi a hug for being the chief cook at dinner.

Mack and I cleaned the kitchen after we ate; Gina called shortly after. Until I talked to her that evening, I thought I was the only one getting hot under the collar when we kissed.

"Justin, I, uh, I've been thinking," Gina said after we'd talked about homework assignments. Actually, I'd been working on mine when she called. I didn't mind the interruption.

"About what?" I said, studying the equation in front of me and attempting to work it out in my head.

"Well, you know, most guys are pushing to have sex after the second date."

"What?" That put the brakes on doing two things at once.

"Well, you know—they are," she said. "Sometimes I don't go out with them after that, because, it's just—you know, uncomfortable."

"Baby, I haven't asked you for that," I began. I had no idea where this had come from and had even less of an idea where it was headed.

"Well, that's, oh, this isn't coming out right," she fussed. "Look, I wouldn't mind. If you did ask, that is. We're both eighteen, and we're responsible. I guess that's what I mean," she finished lamely.

She wanted to have sex? I couldn't breathe for a minute.

"Are you sure?" My voice sounded almost normal, which was a real shock.

"I'm sure. I want your arms around me. I want you to uh, touch me like that. I want you to be the one, Justin. You."

I could have bet that she was blushing. My face felt heated, too. That didn't mean I wanted to turn her down.

Hell, no. I just didn't want to disappoint her.

"Okay," I said after taking a deep breath and releasing it. "Let's just take things slow. I don't want to rush this and risk not making you happy."

"Oh my gosh, Justin, that may be the nicest thing any guy has ever said to me. About sex, anyway."

At that moment, I wanted to pound anybody who'd been rude to her before. I didn't want to *Look* for their names—that would be dangerous. After all, I *could* pound them into pulp if I let my wyvern and my temper get away from me.

I was also grateful that we weren't at Valley High anymore. There were no jeers or whispers about our relationship—no speculation and no gossip. Mack and Sarah knew—that's it.

As for the sex part—I wasn't willing to share that with anyone. That was between Gina and me. I worried that Dad might guess, but then I probably should have a talk with him anyway. Sure—most people my age knew the mechanics of sex, but there was so much more to it than that, and I didn't know where to start.

"You'll need these. Not that you'll really need them," Joey said, handing a box of condoms to me after knocking on my door later. "But it will reassure Gina, and that's what matters most."

"How did you?" I sputtered.

"It's my job," he shrugged with a grin. "And, as your father is so famous for saying, sex is natural between people who care for one another. You're of legal age and nobody expects either of you to remain celibate forever."

"This is unbelievable," I muttered, rubbing my forehead.

"I had no idea what I was doing when I was your age," Joey said. "So you can either let your Dad give you pointers, or your Uncle Lynx. Or Merrill—he's the one who finally gave me the scoop. All good advice, I might add."

"What about you?" I mumbled, lifting my eyes and staring at Joey. He was way too cheerful for my current frame of mind.

"Seriously? I've never had sex with a girl. Sorry, dude. Can't help." Joey was now smiling. *Definitely too cheerful.*

"Well, uh, wow. This is embarrassing." I now rubbed the back of my neck. I realized I didn't want to discuss this with Dad—no way.

The fact that he and Mom—well—she was pregnant, so both of them had to be involved.

"You should probably decide soon, just in case," Joey shrugged. "Your choice."

"All right," I whispered. "Just don't go—announcing it to everybody, okay? What if Mom finds out?"

"Why do you think your mother will mind? As long as it's consensual, you're both of legal age and both enjoy it, why would she mind? Pheligar already says you're sterile and you're not susceptible to diseases."

"Sex complicates things," I huffed, feeling angry that Pheligar knew about my sex life—or lack thereof.

"Says the guy who's never had it," Joey retorted.

"Will you shut up?" I hissed. "I don't think the neighbors half a mile away heard you, yet."

"You're approaching this as if you and Gina are both virgins," Joey began.

"Whuh—what?" That fell on me like a load of bricks.

"You won't be her first. Her mother knows. Mrs. Allen likes you a hell of a lot more than Gina's ex."

"TMI, Joey," I flopped against the wall next to the door, my head in my hands.

"What do you want, then? To go into this blind and just fumble along? Very few people are happy with their first time, Justin. The guy lasts thirty seconds if he's lucky and the girl gets absolutely nothing out of it. Be better than that." He turned to walk down the hall while I dropped my hands and watched him go.

"Your nose is more sensitive than you think," Merrill said.

No, I couldn't sleep, so I went to the back porch to sit a while. The night was nice, fairly cool and I'd found Merrill sitting there having a glass of Scotch. Before I knew it, I blurted out my problem to him.

"But," I began.

"Let it help you," Merrill said. "Keep your eyes open, too. There are signs that tell you—apart from the scent of arousal—that your partner is ready to couple."

That night, a two-thousand-year-old vampire gave me instructions for making love. He wasn't embarrassed in the least and I found it easier and easier to ask questions as he explained things.

"No always means no, but you can ask whether they really want you to stop," Merrill said. "Pull away first and ask your question. Never, ever, manhandle or paw her. Pull away and offer to leave it for another time. It will be extremely frustrating, but a session in the shower is ultimately better than offending."

"Wow. Thanks, Uncle Merrill," I said, rising and stretching. It was nearly two in the morning and I had to get some sleep.

"No problem. Come to me anytime if you have concerns," he said.

Uncle Dragon had his back to me when I walked into the kitchen the following morning, still half asleep after a short night. Even with a short night, I was up before Mack and watched for a moment as Dragon lifted a cup of tea to drink.

"Hey, Uncle Dragon," I said, walking past him and heading toward the fridge for some juice.

"Dragon will be here in a moment—he is speaking with Lion upstairs."

Yeah, I stopped in my tracks and whirled around.

He looked exactly like Uncle Dragon, except for the tattoos of cranes peeking from beneath the rolled-up sleeves of a white shirt.

"Uh, wow. Sorry," I apologized.

"You weren't expecting me, so no apology is necessary. I was often mistaken for my brother in the past," the corners of his eyes crinkled in a smile. "Dragon found it less amusing than I did. I am Crane, former General to the Dragon Warlord."

"Glad to meet you," I bowed my head slightly. He did the same, his dark eyes gleaming as he moved. He never took his eyes off me, either; it was a show of respect.

"I see you've met my brother," Dragon walked into the kitchen with Lion right behind him.

"I thought he was you from behind," I said. "Sorry about that."

"No need to apologize," Dragon waved a hand. "The vampires were called back to Britain last night, so your father and I transported them. A small town in Scotland was destroyed by spawn, so the Vampire Council called their enforcers back. I'd hoped the problem was confined to the U.S. That is no longer true. I brought Crane here afterward, to help with spawn in the absence of our vampire allies."

"Thank you for coming," I said, while the chill of fear and worry went through me. Crane was only one man; how could he replace Radomir, Russell and Will? At least we still had Merrill, Kyle, Daniel and Teddy, but that left us short.

The one advantage Crane had over the vampires was that he could fight in daylight. My concern was this—was he fast enough to fight spawn?

"If you were skilled in bladework, Crane would show you how fast he is," Dragon pulled the thoughts right out of my head. "I would not have asked him to come if he weren't prepared to fight effectively."

"Then we're cool," I said. "Sorry."

"Those questions are the same I'd ask as Warlord," Dragon said. "There is no offense."

"My brother prefers those around him who are skilled in strategy and think for themselves," Crane said. "He invites respectful dissent and argument, as that tends to point out flaws in any plan. It gives time in most circumstances to revise or redesign battle tactics."

"You live longer," Dragon shrugged. Lion grinned and slapped Dragon on the back.

"That is seriously cool," Mack breathed as he walked into the kitchen and studied Dragon and Crane.

"Someday, I will teach you bladework," Crane gave Mack a nod. "My brother has already promised to instruct this one," he gestured in my direction.

"All right," Mack crowed and raised his arms in the air.

"What the hell is anybody doing about breakfast?" Mom walked in dressed in pajamas and looking somewhat rumpled. "Justin, Mack, school starts in an hour," she pointed out.

"I bow to the First," Crane said, giving Mom a deep bow of respect.

"Now see, why can't I get more of that?" she grumped and walked toward the fridge to get eggs and ham out.

Dragon covered a snicker. Lion laughed out loud.

CHAPTER 15

t least it was Friday. Gina had to work at the restaurant after school, though, so any plans for our first lovemaking had to be put on hold. As it turned out, Mack and I had to work, too. Dad got a call from werewolf Agent Renfro, who said the spawn in Memphis were becoming a problem and we needed to come.

"We'll be there just after dark tonight. Will that work?" Dad asked, his cell phone pressed to his ear as he walked into the kitchen. Merrill, who walked in with him, went straight to the coffeepot and set about making coffee for Dad and himself.

"Would you like some green tea, Kiarra?" Dragon asked softly. She was busy scrambling eggs in two skillets in between turning ham slices over in two more.

"Here," Crane took over at the stove while Mom lifted an eyebrow in surprise.

"He cooks?" Mom stared at Dragon. "And yes, tea would be wonderful. Thank you."

"Crane is quite decent at cooking, actually," Dragon said. "Although he prefers meats over vegetables. Have a seat—we'll take care of this."

In no time, everybody had a plate of eggs, ham and toast in front of them, except for Mom, who had eggs, toast and strawberries.

Gina and Sarah found us there, eating and talking before school started that morning. Bearcat, who'd become a regular chauffeur for them, grinned, took a seat and accepted a plate of food.

"Want something to eat, baby?" I asked Gina softly after standing to greet her.

"We had breakfast," she smiled shyly and put an arm around my waist.

"Cool. I need to brush my teeth before class," I said. "Mack does, too."

"Huh?" Mack looked up from his plate in surprise. Sarah giggled.

Adam's Journal

We had one Falchani warrior to replace three vampires; that meant we could be short-handed when facing an unknown quantity of spawn in Memphis. At least these showed up on our radar; the Paranormal Division of the FBI was watching them closely.

I ground my teeth as Justin and Mack dressed for battle before Dragon and I folded them to Memphis.

Justin's Journal

Agents Renfro and White met us at the usual building downtown and showed us a map of our targeted area—an old petroleum storage facility on the river. "We think the employees have been turned to spawn—most of them, anyway. There are a few humans still there, providing product to boats and barges, but we can tell by scent that spawn are there."

"Our surveillance cameras show a few suspected spawn working outside after dark," White broke in. "We've only observed until now, hoping your team might be available to help. We've had word," the vampire Agent raised his hand. "We know the Enforcers have been called back to the UK, so we're prepared to go in with you tonight."

"Good—thank you," Dad said. I could tell he was relieved at the news. Teddy was too; he was worried—more than Mack and I were, I think. At least we had Darzi with us—he stood next to Mack, listening carefully to everything everybody said.

"We tried to get Winkler and some of his wolves to fly in, but he seems to be neck deep in business negotiations in the Corpus area and couldn't come," Renfro said. "Something about buying property and incorporating a new township on the Gulf Coast." Renfro sounded disappointed. So was I—Mr. Winkler had been terrifyingly efficient at killing spawn, as had the wolves with him in Dallas.

I thought Winkler was the Dallas Packmaster, Mack sent. *What's he doing in Corpus Christi?*

No idea, I sent a mental shrug with my words. *Maybe your Dad knows, since he's a Packmaster, too.*

I'm almost afraid to ask about that stuff, Mack shivered. *I had no idea that anybody can challenge a Packmaster at any time. The fight is to the death. Dad told me he's been challenged five times since I was born. Do you know what that means? He could have died.*

That's not scary or anything. I wanted to shiver, too. I didn't, but it was close. *Being a werewolf isn't all fun and games, is it?* I asked.

I figure it might be better than what your parents do, Mack responded. *Or what we're trying to do here,* he added.

Yeah. I hope this time is better than the last time.

You think more of those kapirus things may come out of the river?

"If more of those kapirus things arrive, as you say, I assure you they will not live long." A large hand dropped onto my shoulder while the others, Dad included, almost took a step back.

The only one who didn't seem surprised was Darzi, who offered a respectful nod to the High Demon who stood behind me.

In human form, he was taller than I was, with dark eyes, darker hair and a habit of breathing curls of smoke. I guess if you were classified as a demon, you could do those kinds of things.

"He Kifirin," Darzi nodded toward the High Demon. "We work together, now."

Dragon cursed in his native language and offered Kifirin a bow of respect. Kifirin nodded back, his eyes meeting Dragon's. Dragon knew of Kifirin, at least, even if he didn't recognize him.

Dad's shoulders sagged in relief—he knew something too, he just wasn't saying it.

~

Adam's Journal

What the hell is a god doing here? I sent to Dragon.

I will not question powerful help, Dragon replied. *This one outranks Thorsten, so he cannot be commanded not to help. I fear we may be facing something terrible here, otherwise he would likely have stayed away.*

Why would a god interfere? Has that ever happened before?

It happened in Florida, and your son's life was saved as a result, Dragon observed.

True, I said. *Remind me to thank him for that.*

No thanks are necessary, Kifirin broke into our mental conversation, telling us immediately that even our shielded sendings were open to him.

Do not fear, he added. *I am used to a variety of conversations and your information will stay with me.*

Then I'm grateful we didn't say anything to anger you, I said.

He chuckled aloud.

He not always like that, Darzi informed me, shocking the hell out of me that he had mindspeech. *He much better, now. Stronger. Laugh more. Have better sense.*

Kifirin threw back his head and roared with laughter.

~

Justin's Journal

I wasn't sure what the mental conversation was about, but Kifirin laughed, so it must have been a good one. It made me feel better that he laughed—after all, I'd seen him squeeze a kapirus to death one-handed.

The fact that he could breathe smoke was downright scary, and the way he looked when he changed? Mack would call it poop inducing.

"Is everybody ready?" Agent White asked, pulling us back to the present and our pending mission.

"Ready," Dad nodded. He and Dragon folded us to the old petroleum company near the Mississippi River.

Adam's Journal

Dragon nodded to Crane before he and I left—something passed between those two, letting me know that his twin likely had mindspeech, too. Had Pheligar collected him in the beginning, or had someone more powerful?

I still had no recollection as to who'd rescued Kiarra and me—all I recalled was that we'd died. To me, the fact that we lived now told me that we still had work to do. It angered me, and not for the first time, that Thorsten had bound our hands, now. After all, our mission was to combat spawn and Ra'Ak. It was the very reason the Saa Thalarr existed—why they'd been created.

Someday, perhaps Kiarra and I should talk about the hierarchy of gods and godlings. All I had was a vague awareness, with no idea of Kifirin's place in all of it.

"Earth teas are always too weak," Dragon murmured as he sipped the strongest offering available at the Memphis coffee shop we'd chosen.

"Staying awake for a week isn't very healthy for the local inhabitants," I pointed out. "Plus, lack of sleep makes them cranky. I believe you were born cranky." Normally I wouldn't spar with the Dragon Warlord-turned-Saa Thalarr, but I liked the local tea just fine and it offended me that someone raised on another planet might complain about it.

A dark eyebrow lifted before he snorted a laugh and raised his cup in a mock salute.

~

Justin's Journal

While I would have preferred to approach the building as quietly as I could, Kifirin felt it prudent to announce our presence by stomping toward the rusting metal building, turning to his smaller (according to Darzi) Thifilathi and roaring a challenge.

"Oh, man," Mack breathed beside me. Spawn came boiling from every door, crack and crevice in that building. At least the young, normal-sized ones did. The larger ones burst through the metal as if it were paper and bore down on us, some of which had to be at least twelve feet tall.

That's when I saw Kifirin's Full Thifilathi.

Eighteen feet of angry High Demon braced himself and waited for the spawn to attack.

They did, and it shocked me when I saw what would happen when they touched his scales.

An accident at a fireworks factory might have been less of a distraction. Spawn burned and exploded the second they touched him. Maybe somebody told the spawn to aim for the biggest and baddest of the enemies confronting them—I had no idea.

All I knew is that they attacked Kifirin first and as a result, died in the hundreds.

The few that got knocked away by the explosions of others of their kind were casually destroyed by the rest of us. I learned never to doubt Crane's skills again—both blades were in his hands and spawn were beheaded almost indifferently when they attempted to get near the former Falchani General.

What worried me was the sheer numbers of spawn waiting to attack. There had to be thousands of them. Kifirin stood tall on cracked concrete in the moonlight while spawn exploded in showers of sparks all around him.

It became obvious that heat and fire bothered him less than the spawn did. The big ones? They blew up in huge fireballs after touching him, and the heat, stench and the force of the winds afterward pushed the rest of us backward.

Right into the advancing army of kapiri.

Fly, young one, Kifirin's voice commanded in mindspeech. I was terrified as the first kapirus was met by Merrill, who flew around it so fast it was cut to ribbons before it realized.

I don't know how, I wailed at Kifirin as a kapirus came for Mack's wolf.

How did he do it? Information I'd never known before shoved its way into my mind so fast it gave my wyvern a headache.

Along with the sudden knowledge of how to fly came information on breathing fire. *You are now much more than you were,* Kifirin grunted as another large spawn burst into a fireball behind me. *Fly. Protect your friends.*

Before I took flight for the first time, I roared at the kapirus who'd lifted Mack's wolf like a toy, preparing to bite his throat. My fire hit the monster's feet—I didn't want to aim higher and risk hurting Mack.

Mack yelped when the kapirus dropped him, then rolled away while I roared again, releasing a jet of flame that burned the kapirus' head and shoulders to a crisp.

"Get back, let Justin and the vampires have them," Merrill shouted at the werewolves.

That's when I lifted off the concrete, beating unfurled wings as hard as I could to escape a grasping kapirus; he'd thought to attack and pull me down. I burned him with half a thought while I flapped upward. Yes, I'd blinded the last kapirus who thought to attack me in Florida, but my fire had been weaker, then.

This time, I had the force of a dozen giant flamethrowers at my disposal, and discovered just how vulnerable kapiri were to fire.

Scales and flesh burned and melted as I flew, whipping in and out of their ranks like the swiftest mouse through a familiar maze. At least fifty had been sent to attack us, and with Merrill, Kyle and Agent White working together to cut and kill, we annihilated their numbers.

The last three turned and ran, but they didn't get far. My wyvern had the scent of burning flesh and melting scales in my nostrils that night as I flew after them and took them down.

There were a few wounds to tend after the last of the spawn died—Mack was bruised and had a concussion after being thrown onto hard concrete. Teddy, Agent Renfro and Daniel had cuts and bruises—all vampires showed evidence of their fight with kapiri.

Darzi, Crane and I were the only ones, aside from Kifirin, who came away unscathed. Darzi had killed his share of kapiri by whipping in and biting what Merrill and the others managed to knock down with claw cuts.

Ready to come get us? I sent to Dad.

He and Dragon were there in seconds. Kifirin folded himself away with a nod, while Dragon took the agents back to their office and Dad hauled the rest of us to Fresno.

"Kifirin give gift—bring out wyvern talents," Darzi shrugged, explaining to Dad and Mom how we'd come out of the attack alive.

"Will he demand anything in return?" Mom sounded worried.

"No," Darzi grinned. "He give true gift. No obligations."

"Good," Mom visibly relaxed. I listened to their conversation while I sipped milk and ate my fifth slice of pizza. I had no idea why Kifirin might demand something in return for a gift I hadn't requested, but realized that if he hadn't, half of us could have died.

"Justin, I'm proud of you," Mom smiled at me. "You, too, honey," she hugged Mack. He'd been treated by Karzac before he was allowed to eat, then finished off an entire pizza by himself.

Even injured, he, Daniel, Teddy and Agent Renfro, with help from Crane, continued to kill spawn who thought to get around Kifirin. Altogether, it was a successful night, although we would have lost everything without the High Demon's help.

"I'm just glad Kifirin decided to help us," Mack mumbled. "I think I could sleep a week after this."

"Sleep as long as you want, tomorrow's Saturday," Mom smiled and rubbed his back. "Your dad and your sister are coming for dinner tomorrow night."

"Can I invite Gina?" I blurted.

"Of course. Her mother, too, if you'd like."

"I help cook," Darzi offered.

"Thank you." Mom moved to his chair and gave him a hug. He was very happy about that.

"We go grocery store. Buy things," Darzi grinned and hugged Mom back.

"Tomorrow," She laughed. "What are we buying?"

"Surprise," Darzi shrugged. "Make special for you, too."

"Sounds great," she said. "I'll even buy Dr. Pepper for Mack and Justin, since they're too young to celebrate with champagne."

"I'd rather have Dr. Pepper," I said.

"Me, too," Mack nodded enthusiastically.

"Then I suppose that's settled," Mom said. "I'm going to bed unless anybody needs anything. Good job, everybody. I'd tell Kifirin, too, but he isn't here."

"I let him know," Darzi shrugged.

"Awesome." I lifted my sixth slice of pizza and bit into it.

"Here." Joey handed keys to me just before I went to bed.

"What's this?" I asked, feeling confused.

"Keys to my house," he grinned. "Just in case you need some privacy."

"Seriously?"

"Just in case," he nodded.

He'd been reading my mind, too, because I'd been racking my brain trying to come up with a decent place where Gina and I could be alone. "Uh, thanks," I said, feeling only moderately embarrassed.

I couldn't help feeling philosophical about it, too—that in the midst of overwhelming problems and dangerous conditions, people still wanted sex. Or, perhaps it was *because* things were so dire that sex was a way to escape the fear and worry for a while.

Maybe it was the raging hormones of an eighteen-year-old man. After the events of the past few weeks, added to the fact I'd killed spawn and kapiri to defend my friends and myself, I no longer considered myself a teenager.

That night, I think I went to bed tired and older.

⁓

Adam's Journal

"Sweetheart?" I drew covers over us and pulled Kiarra's head against my shoulder. Her sigh tickled my skin as she exhaled.

"Adam?"

"Feel up to some love?" We hadn't had sex since she'd been attacked in the parking lot of a grocery store. I didn't want to think of the many mistakes I'd made since then.

"Will it take my mind off trying to figure out what the enemy is planning?" She turned her head so she could see my eyes. I leaned in to kiss the tip of her nose.

"I sure hope so," I said when I moved away. "Is that what you were doing while I was gone?"

"Yes. Lion, Marli and I sat on the back porch and discussed every possible scenario we could come up with. So far, I don't think we're even close to the truth."

"Then let's table that discussion until tomorrow. I heard from Martin after we got back—they killed six more spawn not far from the construction site last night.

"That's not good." Kiarra sat up in bed, taking her warmth away from me. "I don't like it that they seem to be honed in on all of us," she added. "I mean, Lion and I both discussed those nuclear warheads that were moved a month ago—you know the ones that were set out on the tarmac of a military base and forgotten for a couple of days?"

"I remember," I agreed. "That could have been disastrous."

"I think the enemy missed their chance there—those warheads

could have destroyed the entire West Coast if somebody had gotten their hands on them—if not directly by the bombs, then by the resulting radiation."

"I can't believe anybody would consider keeping those things to begin with," I said. "They're just too dangerous."

"Case in point—all the chemical weapons created and stockpiled on Tiralia," Kiarra pointed out. "They knew they had enough to kill the entire planet many times over, yet all three sides refused to stand down and destroy what they had. End of story, everybody died because they couldn't get along."

"How big was the planet?" I asked.

"Nearly twice as big as Earth, with three major continents and strings of islands around each. The crystal was only found in great quantities on one continent. Everything was fine until everybody got too greedy."

"Now it all belongs to my wife," I pulled her close and kissed her amorously, nipping gently on her lower lip—the signal to her that my John Thomas was awake and standing tall.

"At least they dismantled all those B53 bombs years ago," she mumbled against my mouth.

Stop talking about nuclear bombs, I sent, kissing her again. *It upsets John Thomas.*

John Thomas is upset? Her hand brushed that part of my anatomy, making it jerk with desire.

Now you have to make him feel better, I said, kissing her neck. I wanted to bite. I held that urge back.

What does John Thomas want?

Soft. Warm. Jane Thomas, I replied.

What if she's not ready?

I'll fix that, I offered a devilish smile and dived beneath the covers.

Justin's Journal

Waking with an urgent erection was becoming too common. That made me want Gina more than ever. Merrill had talked to me about that, too—that women tended not to feel amorous on most mornings because they felt unattractive and had morning breath. He'd smiled and said it didn't matter at all to most men.

"Hey, baby." I'd pulled my cell phone into my hand and called Gina before thinking about it. At least she was already awake. My bedside clock said eleven, so she'd probably been up for a while.

"Want to come to dinner tonight, or do you have to work?" I asked.

"I'm working the early shift, but don't get off until eight."

"I think we can save something for you to eat, and you can bring your mom if you want," I said.

"Let me ask." Gina set the phone down and I could hear her calling her mother. My hearing was definitely sharper after the wyvern made its appearance—I could hear her mother's answer from another room.

"We'll be there as soon as we can," Gina's voice held a smile.

"Awesome. What are the chances we can sneak away alone afterward?"

"I think we might be able to do something. Want to plan a late movie that we manage somehow to miss?"

"I think we can see a movie if you want—from a big, comfortable bed."

"Really?" Gina sounded breathless. "Yes. That sounds great."

"Great," I repeated her word. "Bye, baby. See ya when you get here."

"Bye, Justin." She sounded shy, suddenly.

Merrill talked about that, too. I ignored his lesson for the moment and focused on the body part demanding attention.

"You okay, man? You usually beat me to the kitchen," Mack grinned as I sat beside him with a plate of eggs and bacon.

"Talked with Gina on the phone, dude," I said before stuffing an entire strip of bacon in my mouth. I was hungry.

"Is that all that held you up?"

"All I'll admit to."

"Probably for the best," Mack agreed and crunched into another slice of bacon.

I felt older; Mack sounded older. I guess going to war against spawn and who knew what else would do that for you. Mack had been injured twice and kept fighting both times. He was brave *and* tough.

"Thanks for not frying my fur last night," he added with a sigh.

"I will never fry your fur, dude. I had to aim for that bastard's feet, though. I'm just glad giving him a hotfoot was enough to get him to let you go."

"Understood," Mack grinned.

"And you're welcome. Thanks for guarding my back in Florida."

"No big." Mack speared scrambled eggs and shoved them in his mouth before they could escape his fork.

"You had a broken wrist, dude," I pointed out.

"I still had three good legs," Mack grinned.

"Oh," I tossed up a hand. "Why didn't I think of that?" I added sarcastically.

He laughed. It was a good sound.

"Trading war stories?" Crane asked as he wandered into the kitchen and set about making two cups of tea. I figured he'd be taking the second one to Dragon, so I didn't ask.

"Maybe," Mack said. "We admit nothing."

"Always the prudent thing to do in any war. You tend to stay out of trouble that way," Crane nodded sagely while filling the kettle with hot water.

"Who's the better swordsman, you or Mr. Dragon?" Mack asked. Yeah, he definitely admired both men.

"My brother is the second-best swordsman I've ever seen," Crane said. "I'm slightly behind him. The best I've ever seen trained us."

"Who was that?" Mack asked, sounding almost breathless. I was interested too—somebody was better than Dragon?

"Caylon Black," Crane said. "Died on the northern border when he and his scouts were attacked by a much larger force. He was the last one standing, and the bodies of the enemy were piled around him before he was overwhelmed. Dragon and I had been in the army under our father's command for less than ten years when he fell."

"Wow. That's too bad. I'd like to have seen him fight," Mack breathed.

"We feel privileged to have trained with him," Crane shrugged. "He made warriors out of spoiled Warlord's sons."

"How old were you when you went to war?" I asked.

"Seventeen. That year, Dragon won the Solstice Trials. He fought me for the win."

"What are the Solstice Trials?" I asked, immediately intrigued.

"Consider it the Falchani version of the Olympic Games," Crane smiled. "They are held every year at the summer solstice. You fight with blades only, until the last two are left. The one who wins the final bout receives a prize from the Warlord. Generally, it is gold and a tattoo. Dragon's back tattoo came from that win."

"Who's older?" Mack asked, his eyes shining. I could see he was already imagining himself as a combatant in the Solstice Trials. It would also make a killer video game. I wondered if Joey had considered it, yet.

"I am—by six of your minutes," Crane answered Mack's question as he dropped tea leaves into cups and poured hot water over them. "Sometime soon, Dragon and I will see you trained with blades." He nodded to us before carrying both mugs of steeping tea from the kitchen.

Adam's Journal

"Adam," Kiarra gripped my arm. We'd dropped by a fish market with Darzi—he said he wanted to cook fish for dinner, so I drove both of them to a shop in Clovis. The clerk packed it in ice, so we felt comfortable stopping at a donut shop on the way home—Kiarra was getting her first cravings.

She'd noticed the small television hanging on the wall behind the counter, and was now calling my attention to it. I read the crawler across the bottom of the screen and almost stopped breathing.

Joyce Christian, Texas Congresswoman, killed in accident in Texas, the crawler proclaimed.

Kiarra shouted at the television screen at home whenever Joyce was shown on this news program or that, spouting her warped version of history, politics and religion. Truth never concerned Joyce Christian; she avoided it as often as possible. The problem was that she refused to back down when the truth was pointed out; too many people believed her and she kept getting reelected.

Now she was dead. *I don't know whether to sing or shout with joy first,* Kiarra sent, bringing my attention back to her.

I'd like to hear you sing, I offered, hoping it wouldn't make her angry.

I'll think about it. She gave me a beautiful smile and asked the clerk behind the counter for half a dozen maple bars.

~

Second's Records; Trajan Gibson's reports

"Three people have asked you to move to west Texas and run for Joyce Christian's vacancy," I handed messages to Winkler, who strode casually into the office at his beach house in Port Aransas. We'd been working on getting Star Cove on the map as a new municipality on the Texas Gulf Coast. After a few snags, things finally looked good in that respect.

"One of these is from the Governor," Winkler held the message up, as if I hadn't seen it already. Hell, I'd taken the call in the first place.

"Please tell me you're not thinking about it," I said.

"I'm not, but we'll have to make a valid excuse to the governor—I don't care about the rest of these people." He dropped the messages onto my desk, letting me know to say *no, thank you* in a nicely benign fashion, so nobody would be pissed off.

"The Grand Master would have a cow," Winkler added. It was something Lissa would have said—he and I knew that.

"He'd have a longhorn," I pointed out. The Grand Master didn't want to explain the unexplainable to humans, if a werewolf died under unusual circumstances. That happened more often than not with Packmasters—and their Seconds.

"There's no way in hell I'd want to involve myself in politics. No more than I already am," Winkler shook his head. "I have kids, and it's bad enough that I'm under a microscope. They don't need that pressure. Not to mention what Kellee would do as my ex."

"Enough said," I held up a hand. Kellee was a sore spot with all of Winkler's wolves. The only reason Winkler still tolerated her tantrums was because she was Wayne and Wynter's mother. When they reached their majority, Winkler would likely tell Kellee where to stick it.

I wanted to listen when he did.

"Star Cove is going to be a jewel in the coastal communities," Winkler said. "We can start building next week."

"That sounds good, boss," I grinned and lifted the phone. I had people to call. I'd let them know that Winkler had too many commitments and couldn't consider running for congress.

Justin's Journal

Dinner was amazing. Teddy came with Beth and Mr. Walters. I was beginning to see him as husband material for her; I think Mack was coming around, too. It was easy to see she cared about him—her eyes shone whenever he paid attention to her, and that happened a lot.

Gina, well, I was beginning to see the same thing in her eyes. In fact, I was paying so much attention to Gina that Mack asked me three times to pass the platter of fish so he could get thirds.

Darzi had cooked the best fish I'd ever eaten. Mom didn't make fish often, and nothing like this. Darzi made a sauce that complimented the fish perfectly, and there was fish stew as a beginning course.

Mom got a vegetarian noodle and sauce dish that was outstanding —I tried a bite of it and it was excellent. Darzi could cook anytime he wanted, in my opinion. He was quite humble about the whole thing when everybody complimented him, saying the recipes were borrowed and not his.

I didn't care whose recipes they were; Darzi did a wonderful job preparing them.

Gina touched my hand several times under the table, so I went ahead and cleared the movie idea with Dad and Mom—Gina's mother could drive my old Honda home, and I'd drive Gina home after the movie.

Sure, we could watch a movie from Joey's big king-sized bed, but my mind would be far from the movie, I think.

The Princess Bride is on my DVR, Joey sent mindspeech. *So your movie watching won't be a lie,* he added.

He knew that movie was a favorite of mine. Mack's, too.

That's perfect, I responded. *I can quote that one in my sleep.*

I don't think you'll be sleeping, Joey said.

You got that right, I replied.

CHAPTER 16

*J*ustin's Journal
"Are you sure this is okay?" Gina asked as I led her through Joey's house. It was always neat and tidy—Joey didn't like clutter. I knew the sheets and bedding would be spotless, too, or he wouldn't have invited me to use the bed.

"Oh, yeah," I said.

"This is a nice place," Gina breathed as I led her through Joey's media room. He had a huge screen covering one wall. The thing was, he used that one more for game design than he ever did for watching television.

"The bedroom's just as nice," I took her hand and kissed it before offering a lop-sided grin. "And we can watch *The Princess Bride* on DVR."

"I love that movie," Gina smiled shyly.

"Good. We'll watch that, then," I said and pulled her toward the hallway and Joey's bedroom. If we needed a distraction for her so she'd be comfortable, then one would be provided.

Joey's bedroom is decorated in rich greens, golds and browns. Wood floors were covered in a soft, thick rug that made Gina sigh happily the moment she kicked off her shoes and scrunched her toes into it.

"This is your Uncle Joey's house? He has good taste," Gina smiled at me. I didn't tell her that he'd learned most of his interior decorating from my Dad, who has impeccable taste.

"Yeah," I leaned in to kiss her. She wrapped her arms around my neck, so I stepped closer and held her tightly. The kiss went on for a while.

Merrill told me it wasn't just a mashing of lips, if you wanted to keep your girl. I sucked on her lip, then tickled her mouth with my tongue.

Make love to her with your mouth, Merrill said. I was doing my best.

She tasted good—and she liked what I was doing, meeting my tongue tentatively with hers. That almost drove me wild.

I had no idea my body might get as hard as it did, either. If I didn't slow down, I'd last the predicted ten seconds, just as Merrill said.

"Movie," I mumbled, realizing I needed the distraction as much or more than Gina did.

"Oh, sure," Gina pulled away. I didn't want her to go, so I stole another kiss before lifting her easily in my arms and carrying her to the bed. The pupils of her eyes were wide and dark as she smiled at me.

"You're so strong," she whispered. "Nobody ever picked me up and carried me before."

"First of many, baby," I settled her carefully on the bed and kissed her again.

Fumbling with the remote for a few minutes, I got the movie pulled up and started on the DVR before climbing on the bed and pulling Gina into my arms. For ten minutes, maybe, we sat like that, watching the movie. Gina lifted her face to me, silently asking me to kiss her.

I obliged before letting a hand wander to a breast. Her nipple hardened beneath my fingers—I could feel it through the thin fabric of her blouse. I wanted my mouth on that.

I told her so.

"Yes," she said, her words breathless.

Don't fumble, I kept telling myself as I took my time removing her blouse and unhooking a pretty bra. I'd been instructed to reveal things slowly, although my brain was panting with impatience and my body certainly wanted everything as quickly as possible.

Sucking gently on a nipple the moment I lifted the bra away made Gina moan. *A moan was good. An ouch meant I'd gone too far.* She moaned again when I gave a careful nip. That was as far as I could go. Somehow, I knew that.

My hand wandered to the button of her jeans. Taking my time once more, I unbuttoned them without a hitch.

Great.

Zipper next.

"Your shirt, Justin. Please take it off," Gina's hands touched my face then wandered beneath the fabric of my pullover.

That felt good.

"Anything for you, baby," I breathed against her neck before kissing her there.

The shirt came off, but I didn't rush it.

Her palms lay against my chest. "I've watched you at football practice, playing without your shirt," Gina sighed. "You put those other guys to shame with this," her hands wandered down my body. Yeah, I have a six-pack. I figured it was a combination of sports and working on construction sites for Dad.

Lately, it was fighting spawn, but that was something Gina couldn't know.

My body had never really been a concern and the truth was, Mack was just as built, he was just shorter—at least for the moment. I figured the wolf would see to that. Mack had run track in junior high and high school, and had a few trophies on the shelf in his bedroom. I figured the wolf had helped out with that, too, we just didn't realize it before.

Gina's hand wandered to the button on my jeans.

"Want that open, baby?" I breathed, covering her hand with mine.

"Yes," she mumbled, closing her eyes when I kissed her.

"You got it." I pulled the fabric loop from the button, leaving the zipper up. I let her do that herself.

The second she touched my cock, I thought I was going to come. With a force of will I had no idea I possessed, I kept it from happening.

Her fingers, wrapped around my shaft, drove me wild.

"Justin, this—I've never seen anyone this big," Gina breathed against my mouth. I was desperately attempting to distract her—to keep her from stroking me.

"Your fault," I mumbled against her lips. "All your fault."

"You won't mind that I'm not," she began. She was worried I'd think less of her because she wasn't a virgin.

"Baby, that has nothing to do with us," I said, leaning away. "Now, if you keep touching me there, I'm gonna come, and that means you won't be satisfied like I want to satisfy you. Okay?"

"Can we save it for later, then?"

"Oh, yeah."

I think we made love as Westley rescued Buttercup in the fire swamp. In a way, it was fitting—I dived beneath the covers the moment Westley drew a breath and dived into the lightning sand to save his true love.

Gina came—twice—before I stopped pleasuring her with my mouth. We joined then—after the ceremony of the condom was completed. She did it for me while I watched, her hands sending messages to my body and my brain as I watched it roll down my length.

Her hand guided me into her body after that, and I was grateful not to fumble that.

It couldn't have been more perfect, and my satisfaction was complete at the end of it.

While Gina acted shy after we dressed later, I pulled her chin up so I could see her eyes. "This is our love, Gina," I said. "That means there's nothing to be shy about or feel ashamed of. Nothing is different between us. I just hope you enjoyed it as much as I did."

"I did. Justin, that was—incredible. I really don't have a better word, and there should be one," she said. I kissed her for that.

"It's late and we should go," I said. The credits had rolled half an hour earlier, and I didn't want to keep her out too late.

"Yeah. Mom might worry," she acknowledged. "Thank you, Justin. This was the perfect night."

I drove her home after that, walked her to the door of my old house and kissed her there on the doorstep. The porch light was on, but I didn't care if her mother saw me kissing Gina.

She was my girl.

I handed house keys back to Joey the following morning. He nodded and never said a word. Maybe he knew it went well. Maybe he knew it wasn't any of his business. We didn't discuss it, and that was the right thing to do.

It was Sunday; Mack and I had homework to do—Joey did remind me of that. We had a calculus assignment to turn in and a writing assignment in history for Bearcat.

Lately, that was the story of our lives—punctuating the absolute terror of fighting spawn and kapiri with mundane high school homework.

"Dude, I need to do laundry," I handed the saltshaker to Mack over breakfast that morning. "Almost out of clean jeans."

"Yeah. Sometimes Beth does my stuff at home, but now," Mack shrugged.

"Come on. Grab your stuff and we'll get it done while we do calculus homework."

"Is this how it'll be in college?" Mack grumped.

"I figure it will," Mom walked in and patted Mack's shoulder. "I'm thinking of hiring somebody to help clean this house. I can't do it all myself, especially since I don't have any power at the moment."

I studied Mom—the baby bump looked slightly larger. "Your dad's birthday is coming up," Mom reminded me. "Have you done anything about that?"

"Oh, crap," I said, rubbing my forehead. "It's next Saturday, isn't it?"

"Yep."

"What do you have planned?" I blinked at Mom. "I mean, he already got the cufflinks you ordered for him."

"Before your autocratic father demanded cufflinks, I'd already bought something for him," Mom huffed. "It's not returnable, either, or I might have tried that."

"What's not returnable?" Dad wandered in, a cup of tea in his hand.

"Your real birthday present," I said before Mom could shush me.

"Sweetheart, those cufflinks are worth a king's ransom," Dad began.

"I already bought you something, before you demanded those," Mom said. "Don't ask me about it. I can't return it—you're getting it. End of story."

"How much is a king's ransom?" Mack asked. He and I were curious about how much Tiralian crystal was actually worth.

"Those cufflinks together have six carats of Tiralian crystal," Mom said. "The raw stones are worth twelve million dollars. That doesn't include the cutting, shaping and spelling by Grey House, so you can add another eight million to that. That's what your father got for his birthday," Mom snapped and flounced out of the room.

"Damn," Mack breathed. "Twenty million dollar cufflinks. Well done, Mr. G."

I bent over laughing.

∽

Adam's Journal

If I'd been anyone else, I'd have bought extra insurance and an alarm system for the house—after installing a hidden safe.

With the multiple shields around the house, the other things were not only unnecessary, they'd be redundant.

I suspected the cufflinks were expensive. I just hadn't estimated twenty million dollars' worth.

It made me wonder about the other gifts—while they weren't made of Tiralian crystal, they were gray jewels crafted by Grey House and included gold, platinum and in the case of the boys' watches, chaugis-skin bands. Chaugis skin was highly prized and the species was protected, therefore, only the skin of the naturally deceased animals could be used for anything, including shoes, boots and watchbands.

Those watches were likely worth eight million apiece; I just didn't want the boys to know—they might take them off. They were built to protect their owners, after all, and spelled against wear and tear.

"Dad?" Justin said, bringing me away from my thoughts, "Mack and I need to run errands this afternoon, when we finish laundry and homework. Is there anything you want us to pick up? Flowers, maybe?"

I lifted an eyebrow at my son before nodding. Yes—I owed my wife flowers, in addition to many other things.

"Here," I pulled out my wallet and handed Justin a wad of cash. "Get as many roses as you can carry in that Jeep of yours when you're done with your errands," I said. "I want to fill the pool with rose petals. I can place a stasis spell, so they'll stay fresh as long as I want."

"A stasis spell? That's kind of amazing," Mack said. "Wish I'd known that before I dumped the expired chicken salad last week."

"You—homework," I pointed toward the hall leading to their bedrooms. Mack and Justin snickered as they walked away.

Justin's Journal

Gina had to work, so we didn't get to take her shopping when we went. I had to find something Dad would like—he was picky about his clothes, ties and shoes.

"How about a special box—for his twenty-million-dollar

cufflinks?" Mack suggested as we made a second round through the mall.

"You know, you don't get nearly enough credit for being an almost-genius," I teased.

"I have my moments," Mack grinned. "There's that little specialty shop down at the end, let's go see what they have."

They had plenty, as it turned out. Boxes carved from all kinds of wood, plus a few made of semiprecious stone. Those looked too small to me, so we studied the ones made of wood.

That's where he found us. With everything else that had happened, I'd almost forgotten Randall Pierce. Yes, he was a fugitive who'd broken out of jail, yet here he was, strutting into a small shop at the mall as if he weren't a wanted criminal.

I did the first thing I could think to do under the circumstances. I couldn't attack him—that could get me arrested right along with the asshat who stood three feet away wearing a malicious grin.

Dad, I sent, *Randall Pierce is here at the mall. I don't think he wants to be friendly and apologize, either.*

"Better check all your friends," Randall sneered. Mack growled low in his throat.

"What the hell are you talking about?" I snapped.

"Some we couldn't get to. Not all of them, though," Randall's voice became a snarl. If I hadn't held Mack back at that moment, his wolf would have shredded Randall. As it was, Dad and Uncle Dragon walked into the shop, followed by Officers Francis and Barton.

"You think that jail is gonna hold me a second time?" Randall spat at us as he was handcuffed.

Dad, I think he's done something terrible, or knows about it, I sent while Randall continued to grin at me.

He intended to hurt me in some way. Gina was my first thought, so I texted her immediately.

Justin, I just got to work, her return text read. *I'm fine.*

Stay that way, I texted back. *We just found RP at the mall, and he made some awful threats.*

Did the police show up?

Yeah, but he's saying they won't be able to keep him in jail since he broke out the last time.

That asshole, Gina replied.

I can think up better words, I tapped.

So can I, but autocorrect keeps changing them.

Understood. Be careful, okay?

I will.

"Son?" Dad dropped a hand on my shoulder. He'd watched me text Gina. "What threats did he make?"

"He said we'd better check all our friends," Mack answered for me.

"Gina's fine. Can we ask the police to watch the restaurant?" I asked. I worried about her in such a public place.

"Is there anyone else?" Dragon asked, his dark eyes focusing on me.

"Oh, my God, Sarah," Mack breathed.

"Let's go," Dad said.

The moment he got us out of the mall and away from prying eyes, we folded space.

Sarah lived with her parents not far from our old house. Yeah, the old house was protected with shields; Dad said so. So was Joey's house, where we'd been last night. It was three blocks away from Sarah's house.

I figure Randall's allies wanted to get to Gina and me, but were prevented. Randall had likely named an alternate target.

The minute we landed outside the house, Mack smelled them.

Spawn had been here. Some of the larger ones, too. They'd hit Sarah's house, plus the neighbors on both sides.

All the infected inhabitants wandered out of their houses the moment we appeared, Sarah included. She was dead—only a monster stared through her eyes, now.

"No," Mack breathed, his voice breaking.

"Son, take Mack for a walk. We'll handle this," Dad said softly.

~

Adam's Journal

Dragon and I wouldn't do this ourselves, but we had enough allies to do it for us. Dragon folded Merrill, Daniel and Martin Walters in while I held the newly born spawn at bay.

Nearby neighbors from across the street and houses farther down the block had come out to watch. Some of them already suspected what had happened—after all, there'd been plenty of reports on the news, and everybody had seen the attacks from the silent monsters at the Valley High football game.

"I went to visit this morning. Couldn't get a word out of 'em," one man said as he came to stand beside me. "What can we do? I saw those things attack at the football game."

"I have help on the way," I sighed. I'd have to shield Merrill's claws; Martin and Daniel would appear to be Merrill's vicious, extremely large dogs.

If anyone recorded the attack, they'd see soon enough that these were no longer human—the dusting would be the best indicator of such.

I wanted to weep for the young girl who'd befriended Mack and Justin; she'd been Gina's best friend since first grade.

Her monster stared at me now, blank-eyed, waiting for me to make the first move.

I wouldn't be making it.

Dragon drove up and parked my SUV across the street while Merrill and two large wolves climbed from the vehicle. They were halfway across the street when the spawn recognized them as a threat and attacked.

Seven former humans died in a rapid dusting as the wolves and a vampire defended themselves. Several watchers recorded it on their cell phones.

Dragon recorded it on mine, in case there were any questions. I had something to do, however, when Officers Barton and Francis showed up with several other police officers, blocking the street with their cruisers.

"Everything all right?" Francis asked as he came to stand beside me.

"For the most part," I sighed. "The Pierce boy told Justin to check all his friends. He had something to do with this."

"You think he and his father are friends with those creatures who do this?" Francis swept out a hand, encompassing the spray of dark spawn dust covering the street.

"Innocents died because of them," I nodded. "One family because they befriended my son."

"What do they have against him?" Francis asked.

"My son is standing between us and those monsters bent on destroying all of us," I answered truthfully. "If anyone asks, you will not be able to repeat that information."

"I wouldn't repeat it anyway," Francis shook his head. "If your son has some way to combat this epidemic, then I'm all for it. I'm all for that man and his dogs, too," Francis nodded toward Merrill, who was busy placing compulsion on the officers asking questions.

After all, he was too fast for anyone to record on their cell phones, so only Dragon and I saw him behead four of the seven while Daniel and Martin's wolves crowded in to cover the deed.

With compulsion, the *dogs* in question wouldn't even need a rabies tag. The truth was, however, that I could produce those with power if it became necessary.

My immediate concern was for Justin and Mack.

Then I intended to have a chat with Randall Pierce at the jail. In my eyes, he was guilty of murder and attempted murder. I wondered how he and his father had gotten involved with spawn to begin with, and why those spawn had left them human, when anyone else was bitten or consumed immediately.

That's when Officer Francis' radio began chattering. Not only had the police station been attacked, three officers had been killed and partially eaten by the spawn who'd broken Randall Pierce out of jail a second time.

~

Justin's Journal
Mack and I felt sick. Nauseated as well as sad and weary.

Sarah was gone, and I'd just begun to realize what sort of void she'd leave behind.

How could we tell Gina what happened?

Could we tell Gina what happened?

If the incident was recorded and shown on the news, then she'd know Dad and Uncle Dragon were there on the scene. That meant I'd know, and if I didn't tell her, she'd be even more upset.

How do you tell your girl that her best friend and her parents were taken over by monsters, and then killed by others that most humans would consider monsters as well?

I wanted to find Randall Pierce and show him my monster. Mack probably wanted the same thing.

Son, come back, now. Randall Pierce has managed to escape from jail again, and his spawn allies killed three officers in the process, Dad sent.

"Did you get that?" I asked Mack.

He nodded, keeping his head down and his eyes on the grass at our feet. We stood in a small, neighborhood park two blocks from Sarah's house, while kids played, laughed and squealed around us.

It all sounded so surreal—that people had died not so far away.

Life went on and for a moment, I was witness to all of it—the good and the bad. I wanted to cry, because there wouldn't be another body for Gina to bury.

Mom? I sent as Mack and I walked away from the park toward Sarah's house.

I know already, honey. Your dad told me, Mom said. *This is a horribly sad day for all of us,* she added. *Sarah can't be hurt anymore, but Gina will feel this all her life.*

She was right. The people left behind would suffer the most from such a senseless thing. There was no reason for it, other than the anger and hatred one small-minded boy could pour out toward perceived enemies.

"I want to kill him," Mack clenched his fists beside me.

"You may have to stand in line," I muttered.

Guilt began to eat at me, too. If Randall hadn't focused his hatred on me, Sarah might still be alive. Actually, she would be alive. Randall only attacked her because he couldn't get to Gina. Or me.

"I think we need to convince Gina she's in danger," I said, breaking into a run. The police couldn't protect her from Randall Pierce's spawn buddies.

Mack ran beside me and picked up the pace—he knew I was right.

Adam's Journal

"The police are taking Gina home," I assured Justin. He was convinced now that Sarah's death was his fault and that Gina could be next. I never thought to see my son break down like this, but he was close to tears.

Kiarra and I had pulled him and Mack into my study the moment I got both of them home, attempting to tell him that he wasn't at fault— Randall Pierce was deranged in his anger, and likely encouraged by those who held power over the spawn he considered allies. I couldn't disagree, however, that Gina was likely in danger as a result.

"There is no logic or reason left in him or his father," Kiarra rubbed Justin's back. "The blame is his. The guilt is his. Don't take it upon yourself; you had no part in it."

"What can we do, Dad?" Justin's eyes glittered with unshed tears.

"Why don't you let me think on that, with your Uncle Dragon and Uncle Lion? We may be able to come up with something."

I could tell he wasn't convinced. After all, my hands—and the hands of every other Saa Thalarr—had been effectively tied. The only hope I had was that Thorsten's edict concerned spawn.

Randall Pierce was still human, and he'd threatened my family.

According to the rules, I was allowed to protect my family and myself. I just needed a way to get Randall Pierce to attack one of us openly.

I'd missed my chance when Raymond Pierce attacked Kiarra in a grocery store parking lot.

I didn't intend to let the opportunity slip away a second time.

"We'll figure this out, honey," Kiarra hugged Justin. "It may take a while, but it'll happen."

"I sure hope you're right," Justin mumbled.

～

Home now, Gina texted me. *I can't believe she's gone.*

I'm so sorry, baby. I can't believe it, either, I texted back.

The police told me Randall Pierce was in on that. He's a murdering bastard.

He's done his best to wipe all of us out, I agreed. *I promise I won't let anything happen to you. I promise. I swear I'll kill him if he comes anywhere near you.*

Justin, stay away from him. He's dangerous, Gina said. *I'm sorry, I can barely see the screen. I keep wiping tears away,* she added.

Baby, please don't cry, I wiped away tears of my own. *This is so awful.*

I know. I have to go.

Tossing the cell phone onto my bed, I stood there for a moment, feeling lost. Out of place. As if my slot in the universe had closed up, pushing me out and leaving me behind.

I wanted to hunt Randall down and crush the life out of him.

Something in me said that was wrong, but I barely listened to it.

"Come on, let's do laundry," Mack gripped my arm. "Maybe we can figure this out on our own while we fold jeans."

"Sure." I didn't mean it, but I followed Mack to the laundry room anyway. We found Mom there ahead of us, moving clothes from the washer to the dryer.

"We'll get this, Mom, you don't have to pick up after us," Mack said, giving her a big hug. "I talked to Dad a few minutes ago. He said they did what they had to, but he didn't feel good about any of it."

"I know, honey," Mom rubbed his back before pulling away. "Will you be okay? Tell me if you need Dr. Karzac, all right?"

"I will."

"Why don't we get in the pool?" she asked, once the washed clothes were drying and a new load was in the washer.

"Yeah. I think I could use a warm soak," Mack agreed. "Dude?" He turned to me.

"Sure," I said. I still felt lost and wanted to cling to all I had left, which happened to be my family.

If any of them died because of me, I didn't think there was a safe place anywhere for Randall Pierce.

~

Sorry about the roses, I sent to Dad when Mack and I got in the pool a few minutes later with Mom.

We'll do it another time, Dad replied. *I'll come sit by the pool*, he added.

He brought his tablet and phone and took a seat in a comfortable chair to get work done while Mom floated by and Mack and I swam a few laps.

Lion and Marlianna showed up after a bit, then Dragon and Crane came. I'd never seen Dragon with his hair wet before, but he and Crane dived into the water on the deep end as if they'd been doing it every day.

Darzi arrived, became the snake immediately, allowed his clothes to fall in a puddle around him, then dropped into the water from the side of the pool. I guess lion snakes like to swim—he was enjoying himself as he lazily wriggled past Mack and me.

The last one to arrive and get in the pool, shocking all of us, was Pheligar. I guess Larentii like warm water, too. He sat in a corner on one end of the pool, where the water level was chest-high.

With his eyes half-closed, he nodded to Mom and Uncle Dragon. I understood they were having mindspeech.

That's when Mom, Dragon, Crane, Lion and Dad began their conversation on how to find Randall Pierce. Mack and I stopped swimming so we could listen. It became apparent that we all wanted the same thing—Randall Pierce and his father, plus the spawn who were working with them.

We can only discuss this while Pheligar shields our conversation, Dad informed me after a while. I wasn't sure I understood that completely, but nodded anyway.

"I've been *Looking*," Mom said. "We likely can't find them if they're in close proximity to a Sirenali."

Pheligar slowly nodded his assent, his bright-blue eyes still half-closed.

Did I say he was naked?

He was. It didn't seem to bother him a bit. Larentii look humanoid, minus the body hair. If you added sky-blue skin, blond hair and bright blue eyes, he could be a bodybuilder from another world. Every muscle was defined and evident. I didn't see anything that wasn't perfect.

It's the way they're made, Mom read my mind. *He can read your mind, too, you know.*

Do not be embarrassed, Pheligar sent. *Curiosity is quite natural. We have our physique naturally as we feed on energy, consisting mainly of sunlight. It sustains us and maintains our bodies.*

That is seriously cool, I returned.

I watched as the corner of Pheligar's mouth curved slightly. He was smiling.

"Randall Pierce doesn't stay within range of the Sirenali all the time—we found him easily enough at the mall," Dragon pointed out.

"I suggest nexus echo," Pheligar said, surprising everybody.

"What will we listen for?" Mom asked.

"Your child's name, and that of the young werewolf, there," Pheligar indicated Mack. "You can focus the nexus echo so it will be tuned to one individual, or in this case, two."

"We may need your help to do it," Dragon observed.

"Then you will have that. The young one who died should not have."

I am in total agreement, I sent to Pheligar. Yes, it was probably presumptuous of me to think I could just mindspeak him anytime, but he didn't seem to mind. In fact, he probably knew I was seething over Sarah's death. As Pheligar said—it shouldn't have happened.

We will speak later, he sent, shocking me completely.

No, he didn't sound angry. Somehow, his words held a promise— as if he wanted to help me in some way. I had no idea what a Larentii might do to help, but I wanted to stop Randall Pierce. If Pheligar had ideas on that, I was ready to listen.

∾

"So everybody is using that nexus thing to listen for Randall to say our names?" Mack shook his head later as I hung jeans and shirts in my closet. Mack had settled on my bed, his back against the headboard, toying with his cell phone while I worked.

"Yeah. I guess," I shrugged. It was time for bed—for a normal Sunday night. With Sarah's death, our classes were cancelled for three days. Gina needed the time to mourn. I needed the time to plan.

That's when Pheligar came to visit. I don't know what he said to Mack in mindspeech, but Mack slid off my bed without a word and went to his bedroom. I heard his door shut only a few seconds later.

"Please sit, I wish to assess your talents," Pheligar said. I stared stupidly at him for a few seconds before doing as he asked. I took Mack's spot on the bed before nodding to the tall, blue Larentii.

He placed both hands on my head and closed his eyes, as if concentrating. While a human's hands would have felt warm or perhaps hot after a while, Pheligar's remained cool and comfortable.

What made me uncomfortable was the fact that he was examining me so closely. I wasn't sure how to feel about it. After several minutes passed, his hands moved away and he stepped back from my bed.

"You have received extraordinary gifts from the High Demon god," Pheligar sighed.

"What does that mean?" I blurted.

"It means you can fold space, young one. Among other things."

"But I don't know how," I whispered. *I could fold space?* That sounded preposterous.

"I am shielding us, so no others will know of this," he added. "This secret would be best kept to yourself, unless it is needed in the direst of circumstances. I must think on this." He disappeared before I could ask any questions.

If I'd been tired and sleepy before, a Larentii had just given me a jolt, ensuring that I'd be awake most of the night.

CHAPTER 17

*J*ustin's Journal
   The last time I looked at the bedside clock before falling asleep was at four-ten in the morning. My eyes popped open at seven, though, as if I'd had a full night's sleep. Immediately, my mind began its race again, troubled over what Pheligar had discovered.

What had Kifirin done to me?

Why had he done it? I was struggling with that one.

Darzi said it was a true gift, and there were no strings. What did that mean?

My quilt lay on the floor when I moved to slide off the bed; I'd kicked the heavy cover off sometime during the night. The bedframe squeaked softly as I rose from the mattress, standing and stretching to my full height.

I'd never really wanted coffee, but considered it now—I needed to wake up and contemplate everything with a clear head.

Darzi was the only one in the kitchen when I shuffled in, my bare feet scooting across the tiled kitchen floor. Dad said the tile was Italian. The polished stone was cool and comforting to my bare feet, and that was the most important thing to me.

"You wonder about things," Darzi said, sipping tea from a souvenir mug we'd bought on a trip to Yosemite years ago.

"Huh?" I didn't know whether to stop and ask questions or go ahead and find something to drink, first.

"Get drink. We talk. Conversation remain secret."

"Okay." I didn't want to argue, and my head needed serious clearing. For the first time ever, I made coffee for myself, poured half-and-half in it to make it almost white and then stirred several teaspoons of sugar into the cup.

"That wake you up," Darzi snorted as I set the cup on the island and took the barstool next to his.

"What are we talking about?" I asked, sipping the hot coffee and almost grimacing at the taste and heat of it. I ignored that and sipped again, hoping the combination of caffeine and sugar would work at something close to the speed of light.

"Drink more," Darzi encouraged.

I did.

"Things happening," Darzi began. "Not supposed to happen."

"Yeah," I snorted into my cup before drinking more coffee. Sarah's death had settled on my shoulders like the heavy quilt on my bed. I couldn't kick that weight off as easily, however.

Pheligar's discovery had me befuddled, too. What good was any particular talent, if you didn't understand how to use it? He'd said to keep it to myself, too. What about Mack? Mom and Dad?

"Stop worry." Darzi placed a hand on my shoulder. "Things happen in own time. Kifirin give gift. He not do lightly. Someone else ask him to do this."

"Who?" I huffed. I couldn't imagine why anyone might take an interest in me.

"Mighty one," Darzi shrugged. "Have reason."

I had no idea what any of that meant, and when I *Looked* for information, nothing came up.

That was interesting.

"Kifirin move time," Darzi said. "With me. Not from now. He asleep now."

"What does that mean?" If Darzi meant to explain things, he was only confusing me more.

"You," he tapped a finger against my forehead, "past. Me," he tapped his chest with the same finger, "future."

"You're saying you're from the future?" I shook my head. After little sleep and a likely overdose of coffee and sugar, perplexed might best describe how I felt.

"Exact," Darzi's nod was emphatic. "Things change, your past. I come. Help."

"Do you mean that this isn't how the past was supposed to be?" I almost stopped breathing.

"Yes. You hit nail. Exact."

"Why are you telling me this?" I asked after drawing in an unsteady breath.

"You different this time," Darzi sighed and drank more of his tea. "More. Have to be."

"You make it sound like these things have already happened once," I said.

"Exact."

I probably shouldn't have tried it, but Yosemite was closed to visitors after the spawn attacks only a few weeks earlier. So many things had happened since then.

I folded space to Yosemite, discovering it was easy.

I needed to fly. I'd gotten a taste of it, and hadn't had time to savor or enjoy it. I did so now, riding thermals above Half Dome and El Capitan. Grasses in the valleys below those mountains had gone yellow with the season and shone golden in the early-morning sun.

I imagined what it might be like to fly over the Fresno pack on a full moon, so I could watch Mack, Beth and the others run. I'd seen Dragon flying over the ocean on Mom's private planet.

I wanted to do that, too.

More than anything, though, I wanted to take Randall Pierce down. He and his father had stepped over the line long ago, I imagined. Who knows if Raymond Pierce had locked Mack in a cell with a known killer on his own volition, or whether those he'd befriended had instructed him to do so?

It didn't matter—Mack almost died.

Sarah did die—a stupid, useless death. Randall, his dad and those they'd allied with wanted to hurt me in any way they could. Their focus had shifted from Mack to me, almost in a blink.

Why?

I wasn't sure anybody had an answer for that.

Time to go home, a voice filtered into my head. I'd never heard that voice before. It didn't speak to me again. The thing was, I'm not sure I could have disobeyed it, anyway. I folded space to Fresno.

Adam's Journal

"I'm surprised they haven't attacked other small towns by now," Kiarra said. She drank orange juice and rubbed her slightly-swollen belly, as if she were comforting our daughter.

"I'm surprised, too, but I don't want to examine that gift too closely," I said. Darzi was busy at the stove, making poached eggs for Kiarra, who'd had a craving for them.

"What if all that was just a distraction?" she asked.

"A distraction from what?" I flung up a hand.

"I don't know," Kiarra grumbled. "Where's Justin?"

"Here," he walked into the kitchen, smelling of sunlight.

"Where have you been?" I demanded to know.

"Uh, outside," he hedged.

"You didn't go to Gina's did you?"

"No, Dad. I didn't go to Gina's, as much as I'd like to," he said. "I just went outside for a while, to be alone and think."

"If you go outside the walls, someone should be with you," I ordered. I hated to confine him like that, but I was terrified for my family. Sarah's death had come too close to all of us. It could easily have been Gina. It almost was Kiarra. I was furious that I couldn't protect them as well as I might.

"I'll let you know, Dad," Justin held up a hand to stave off my growing anger.

"I'm not mad at you, Son," I said apologetically. "These recent events have me on edge, and I have no idea how to react."

"Yeah. I hear that," Justin said before pulling a glass from a cabinet and getting cold water from the fridge.

"What's for breakfast?" Mack wandered in, his hair ruffled, an oversized T-shirt hanging loosely about his shoulders and wearing relatively new jeans, which were rapidly becoming too short.

"Poached eggs," Kiarra said. "Have a seat. I'll help Darzi with the plates."

"I love poached eggs," Mack proclaimed and slipped onto a barstool at the island.

"Dude, that shirt is three sizes too big," Justin pointed out.

"Yeah. My mom sent it to me for my birthday."

I knew what that meant—Martin's ex-wife hadn't bothered to check what clothing sizes Mack needed.

"It's good to sleep in," Mack added. Kiarra put a plate of food in front of him, so he cut into his eggs immediately.

"Adam," Kiarra looked at me, lifting an eyebrow and then nodding toward Mack's overly-large shirt.

"I can fix that if you want, so it'll fit," I offered.

"That would be cool, Mr. G."

I altered the shirt with power, so it fit properly. Mack grinned as he touched the hem of the shirt—it no longer hung too low on his body and the shoulders, chest and waist were proportional to his size. I'd also lengthened the jeans—they weren't riding above his ankles, now.

"That might be the coolest talent ever," Mack said before going back to his eggs. "If Beth could do that, she wouldn't have to worry about her fat jeans fitting anymore." He lifted a wedge of toast and crunched into it with a grin.

Kiarra hid a smile and rubbed his back affectionately.

Justin's Journal

"I'm off work until next Friday," Gina said over the phone. "Will you come over?" She sounded lonely. Sad. I wanted to hold her.

"I have to check with Dad—he says we're all in danger," I pointed out. Two months earlier, I'd have asked the obligatory question, then jumped in my car and gone because my parents would have said yes without question.

Things were much more serious now.

"Will you ask?" I could tell she was crying.

"Yeah. Don't cry, baby. I'll come if I can."

By the time I found Mom and Dad sitting by the pool and talking with Uncle Lion and Uncle Dragon, Gina's mom was calling mine.

"They want to go to the mall," Mom sighed, covering dad's phone with a hand. I stopped in my tracks. It was one thing to go to the old house, which was protected. It was another to go out in public, which was not protected.

"But," I mumbled. *Why did they want to go to the mall?*

"There's a memorial service tomorrow at their church," Mom said. "For Sarah. They don't have anything appropriate to wear and they're asking if you can go with them. For protection."

Yeah, they thought human protection might be enough. I guess it was a good thing I wasn't. Human, that is.

"I think I want to go, too," Mom lifted off her lounge chair and stretched after standing straight.

"What?" Dad sputtered.

"If you don't want to go, Merrill will come," Mom said.

"Then take Merrill. See if Mack wishes to go," Dad growled. He wasn't happy about the whole thing, but he didn't want to argue about it with Mom.

"Good." Mom handed the phone to me and stalked out of the room.

"Uh, hi, Mrs. Allen," I croaked into Dad's cell phone. "I think we're coming to get you in a few."

"Are those warheads ready to go?" The General asked.

"They are," Acrimus bowed his head respectfully.

"I find it humorous that they were never checked after their rediscovery at the military base," the General chuckled. "So easy to substitute the inner workings of more, shall we say, deadly explosives? I love the idea of hitting Texas and Oklahoma with ranos missiles instead of nuclear bombs."

"They'll be obliterated—we have enough warheads for that," Acrimus agreed. "Now that our servant is dead in Texas, there's no real need to preserve the state. Oklahoma, well, we know something is there, through the Elemaiya. We just don't know what it is. Nevertheless, we'll take two states with eight birds, eh?"

"Two for Oklahoma, six for Texas," the General agreed. "Time may be short—I anticipate moving when the woman and her child are eliminated."

"The opportunity has arrived, according to Calhoun," Acrimus reported the mindspeech he'd just received. "I hear they've left their protected compound. How fortunate that Thorsten can retain his blameless state in this and remain in his position over the others. It is only a matter of time before the entire race is gone."

"Fortunate, indeed," the General nodded.

Justin's Journal

Merrill drove Dad's SUV with Mack in the front passenger seat. Mom, Darzi and Mrs. Allen sat in the second row; Gina and I sat in the little-used third row on our way to the mall.

Mack was happy to get out of the house, I could tell—I guess he'd felt like a caged wolf since Memphis.

Merrill was happy to get out, too—even if he seldom did anything as mundane as going to a mall.

His clothes sure didn't come from any mall. Dad said Merrill shopped at exclusive clothiers in Britain. He had good taste, too, although he wasn't nearly as stiff and unrelenting as Dad was about what he wore.

I'd seen Merrill in jeans when he fought spawn. I'd seldom seen Dad in jeans, he never wore T-shirts and getting him into athletic shoes took an act of congress. To top it off, he never, ever wanted to wear shorts. Swim trunks was the closest he'd come, and he really didn't like those, either.

That's where I was—holding Gina's hand and thinking about Dad's aversion to any clothing that rose above his ankles when Merrill pulled up at a stoplight on the way to the mall.

The earthquake came first, and it was the worst one I'd ever experienced.

~

"Our targets are locked. Turn the keys and begin the countdown," the silo commanders spoke.

~

Justin's Journal

I'd only seen photographs before.

This was the reality. While the ground shook about us, fissures began opening in the streets, with concrete and debris falling into deep crevices. People screamed and attempted to escape their vehicles the moment they realized what was happening.

That was a mistake.

Following the appearance of the giant, copper serpent on a street corner not far from our house, spawn began crawling from the fissures opening in the streets, moving as swiftly as angry insects when their nest has been disturbed.

Those spawn fell on any brave enough to leave their cars behind and run. Other cars, still occupied, fell into the gaping holes opening beneath them with a crash. Gina screamed beside me when a truck close by burst into flames as it was swallowed by still-shaking ground.

Shining, copper scales glinted in the sun as the serpent watched spawn devour fleeing humans. *Everything about them is poisonous. Scales, teeth, spikes, all of it,* I recalled. Some people ran right past the Ra'Ak. A few ran into him, likely dooming themselves with the poison on his scales.

He paid them little mind.

The Ra'Ak hadn't come for them.

He'd come for us.

If I'd bothered to *Look* right then, I still wouldn't have seen the giant serpent. Something blocked his presence—whether from inside or outside his body, I had no clue.

Mom did what she could, telling Gina and Mrs. Allen to wait until we were out of the vehicle before getting out behind us—so we could protect them. We were forced to get out, after all—a crevice had opened in front of the SUV and we'd fall into it if we didn't leave the vehicle behind. That meant that Merrill, Darzi, Mack and I would face the worst monster we'd ever seen while trying to save our lives.

Fifty feet, from snout to tail, he roared at us as we opened doors slowly and stepped from the car, his fangs too many to count and dripping with venom. *Teeth or spike injuries can be fatal if they're not treated immediately after the Ra'Ak dies.*

The worst poison of all—teeth or spikes. I saw the spikes, then— the Ra'Ak's tail whipped about, knocking cars across multiple lanes of traffic before falling into widening cracks. Mack cringed; the monster's roar was deafening.

Behind me, Gina screamed again.

I go, Darzi spoke into my mind. *Stop bombs. Have to. No choice.*

He disappeared, causing Mack to shout his name. We needed the tough, lion snake shapeshifter.

There were three of us left, now, to combat a Ra'Ak and too many spawn to count.

I've already tried to send mindspeech, Mom informed me. *It's bouncing back, just as it did for you in Florida. I think our Ra'Ak friend, there, was Sirenali when he was turned. He's keeping everything blocked. We're on our own, honey.*

The SUV dropped into the crevice with a crash behind me, its horn blaring relentlessly as Gina and Mrs. Allen screamed.

"Mr. President, sir, there are six warbirds heading toward Texas, and another two toward Oklahoma," the Chief of Staff interrupted a meeting to inform the President.

"What the hell is going on?" The President stood, demanding answers.

"I don't know. There are no communications getting through to the silos. Sir, there's something else you need to know," the Chief of Staff said.

"What's that?"

"Those bombs have been altered."

"What?"

"I only have sketchy information, from photographs taken by our Air Force jets," the Chief of Staff replied. "But our experts confirm this —the guidance system is different and they can't explain it. It's likely these substituted bombs are much more dangerous than the original warheads. We have no idea who is responsible, or what we're about to be hit with, Mr. President. If we fire on them while in midair, we could cause Armageddon."

"How much time do we have?" The President asked.

"As of now, less than ten minutes. If these are nuclear, the fallout alone can kill millions."

∿

Justin's Journal

Mack fought his way out of his clothes and became wolf. Merrill's claws and fangs were already out. I had no choice—the wyvern told me so.

When Gina screamed again behind us, I imagined she was terrified of the Ra'Ak and the spawn closing in on us. She wasn't alone—I was terrified, too.

What I didn't expect was what happened when the giant serpent lunged toward Merrill, who was doing his best to stand between it and Mom.

Merrill's spelled ring blasted the Ra'Ak backward when it activated, the Ra'Ak's head jerking back as if it had been punched on the snout by a giant hand.

Anybody else might have gone down right then and not gotten up again.

It was merely the opening volley for a Ra'Ak, as it turns out, who snapped back at Merrill so fast it was blinding. If he hadn't been vampire, he'd have died.

∿

Adam's Journal

Mindspeech from Darzi might have been the last thing I expected. Not only did he send words, he sent images, forcing me to my feet so fast it might make anyone else dizzy.

Dragon and Lion, who'd been discussing the current state of affairs with me by the pool, were included in the lion snake's sendings.

Without a word, all of us folded space to an intersection in Fresno, where things had already gone critical. There we found Kiarra, Gina and Marie Allen, Mack's wolf, Justin's wyvern and Merrill, whose claws and fangs were evident, standing on an island of concrete.

Around them lay a deep, rough fissure filled with spawn, wrecked vehicles and fire. "There's a shield up," Dragon growled.

He was right. It was as if someone had dumped a huge, impermeable glass bowl on top of that island, trapping all of them inside with a Ra'Ak.

Outside the bowl, spawn raced after humans attempting to run away. I nodded to Dragon and Lion—if we combined our energy, perhaps we could penetrate the shield. I was terrified that my family would die while I watched, helpless to do anything but weep.

∾

Darzi's Journal

Nenzi best at fixing machines. I not as good. Still know some things. *Look.* Find Ranos missiles inside bombs. Not good. I have to fix.

Fast.

∾

Adam's Journal

We threw our best at it, and even attempted to come from beneath the concrete. The shield was a sphere we couldn't damage or destroy. Mindspeech was useless as I watched Merrill, with blinding speed, whirl around the Ra'Ak's torso so swiftly he left gaping wounds and strings of cuts upon the serpent's body.

Merrill had no shielding capability. If he allowed any of the Ra'Ak's greenish blood to touch his skin, he'd be poisoned by it. He was there, protecting Kiarra and the others with everything he had. That should be me. I was equipped to handle the monster, after all.

Kiarra had pushed Marie and Gina as tightly against the side of the bubble shield as she could, to keep them out of harm's way. For the moment, Merrill kept the monster occupied. The moment he tired, he'd be dead.

The moment he tired, they'd all be dead.

~

Justin's Journal

Things might move as fast as Merrill in the movies or in a few cartoons I'd seen. I never imagined seeing it in person, under such dire circumstances.

The Ra'Ak snapped repeatedly at Merrill, but his teeth always closed on empty air—where Merrill had been less than a blink before.

What would happen when Merrill tired?

He'd die.

The Ra'Ak wanted all of us dead, that was plain to see, he was merely waiting for the right moment to take Merrill, thinking the rest of us would be easy targets.

Merrill had one spelled stone in his ring, and it had already emptied itself.

Mom had two stones in the earrings she wore.

Mack and I wore wristwatches with a dozen stones fixed to the bands. What would that do to the Ra'Ak?

Could we get Merrill safely away so we could attack the monster?

A part of me realized that Mack and I would likely die attacking a powerful Ra'Ak. The thing was—if we took it down with us, the trade would be worth it. Our lives for his.

Dude, Mack's mindspeech came. *You thinking what I'm thinking?*

At least the nearby mindspeech worked, just as it had in Florida.

If you're thinking of jumping that thing to activate our spelled watches, then yes.

You know what that means?

Yeah. Take him down, man. Whatever it takes.

Exactly. You think we can get Merrill out of the way first?

I'm not sure we have time. Let me send mindspeech. See what he says.

I sent mindspeech to a vampire flying so fast around a Ra'Ak's body, he was a blur.

Don't wait, Justin. Attack now, Merrill replied.

He was tiring, and only the force of his will kept him moving so swiftly.

Let's go. My wyvern nodded to Mack's wolf. Together, we leapt toward the enemy.

~

Adam's Journal

I'd seen Dragon use the same tactics before, only he could shield his teeth, tongue and mouth from Ra'Ak blood and poison when he did it.

Justin and Mack, almost without warning, leapt on the monster, their teeth fastening on the serpent's throat, just below the head. Merrill stopped still and buried all ten claws into the creature—to the tips of his fingers and past that, I think.

That's when two dozen Grey House jewels activated, causing the explosion inside the bubble shield and spewing huge chunks of Ra'Ak dust against the surface. I screamed my fear and sadness to the world as I watched the shield fall with the Ra'Ak.

Everything inside the perimeter was covered in Ra'Ak dust and unmoving.

~

Darzi's Journal

Tiny seconds. All I had. Used them.

Changed insides to harmless.

Nenzi be proud.

~

"Impact in ten seconds, Mr. President."

"Nine."
"Eight."
"Seven."
"Six."
"Five."
"Four."
"Three."
"Two."
"One."

CHAPTER 18

"What the hell?" The President stood, watching in disbelief as warhead after warhead hit the ground across two states, bounced, broke apart and threw up sprays of dirt, rock and debris before the pieces came to rest.

A few of those pieces lay on the lawns of the capitals in Oklahoma and Texas.

Rescue workers and military vehicles were on the way, with everyone dressed in haz-mat suits, but they weren't needed.

"What the bloody hell," the President repeated wearily before dropping onto his chair with a sigh.

~

Adam's Journal

"Adam?" Dragon's hand dropped to my shoulder. I realized then that I sat on a tiny pier of concrete in the middle of what used to be a busy Fresno intersection.

"We've checked the rubble. There's nothing there," he said.

"No," I moaned, dropping my face into shaking hands.

They were gone. *All gone.*

Dragon dropped to the concrete beside me and brushed tears away. The chop-chop of a helicopter sounded in the distance. To my ears, it appeared to be having mechanical problems. Probably a poorly maintained news chopper, coming to record the grisly wreckage for six o'clock entertainment.

"The spawn disappeared—when the Ra'Ak dusted," Lion sat on my other side, his boots scraping against damaged concrete as he settled there. Pain was etched across his face as he studied the scene before us.

"Bombs gone," Darzi said, appearing before us. "Find Larentii. Need."

"Are you hurt? What bombs?" Dragon croaked. Darzi didn't look injured, but in my numbed state, what did I know?

"Ranos missiles, like nuclear bombs. Enemy try to kill Texas. Oklahoma. Cannot say why."

"They were sending bombs at the same time they attacked here?" Lion asked, shaking his head.

"Yes. Exact."

"Holy, fucking hell," I mumbled. My profanity was the proper response, there just wasn't any feeling behind it—I was too numb.

"Why do we need the Larentii? To see how we failed in all this?" Dragon shook his head.

"To fix. Heal. They come."

∽

Justin's Journal

I didn't have enough power to fold space a second time. Likely, it was the Ra'Ak poison coursing through my body. I felt it—knew it was there. Still I flew, my wings making an uneven noise as I carried the bubble containing Mom, Mrs. Allen, Gina, Mack and Merrill back from Yosemite.

I'd folded there earlier, when the Ra'Ak exploded—the location was still fresh in my mind and was an almost automatic destination when it became necessary to find one. If I hadn't folded away, the Ra'Ak's dusting could have killed me.

The bubble I gripped carefully in my claws? That's what Mom's earrings had done at the last, when the Ra'Ak dusted—protected the others, encasing them in a small bubble shield.

I'd had a shield for my body—I learned that at the last, but didn't think fast enough to shield my teeth and tongue.

That's how the poison entered my body.

Mack and Merrill were in the same boat—the three of us were dying after coming in contact with the Ra'Ak. Mom wept as she held both of them close; I gripped the bubble tighter in my claws, hoping to land in Fresno before I lost consciousness and fell out of the sky.

I could see Dad, Lion, Dragon and Darzi in the distance as my flight wobbled. Struggling to remain aloft, I worked to glide the last few hundred feet.

Somehow, it had been possible to fold space out of the Ra'Ak's shield, just not inside it. Like one-way glass or something.

The Ra'Ak planned to get away like that, after he killed the rest of us. It ended up just the opposite, except three of us would still die.

With limited knowledge of Ra'Ak poison, I had no idea how much time we had left.

I don't remember touching the ground.

~

Adam's Journal

Justin crashed onto the street behind us while Lion, Dragon and I threw shields to cushion the landing.

What appeared next I may never have an explanation for.

Pheligar arrived, with an army of Larentii. All I recalled later was a sea of tall, blue men as bodies were lifted and folded away, including mine.

~

Kifirin

More than twelve thousand spawn, all obsessed by a Ra'Ak who'd been Sirenali, once. Those spawn would carry their obsessions until they died.

I watched them, now—they'd scattered across the wasted landscape that had once been Tiralia.

This was the proper place for them. I held shields about myself—even I wouldn't risk the poisoned air about the planet. The spawn had no such capability and would die within a day.

It was fitting. They were more than dangerous, and I wanted none of them to fall into other enemy hands. I'd gotten permission from the one who owned the planet to place these here, so they would no longer trouble anyone by their existence.

My word is law, she'd said. *As is mine*, I'd responded.

❧

Justin's Journal

"Where's Gina?"

Those were the first words I spoke when I opened my eyes.

"She's at home—she and her mother weren't hurt," Mom said, taking my hand. "Justin, she, uh, saw your wyvern."

"So?" I croaked. I was thirsty and dry as a Nevada desert. Still, I wanted to know about my girl, first. Explanations concerning my miraculous recovery could wait until later.

"Honey, this should wait; you're still recovering," Mom said.

What was going on? Something was up, that's for sure. "Tell me," I said. "I have to know."

Mom hesitated, ducking her head and shaking it. That meant the news wasn't good.

"You said they weren't hurt," I accused.

"Justin, that's not it." She closed her eyes for a moment, as if what she had to say hurt her.

"She called you a monster, and says she doesn't want to see you again," Mom blurted, gripping my fingers. I could tell she was really upset by what she had to tell me, too.

"That makes things a bit awkward, as she's still living in our old house," Mom added. "Agent White called your father this morning—he said Gina's father's remains are on their way home." Mom helped me sit up and handed me a glass of ice water. "I went ahead and just sent money to the proper people, so they'd release the remains."

I ignored that and went straight to the thing causing the most pain. "She called me a monster? Mom, that can't be right," I struggled to push covers back and almost spilled the water. I drank the whole glass while waiting for Mom's answer. What she was saying couldn't be right.

Couldn't be.

"Justin, sometimes people don't know how to react," Mom said, looking away uncomfortably. "I can have your father play the entire conversation for you—he can do that with power."

"She called me a monster?" I croaked, wishing for a second glass of water.

"After you saved her life—and her mother's life. I know you care about her. I'm sorry it turned out this way, honey."

"What about Mack?" I felt like crying and did my best not to let that happen.

"Mack is recovering, just as you and Merrill are. If the Larentii hadn't come to help, you'd all have died. I tried to explain that to Gina, too. I think she was just too traumatized—after all, her best friend was killed by a monster. Perception colors everything, I'm sad to say."

"She couldn't tell me this in person?"

"Honey, she said she wanted no contact. We have to abide by that."

"What about her mother?"

"Mrs. Allen sends her apologies, but she wants no contact, either. You were more than brave, sweetheart. We've all been hit by this blow. Compulsion had to be laid, and Randall and Raymond Pierce are still out there somewhere. The police are looking for them. I think your Dad can find them, now; their allies have disappeared."

I no longer cared about any of that. My girl—whom I'd just begun to love, had called me a name and walked away.

～

Adam's Journal

I felt like the prize idiot when Kiarra handed my official birthday present to me. Justin, Mack and Merrill had only begun to wake after several days of unconsciousness following the attack. The Larentii had done exceptional healing, however.

If they hadn't, all three would be dead.

"What's this?" I asked, accepting the large, manila envelope from my wife.

"The deed. To your family home in England," Kiarra said and walked away from me.

I almost dropped the envelope, I'd gone so numb. She'd bought the damn thing for me? I felt like more than a fool.

"Sweetheart, no," I ran after her. If she'd been able to fold space, I might not have caught up with her. Instead, I lifted her in my arms and began kissing every inch of her face.

Fuck the deed. Fuck the property. Fuck everything else except what really mattered. Her. She mattered. Justin mattered. Mack and Merrill mattered. They'd taken on the enemy and defeated them with few assets and a universe of courage.

"Adam, you're tickling my nose," Kiarra complained when I kissed it for the third time.

"I love you. My God, I love you so much," I mumbled.

～

"You think they'll be back?" Randall Pierce tossed rabbit bones onto the campfire before wiping greasy fingers on his jeans.

"No idea. Made a lot of promises. You see where we are now," Raymond Pierce complained. "Supposed to get a cabin up here. A big one, with a fat bank account."

"Hey, something just bit me," Randall shouted, standing up.

The snake bit his father, too, before Randall died during his fall to the ground.

Justin's Journal

Eight months later...

Mack and I finished our senior year classes with Joey and Bearcat, and with special permission, were allowed to graduate with our former class at Valley High. Roughly a month earlier my sister, Anna Kay Griffin, joined the family. Barely a week later, Lion and Marlianna became parents to twins—Rush and Rachel.

Today was graduation day.

Dad shaded Mom and little Anna Kay with power where they sat in the bleachers, while Mack and I stood in the sun—on the same football field where we'd fought spawn the first time. Things had settled down after the Ra'Ak incident in late September the year before, but Mom said not to get comfortable. We were targets, and the enemy doesn't forget.

She also said there was a surprise when we got home, but I couldn't imagine what that might be.

Maybe we'd move again. Who knew?

I watched Gina from where I stood, waiting for my name to be announced so I could cross the stage and get my diploma. She'd glanced my way a time or two, but that's it.

No awkward hellos, only painful good-byes.

I considered, too, that the world had been in danger and Mack and I had helped save it. I listened while lists of accomplishments and awards were named when former classmates were summoned to receive their diplomas. World saving wasn't one of the things listed when Mack's name—and then mine—were called.

Gina found me when the ceremony was over. Mack and I were removing our caps and gowns in a classroom so we could return them before we left.

"I'll, uh, just go see what the others are doing," Mack said and walked out the door.

"Justin," Gina said. I watched her fingers twist together while she ducked her head—she was uncomfortable talking to me.

"Gina."

"I heard that Randall Pierce and his father were found up in the mountains. At least their remains were found. The coroner thinks they were bitten by a snake of some kind, and that's what killed them."

I ducked my head to hide the half smile. Darzi had done what we'd all wanted to do. "Does this mean you want to be friends again?" I lifted my head to look at her—she wouldn't meet my eyes, still.

"Justin, I know it's not fair. I know you and your Uncle and Mack saved our lives. I—I just can't deal with that. Being with somebody who isn't human. Whose family isn't human."

"If we'd been human, Mack, Merrill and I, we'd all be dead," I pointed out. We almost were anyway, but I didn't say it.

"A part of me understands that. Please try to see it from my perspective. I have plans, Justin, for my life."

"And those plans don't include a wyvern, do they?"

"Is that what it is? I thought it was a dragon."

"No. Uncle Dragon is a dragon. You should see that," I snapped. "He's bigger and better than I'll ever be."

"Look, I just wanted to say thank you, and leave it at that. I didn't want to fight with you," Gina sighed, her shoulders sagging. Finally, she looked at me. "It's always so trite to say it's me and not you. In this case, though, it's true. I can't help that I'm human, Justin. You can't help that you're a wyvern."

"And to you, that means we can't be together, is that right?"

"For me, it is. I'm sorry. I really need to go."

I watched her leave, steeling myself against the pain of it.

Things could have been so different.

I'll never forget what Darzi said, though, before he left.

"Better coming," he said. "Not worry."

"Justin, Mack, this is Belen," Mom said, smiling at Mack and me. We'd just gotten home and Mack and I were headed to the kitchen for a celebratory soda when Mom made her announcement. I blinked. Belen was so bright, I almost couldn't look at him.

"Not unusual," Belen smiled before extending his hand.

"I name you auxiliary Saa Thalarr," he proclaimed, placing his hand on my head. "You and Mack, here," he touched Mack's head, too. "You will fight spawn for us when needed, and in exchange, you will be granted power and abilities only the Saa Thalarr hold."

I stared at Mom, who was joined by Dad and Merrill.

Merrill shone, too.

"He's new—joined the Saa Thalarr yesterday," Mom said, her smile widening. "He's the Snow Leopard and Ranked Fifth. We're up to ten, now. Isn't that amazing?"

Dad grinned. "Pack up, son, we're moving to England," he said.

EPILOGUE

$\mathcal{T}$horsten stood on a cliff near the home he'd chosen long ago —when he'd been named supervisor of the Saa Thalarr. None of them knew where it was, by design.

"Interfere like that again, regardless of what your maker says, and I'll destroy you myself." Thorsten whirled to see who'd spoken, before dropping to his knees and bowing.

"Yes, Mighty One," he groveled.

"Do your job—the one you were instructed to do. Stray from that path and I'll kill you before he can, do you understand?"

"Yes, Mighty One."

"If they'd died, you'd be dead already. You understand now how important it is to keep them alive?"

"Yes, Mighty One."

"You will not recall this visit, if anyone asks."

"Yes, Mighty One."

Larentii Archives

History has been written—twice—within my lifetime. It is my guess, unconfirmed, of course, that if I were to gaze into the eyes of the Mighty, I might see that it has been written too many times to count—*Nefrigar of the Larentii*

The End

Made in the USA
Thornton, CO
12/11/22 21:59:39

393f4735-02d7-40fe-ad9b-4d930283d58eR02